AN ANNIE COLLINS MYSTERY

THE WEIGHT OF GUILT

HELEN STARBUCK

Routt Street Press

2025

The Weight of Guilt
An Annie Collins Mystery
Published by Routt Street Press LLC.
Arvada, CO

Names: Starbuck, Helen, author. Title: The weight of guilt / Helen Starbuck. Description: Arvada, CO : Routt Street Press LLC, [2025] | Series: An Annie Collins mystery ; book 5. Identifiers: ISBN: 978-0-9992461-9-1
Subjects: LCSH: Women detectives--Colorado--Denver--Fiction. | Murder--Investigation--Fiction. | Evidence, Circumstantial--United States--Fiction. | Trials (Murder)--United States--Fiction. | Lawyers--United States--Fiction. | Operating room nurses--United States--Fiction. | Operating rooms--United States--Fiction. | Man-woman relationships--Fiction. | LCGFT: Detective and mystery fiction. | BISAC: FICTION / Mystery & Detective / Women Sleuths. Classification: LCC: PS3619.T3727 W45 2025 | DDC: 813/.6--dc23

Cover and Interior design by Victoria Wolf, wolfdesignandmarketing.com.

For information, email info@routtstreetpress.com.

All rights reserved by Helen Starbuck and Routt Street Press LLC.

Routt Street Press

Arvada. CO
info@routtstreetpress.com

ALSO BY HELEN STARBUCK

THE ANNIE COLLINS MYSTERY SERIES
The Mad Hatter's Son
No Pity in Death
The Burden of Hate
A Cold Case of Conscience

STANDALONE ROMANTIC SUSPENSE
Legacy of Secrets

DENVER MAJOR CRIMES NOVELS
Finding Alex
The Woman He Used to Know
The Killer Without A Face

Guilt is always hungry; don't let it consume you.

—Terri Guillemets

PROLOGUE

WAS MIA STEWART CAPABLE OF STABBING a man to death, or had she simply been in the wrong place at the wrong time? That question colored everything about Mia from the first time I met her. She was unlikable and evasive, with the seriously entitled attitude that seemed to be the norm if you came from a rich, well-connected family. It was hard to figure out who we were dealing with.

One minute, she was teary-eyed and helpless, swearing she didn't kill the victim and vowing to do whatever it took to avoid conviction; the next moment, she lashed out if questioned or challenged. Her claim of innocence, however, never wavered. I had to take her at her word and hope I could find a way to prove it.

ONE

MAY 2023

I **LEANED OVER MY HUSBAND'S SHOULDER** and watched as he slowly sorted through the crime scene photos on his desk. I had stopped by the seventeenth floor office of the criminal defense practice where he worked to see what his plans were for the rest of the day and had been intrigued by the photos he was reviewing. A blond, good looking man with a carefully trimmed beard who, based on the dusting of gray in his hair and beard, looked to be in his mid-forties lay on the floor in a large pool of blood from a stab wound of the abdomen, his surgical scrubs were blood soaked.

The body lay near the two automatic OR entrance doors that had been blocked by one of his legs. As a result, the doors had opened and closed when they encountered his leg, creating smeared fans of blood on the floor. In the crime scene photos, both automatic doors had been pushed back to engage the magnetic locks on the wall that would hold them open and prevent them closing on the body. There were bloody handprints and smeared footprints surrounding the body and an osteo-tome—a chisel for working on bone—was lying next to it.

It looked as if the area where his body lay was only a couple hundred feet from where operating rooms were and where OR staff were undoubtably working. How frightening to know your life was seeping away with every pulse of your heart and that help was so close yet would never arrive in time to save you. It made my heart ache.

"Remember those photos I showed you earlier today? I could use some help with the case, if you and Frost are interested. You in particular," my husband Angel Cisneros said over a late dinner.

I'm Annie Collins, and I work as a private investigator with my partner in crime Frost, the retired Denver homicide detective I've known (and often frustrated) for several years. Long before that he became my mentor and a part of my family. I'm also a nurse who used to work in the OR—I still do, if the PI business hits a slow spot. There are times during the year when work slows down considerably and other times during the year when it heats up. It's unpredictable and working for an agency allows me to fill in those gaps.

Most of what Frost and I did was the routine bread and butter of PI work, which was rarely as exciting as most TV shows make it out to be. We followed significant others around to determine if they were cheating—most of them were. It seemed to me if you came to a PI thinking it was worth the money to find out if someone was cheating, then they most likely were. I guess it's hard to accept that without proof, and that was what we provided.

We did background checks, and found, or tried to find, people for estates in probate as well as those who had just plain disappeared because of legal or family issues. Sometimes we tried to find runaways. Those were the heartbreaking cases and not many had happy endings. We delivered subpoenas and tried to find those who'd jumped bail. In the midst of all this excitement, Angel periodically asked us to help him investigate cases he was handling.

"What happened—other than the guy being murdered?"

"An OR nurse is accused of stabbing a surgeon to death with something called an osteotome. No idea what that is other than it was lethal."

"Wow. I've never heard of one being used as a weapon. It'd make a good one, but an odd choice. They're big chisels used to work on bone, and they'd be hard to conceal. How'd you get the case?"

"Owen is the nurse's uncle. She's his sister's kid."

Owen Cameron was Angel's senior partner, the criminal defense lawyer who'd offered Angel a job he felt he couldn't refuse. Although Cameron wasn't an Italian mafioso, his offer had been like those in the *Godfather*, hard to resist at a time when Angel was frustrated with his job at the DA's office. As with deals like the ones in the *Godfather*, there were strings. The strings weren't immediately obvious, and by the time they were, Angel was locked in. Much to his annoyance, Owen had kept him on a short leash for the two years he'd been at the firm. It was never clear why, Angel had never needed supervision.

I wasn't convinced practicing criminal defense had been a good move for a former prosecutor with the Denver DA's office, but Angel had been doing it for two years now so the likelihood it would change was low and he seemed happy as far as I could tell. Angel was good at keeping things close, though, probably because he was a lawyer. If he was unhappy he hadn't said anything, and as his grandmother had told me once, Angel rarely did anything he didn't want to do.

"Owen handled her arrest and booking, but he asked that I take over because of his conflict of interest. She claims she found the surgeon bleeding out and tried to help him. She was kneeling next to him, her hands, shirt, and the knees of her scrubs were all covered in his blood, which could have happened if she was helping him. Of course the police and the prosecution think it's because she stabbed him. There was a bloody handprint on her face and on the osteotome handle. The one on the osteotome matches hers for size, but Forensics couldn't pull prints off the osteotome handle. I guess its textured for a better grip—which is a relief—but apparently she had a conflicted relationship with him which adds to motive."

"Conflicted? What does that mean?"

"I've got to get up to speed on the case, but from what Owen told me, the surgeon pursued her despite her telling him she wasn't interested. It seems he wasn't used to women telling him no."

"Did he force himself on her?"

"No, I don't think so, but I haven't talked to her yet. Owen didn't mention anything like that. She's in the Denver Detention Center awaiting a bond hearing in two days. I need to interview her tomorrow. When I do, I thought you could come with me. Your OR experience will come in handy and Frost could investigate the cop side of it. That's assuming Frost will cooperate." Angel said.

Frost's attitude annoyed Angel no end. He had retired from the Denver Police Department a year ago after thirty some years on the force and more than twenty as a homicide detective. He'd finally, grudgingly, adjusted to what he saw as Angel's defection from assistant DA to the 'dark side' as Frost—and most cops—characterized criminal defense work. But it never sat well with him; he'd been a cop for far too long. It had taken me a while to adjust to Angel doing defense work, and I still wasn't entirely used to it. It was good money ... but. There was always a 'but.'

Frost and I worked well together, although it had taken both of us a while to adjust to each other's way of approaching investigations. We had finally arrived at a system that we could live with. He had his lines in the sand regarding working with Angel. If Frost thought a client of Angel's was guilty, he refused to help. He based his decisions on gut feelings and buzzes about the client or the case and chats with his younger cronies who were still on the force. It wasn't usually anything concrete, but there was no talking him out of it once he thought the person was guilty. Angel had yet to adjust to Frost's attitude.

I didn't voice it to Angel or ask Frost, but I suspected that if Frost was really convinced of the client's guilt he'd probably set out to prove it and give whatever he found to the prosecution. His ethics demanded it, regardless of how uncomfortable it made things for me. I didn't blame him, but being caught between my husband and Frost was not a pleasant place to be. It's where I live and I've sort of gotten used to it. Sort of. The last couple years had been adventure in adjusting to change.

"I'll talk to him. What did you need to find out?"

"You're an OR nurse, you know the ropes, if you could interview her coworkers and those involved, that'd be helpful, see what you can find out about the surgeon. I'll have a better idea of what I need from you after we talk to her."

I heard a small voice call for me. I set my wine glass on the table and stood up. "I'll go check on Teo."

Angel grabbed my hand. "I'll go, *chica*. I think he heard my voice. Maybe I can convince him to go back to sleep."

I grinned. "Good luck with that."

Teo. Yeah that was a whole other story and probably the biggest change for both of us.

TWO

I **CRADLED MY TWELVE-WEEK-OLD SON** against my shoulder as I sat in the church pew and watched the pallbearers—Angel, his brother, father, and three other relatives—roll the flower-draped coffin of Angel's *abuelita*, Maria Sandoval, to the head of the main aisle of the Cathedral Basilica of the Immaculate Conception in Denver. A new life had begun and another had ended. Maria had finally succumbed to her pancreatic cancer. She held on until the baby was born and she'd had a chance to get to know him during his first few weeks of life before she went into a final rapid decline. I was both grateful she'd lived to see him and crushed that she was gone.

In the last few years, there had been three important people in my life—Angel, his grandmother Maria, and Frost. The list had now expanded to include our son. But despite this addition, her loss had left a deep hole in my heart that might never be filled.

She had assured me that our loved ones were always with us, as she would be, but at the moment I couldn't feel her with me, and I couldn't think about her being in the coffin. I wished more than anything I could have avoided the funeral. To see the coffin, know her body was in there, and then to see it lowered into the ground was more than I thought I could bear. I wasn't sure a cremation would have been any better—all that kindness, wisdom, and love reduced to ashes didn't seem any better than this ritual and burial. I wasn't sure anything would make her passing better. If I'd had my say she'd still be with us, but we rarely get what we want.

I fought to keep from bursting into tears afraid I wouldn't be able to stop, afraid I would upset the baby and he'd begin crying. Instead I surreptitiously wiped at tears as they began to fall. If I thought I had been emotionally labile since the baby's birth, it was worse now. Aside from the insanity of postpartum hormone storms, I was sleep deprived—both from caring for the baby and helping to care for Maria.

We hadn't chosen a name for him by the time he was born and he'd gone without one for nearly a week, much to Angel's mother Sophia's horror. Angel had sent me a text one afternoon with a suggestion.

<What do you think about Teo?>

<Tee oh?> I texted back thinking he'd lost his mind.

<No, it's pronounced Tay-oh. It was my grandfather's name.>

It had appealed to both of us, so, after mulling it over, we finally named him Teo. Angel's mother was relieved her grandson finally had a name and could be baptized and thrilled at the choice. I hadn't realized that the name Teo meant gift from God in Spanish. Angel hadn't given the meaning of the name any thought either. To him, it was simply his grandfather's name. In Sophia's mind the name was perfect—Teo was a gift from God. There was no question he was a surprise. *God must have a sense of humor, it was the only explanation for how we became parents,* I thought as I let my mind drift to avoid paying attention to what was happening.

We'd moved into a new house the previous year and, not long after a week's vacation in Hawaii, I discovered I was pregnant. It had been a huge shock to both of us. I remembered telling Angel.

"I'm late," I said. I had taken four at-home pregnancy tests in the last few days and all had been positive.

Angel looked up from his dinner with eyebrows raised. "Yeah, for what?"

"For my period."

We stared at each other for a few seconds. His face was blank, his mouth slightly open, he held his fork in the air over his plate.

"But ... you're on the pill."

"I'm still late, my period didn't start like it should have and the home tests say I'm pregnant."

"How did *that* happen?" He looked truly puzzled and a little stunned as he lay his fork on the table.

"Pretty sure you're old enough to know how *'that'* happens," I said irritably and then sighed. "All I can figure out is that I was on antibiotics for that bronchitis when we left for Hawaii and it screwed with the birth control pills. Antibiotics can do that. I'd forgotten about that, and we didn't take any additional precautions."

Of course additional precautions would have required owning a condom factory. The relaxing peacefulness of the nearby ocean, the warm sun-filled days, and no work or other agendas looming had given both of us a chance to relax and enjoy each other without interruption.

He smiled as he reached out and took my hand. We sat in silence watching each other and the pregnancy hovered in the air between us.

"I knew at some point you'd want kids, and that was fine, but I thought we'd have time to plan for it and ... talk about it." I slipped my hand out from under his and watched him anxiously. "I don't know if I'm ready for this."

Angel sat back and stopped smiling. He stood up and walked away from the table and paced, something he did when he was trying to think or calm down. "I don't think either of us was ready for this, I'm not sure most people are. It's always seemed like something we'd do ... later, not something we needed to deal with right now," he said. He sat down again and pushed his plate out of the way. Elbows on the table he frowned, leaned toward me, and said, "If you're really opposed to it, it's your decision. I'll support you whatever you decide."

I knew saying that cost him. It went against everything he'd been raised to believe, but we were partners—he had my back and I had his—and I knew he'd support me regardless of my decision. It was one of the many reasons I loved him.

He reached out for my hand again. "I know this isn't something we planned, and it's a shock, but what are you worried about?"

I closed my eyes and rubbed my forehead. All I knew was I was panicked. "I'm scared. I'm scared I won't be a good mother. I'm scared that if we go through with the pregnancy, it will change everything for us."

"Annie, it will change things." I started to pull my hand out of his. My heart fluttered in my chest and I could feel the anxiety growing. I wanted to pace now. He held onto my hand tightly. "But, if you're willing, we'll figure it out as we go, just like all the other parents in the world."

"I … I kept repeating the test because I just couldn't wrap my head around it."

"Yeah, it's a lot to take in. But I'm serious, I don't want you to feel like you have to do it."

"I know. I'm just freaked out about it."

He got up from the table, walked over to me, and pulled me up against him. "It's a surprise," he huffed out a brief laugh. "And a terrifying one, but *Corazón*," he added with a grin, "We have a basement."

That made me laugh. He'd always joked that if we had a kid who misbehaved we could lock them in the basement until they were twenty-one. Suddenly, I felt a little better about the whole debacle.

Feeling Teo squirm and fuss a bit brought me out of my reminiscences. Angel walked from where he and the other pallbearer's had stationed Maria's casket toward where I sat patting the baby on the back. His face was gray with exhaustion and grief. Neither of us had been getting much sleep. Trying to deal with a newborn who woke every two hours hungry or wet or just generally annoyed with the state of the world on top of caring for Maria had been overwhelming. Angel had been dealing with all this and trying to work. He was probably closer to his grandmother than to his mother and he was taking her death hard. All either of us wanted to do was hand the baby off to his mother, go somewhere quiet to mourn Maria's death, and sleep for a week.

He sat down next to me and reached for the baby as if to comfort himself. Teo objected, fussing briefly, and then settled down against Angel's shoulder. I watched as he rubbed his cheek against the top of Teo's head and closed his eyes. A tear dropped onto the baby's tiny head. I reached out and squeezed his thigh giving him a tenuous teary smile.

After the service, standing in the cathedral's vestibule holding the baby, he turned to me. "I'm not sure I can stand watching them put her in the ground, I've always hated that part of a funeral. I'd rather remember her alive and well."

"I can talk to your mother, if you want."

"No, *Corazón*." His voice was ragged and his eyes were reddened. "I have to see *Abuelita* laid to rest."

"Are you sure? There are plenty of relatives who could take your place."

He closed his eyes and shook his head. "No. She was always there for me. I have to see this through. I need to help," he said handing Teo back to me as the hearse pulled into the parking lot.

"Okay. We can leave whenever you need to. I love you." I leaned into him and kissed his cheek.

His brows scrunched together, his eyes tightly closed, and he looked as if he was going to cry. "*Tu eres mi Corazón*," he whispered.

"You're my heart, too," I said as I watched him walk toward the other pall bearers waiting by Maria's casket.

We got through it and, at last, it was over. I left Angel standing at the grave site and made my way through the crowd of relatives to find Sophia.

"We're not coming to the wake. The baby's fussy and Angel and I are exhausted so we're going home." Teo was cooperating at the moment by crying as I held him in my arms.

Sophia frowned. She never liked her plans disrupted. "She is his grandmother and he's her eldest grandson. He should be there, you too."

I sighed. I hadn't figured this would be easy. She'd orchestrated a huge gathering at the family home and no doubt had planned to show off her newest grandchild. I didn't want to go for a number of reasons, foremost because I had no intention of exposing a twelve-week old to all those people. Angel and I had debated not bringing him to the funeral, but the entire family was going and our supply of babysitters had dried up. It felt like too much work trying to find someone else to take over, so we'd brought him.

"Sophia, cut him a little slack, he's heartbroken, and neither of us has gotten more than two hours sleep at a time since the baby was born."

"He should be ashamed. He's a man, not a child."

I took a deep breath and closed my eyes. "That's just mean and don't you dare repeat that to him. I'm exhausted and so is he. Aside from that, Teo is way too young to be exposed to all those people wanting to pick him up and kiss him and pass him around. I'm not going to fight with you about this. I'm sorry if it upsets you, but we're going home."

She made one last stab at guilting me. "She would want him there."

"Trust me, Maria would understand."

THREE

MAY 2023

MIA STEWART'S SHOULDER-LENGTH straight brown hair was lank and looked as if it could use a good wash. Her face was pale. I'd only been in the Denver Detention Center once, it had not been a good experience then and not much had changed. That strong institutional smell of disinfectant that hung in the air never quite managed to cover up the underlying scent of … I wasn't sure what the smell was other than despair. She chewed on her thumb, and an anxious frown emphasized the dark circles under her eyes. The jail uniform didn't do much to improve things, but jail was not meant to be a vacation. It was a bad place filled with bad people, as Frost constantly reminded anyone who was listening. Angel introduced me, but I was the least of her concerns and received only a brief nod of acknowledgment.

"When can I get out of here?" The urgency in her voice was hard to miss.

Angel pressed his lips together. "You've been charged with first-degree murder. Bail is highly unlikely—"

"You mean I have to *stay here*?" Her voice took on an edge of hysteria.

"I will do my best, but I can't guarantee the judge will agree to bail. If they do, then it will most likely be quite high."

She jolted out of her chair. "I can't stay here. *I can't*. I didn't kill him. I tried to help him! My parents and Uncle Owen said you were a good lawyer. What good are you if you can't get me out of here?"

"Mia, please sit down," Angel said, gesturing to the chair across the table from him. "I need you to talk me through what happened. Let's focus on that for now."

Her face crumpled as she dropped into the chair and began to cry. "I didn't kill him."

Taking a legal pad and a pen out of his briefcase, Angel said, "Tell me what kind of relationship you had with him."

There were no tissues in the room, so she ran her fingers under her eyes and wiped them on her jail scrub pants. Her eyes darted around, refusing to look at Angel, and she shifted in her chair. I watched, remembering a detective who said one tell that a person might be preparing to lie was shifting in their seat and not making eye contact.

"There was no personal relationship."

It's not good if she starts off lying, I thought, adding, "find out if she had a relationship with him" to my mental to-do list.

"I worked with him in the OR. I circulated on his cases and sometimes scrubbed in on them. He had a reputation for hitting on women in the unit—well, I guess on any unit where his patients were. He was an attractive guy, physically. Personally, not so much. But it didn't seem to matter."

"Why do you say that?"

"Oh, come on, you know what I mean. You're a good-looking guy. Women will overlook a lot of crappy behavior if you're good looking."

"Did he have a reputation for crappy behavior?"

"He was a surgeon."

I snorted, and she glared at me. "I've worked in the OR for years," I said in explanation.

She gave me a faint smile and nodded. "He brought in lots of money for the hospital because of all the cases he did. He was their golden boy.

He treated his residents and fellows like slaves, but none of them would complain. Those positions were prestigious and highly sought after. The women in the department either welcomed his attention—and a lot did—or did their best to avoid him."

"Did he come on to you?"

She nodded.

"I take it you didn't encourage or appreciate his overtures?"

"No, I did not." Again, she shifted uneasily in her chair. Whether that was a lie or an attempt to get comfortable in a surprisingly uncomfortable chair remained to be seen. "He's married. But he was persistent even in the face of me telling him bluntly to go away."

"Did you file a complaint?"

She rolled her eyes and shook her head. "It would have been one of those he said, she said situations. He was always careful to avoid witnesses and phrased his offers in a way that could be interpreted as a joke. If I'd reported him, he'd have claimed I came on to him and changed my mind or had misunderstood him. So no, I didn't."

"Tell me what led up to the night he was killed."

She heaved a sigh. "I don't know what to tell you. He got it into his head he liked me, and he kept pestering me for a date. He was married. There's no point in having anything to do with a married man. Aside from the whole 'don't do something you wouldn't want done to you' issue, they rarely leave their wives, or if they do, they end up cheating on you. It's not worth it."

She fiddled with a lock of hair. "I overheard a conversation between two of the women I work with—Alicia Harvey and Joanne Wilson—not long before he was killed. Alicia is … up for anything with anyone, I guess is how I'd put it. Joanne is more reserved." She gave Angel a smug look.

I tried not to show it, but I've always hated it when people, women in particular, come down on other women for having an active sex life. Men, my husband included before we got together, play around with multiple partners and no one blinks an eye, or they're admired for their conquests. Women do it, and they're loose, easy, promiscuous, or sluts. I sighed. *We have a long way to go*, I thought as I turned my attention back to Mia.

"What I heard them discussing was that Joanne had been hit on by one of the surgeons, and I'm pretty sure it was Hudson. Alicia told Joanne that the guy was good looking and rich and it would be fun. He may have hit up Alicia. Maybe he approached both of them. I don't know. It'd be just like Alicia to tell Joanne to have an affair with him." She shrugged, quirked her mouth up, and frowned in disgust. Presumably the disgust was aimed at Alicia, or maybe it was for Geoff Hudson—maybe both. "I wasn't the only woman in the department he was chasing."

"Okay. Did you do anything he might have seen as encouragement? Something that would have led him to believe you would be interested in an affair?"

I'd helped Angel with enough investigations that I knew he had to ask questions that clients didn't like, but most understood why he had to ask them. She didn't.

Her eyes flashed, and she scowled. "For God's sake, this is like the 'she was asking for it' defense men use to excuse rape. No, I didn't *do* anything. All you had to do was be female and attractive for Hudson to hit on you." She clearly had a temper; whether it extended to the point of killing someone was the question.

"Please understand, I'm not placing any blame on you. These are questions I have to ask, and you can be sure the prosecution will ask other people about this and bring it up at trial. If you take the stand, which I'll try to prevent, they could grill you about it. The problem is, the prosecution could in fact call you to the stand, and I might not be able to stop them. So I need you to tell me the truth."

She nodded and gave her head a vigorous scratch. "Sorry, I'm just tired. I haven't slept since they arrested me. It's so noisy, and they never seem to turn the lights out. I don't know how anyone can sleep." She scratched her arm. "I feel like I'll never be clean, like I'll have to be deloused once I get out. It's disgusting here."

"I understand. It's not the Ritz by any means." He sat back a bit in his chair, then picked up his pen again. "Mia, right now I need to get a sense of what was going on up to and including the night he was killed so my staff and I can investigate and mount a defense."

"We worked together a lot, and he liked having me scrub on his cases, but it had been professional for the most part. He was funny and flirty with all the women in the department. As far as I was concerned, I think I was just there, to be honest. He knew me and liked me, so why not hit on me?"

Her eyes drifted up as she thought. "He'd been under stress of some sort recently. Maybe that was behind it all. He was horrible to his resident, Ted Nichols. He didn't tolerate fools and could be merciless if someone screwed up or got in his way, and Ted ... well, Ted wasn't cut out to be a surgeon, and that's putting it nicely. But the last month or so, it hadn't taken much to set Hudson off, and everyone had been a target."

"You have no idea what was bothering him?"

"No. He'd always been a pleasant surgeon to work with, unless you couldn't keep up with him or screwed up during a case, but whatever was bothering him changed that. Something had changed." She watched Angel as if trying to determine if he believed her.

"And you have no idea why, if other women took him up on his offers, he would pursue you?"

"Based on our interactions, I can't think of any reason he'd think I'd be interested. But he acted like I was playing coy, that I was interested but refusing him to ... I don't know. I think he pursued me because I told him I wasn't interested. I think he was one of those men who can't take no for an answer. Maybe pursuing me was a way to self-soothe the stress he seemed to be under. I don't honestly know."

"And he never forced himself on you?"

"No."

"So, what d'you think? Wanna help or not?" I asked Frost.

We sat at our desks in the tiny office space we rented for our PI business—Frost and Collins Investigations. I'd joked we should replace the plain door with one that had a frosted glass window with our business's name on it so we could be like Sam Spade. I said he should get a fedora and I should dress in forties outfits. Those suggestions resulted in a roll of his eyes and a disbelieving shake of his head. I could almost hear him thinking, *The things I have to put up with.*

The office was in an old three-story house in the Capitol Hill neighborhood that had been converted into offices. Ours was on the third floor, which was one reason we got a break on rent. The three flights of stairs were killer, and not many people wanted to rent the two small rooms at the top. It did have a nice treetop view of the Front Range from the small windows on either side of a defunct fireplace. There was a tiny two-person elevator that honestly was more terrifying than the prospect of a heart attack on the stairs, but as Frost assured me, our work, unlike that of Sam Spade, wasn't walk-in business. Clients came from the internet, and referrals came via professional connections.

"It's interesting." Frost tapped a pencil on his desk and cocked his head from side to side, clearly weighing the options. "Ah sure, let's help your boy. Tell me what the client told him at the jail."

So far so good, I thought. Whether he'd continue to help was the question.

FOUR

ANGEL HAD GONE BACK TO THE OFFICE after we spoke with Mia, and he was late getting home. He had always worked unpredictable hours, even in the DA's office. Some days he'd be home by six, other days, depending on what was happening with clients, I wouldn't see him before eight or nine in the evening. I had kept our food warm, and Teo was sound asleep. It was a nice chance to have dinner alone, just the two of us. That didn't happen often. Between my work schedule and Angel's and having a two-year-old, a quiet, uninterrupted dinner together was rare. In the course of dinner conversation, we talked about the details of the case and what he had gleaned during our interview.

"I hesitate to jump to a conclusion, but what she related is absolutely believable," I said. "I don't think she's being completely honest about her and Hudson, though. If he was screwing around as much as she said he was, why would he care if one woman turned him down? According to her, there were plenty who would have been happy to play. I think there was more going on there than what she said. However, I don't think she's lying about not killing him. What did you think?"

"I think there was more going on between her and Hudson, too. You're the OR nurse, does it jibe with what you know about working in that area?"

"Yeah, pretty much. The OR is a restricted area. It's this isolated world that's closed off to the outside, and the 'inmates,' for lack of a better term, are often under pressure with lots at stake. Especially in a main OR. Patients may have serious health problems and are there for more serious surgeries than you see in an outpatient surgery. People do a lot of things to relieve the pressure and the stress. Sometimes relieving stress ends up being inappropriate comments or liaisons."

I took a drink of wine and continued, "Usually staff handle it well and things go smoothly, but when situations deteriorate, behavior can run the gamut from bullying to temper tantrums or harassment. There can be a lot of flirting and joking as well. All of it is mostly invisible to the world outside the OR. Managers and hospitals take harassment and bullying much more seriously these days and intervene, but a lot goes on that never reaches management's attention or is never reported.

"Privately, affairs and one-night stands after social events sometimes happen. Like Mia said, though, reporting his behavior would have been her word against his, and hospitals don't like to piss off money-making surgeons without hard evidence. A lot of docs carry on affairs with staff members, whether they're married or not."

"True, there are plenty of people who're willing to play and don't care who they play with. Seems like if that was what you wanted, there'd be no point in getting married."

"You played around quite a bit."

"I did, but I wasn't married, and the women I hooked up with weren't either. That was my line in the sand, although I got approached by a lot of married women." Angel ate for a bit, then asked, "Do you worry about me cheating on you?"

I laughed. "No. But you never know—things change, people change."

"Not for me, not like that."

"My eternal romantic," I said, smiling at him.

He glowered at me. "Don't blow me off. What do you think's going to change?"

"Angel, it was just a comment. Everything changes, you know that. Our lives are already different than they were initially. Teo has completely altered our relationship and our relationships with family and everyone we know. In a good way most of the time, but we've been through hell before Teo arrived. Fortunately, we managed to survive, but no one can say for certain how things will turn out."

He continued to frown as I talked. The hole I was digging just kept getting deeper, but I continued. "Look at how many spouses Frost and I spy on to see if they're cheating, and at least three-quarters of them are. My guess is most of the people who cheat probably loved their partner at one point, maybe even believed in happily ever after. It doesn't mean it can't happen, but the divorce rate would say otherwise, don't you think?"

For the life of me, I couldn't figure out why I was even pursuing this. Maybe to see what he thought. I didn't worry about him cheating, but I had to admit, there were times when I wondered why he was attracted to me at all. My insecurity was my Achilles' heel when it came to Angel.

He finished the last bite of his dinner and sat back, continuing to stare at me. I wished now we hadn't gotten off on this topic. "Yeah, it does, but it doesn't say anything about the couples who remain married."

He held up a hand to stop my response. "I know what you're going to say—half of those who don't divorce probably are bored or hate their partners—and you may be right, but not all of them feel that way. I agree that things change and not always for the better. One thing you can count on, if I get bored or something seriously changes, I'll tell you. I won't go out and cheat on you." He paused, started to say something, then stopped, took a deep breath, and asked, "Would you cheat on me?"

I was a bit taken aback. He'd never asked me that. Without thinking, I said, "No, who would I cheat with? You have no competition."

I realized my mistake when his mouth dropped open and he frowned. "Would you cheat on me if there was competition?" he demanded.

"No, of course not. That came out wrong." I reached over and took his hand. "I have never cheated on anyone I've been involved with, and I would never cheat on you. I'll tell you if things change as well."

Telling someone you weren't happy with a relationship, though, was a serious and dangerous conversation for most couples, and from past experience with a guy I was involved with, I knew cheating was sometimes easier than talking. Until you got caught, then all hell broke loose. Which is exactly what had happened when I discovered what he was up to.

Angel took our commitment to each other seriously. I did, too, and wanted to reassure him. "I don't see myself getting bored or not loving you, but I'd rather know up front if that changes for you than find out you're cheating on me. That'd really piss me off. I have a gun, and I know how to handle dead bodies. Something for you to keep in mind."

That got a laugh at last and seemed to break the mood. "Yeah, I'll keep it in mind. I've been shot twice since hooking up with you. I'd just as soon not make it three times." We were silent as we sipped our wine. I wasn't sure what he was contemplating, but the slight frown on his face made me think he was remembering our last confrontation with Ian Patterson, an escaped felon, and how we'd barely escaped with our lives. I know I was.

At last, he said, "It does make you wonder, though, what changes—what makes someone break their vows? It can't just be boredom. That's fixable, I think."

"I don't know. Some people don't take the vows seriously from the start, and some can't resist temptation. Some people don't know how to tell their partner they don't want to be in a relationship with them anymore, so cheating seems easier. One of my coworkers at my first job out of school was on husband number four. She maintained that, at some point, all husbands become boring. Then it's time to move on."

I watched as he picked up our plates and took them to the kitchen. The conversation brought to mind my friend Libby Matheisen, who'd cajoled me into trying to find out what was wrong with her a few years back. It hadn't had a happy ending for either of us.

"While I was taking care of Libby, she said she believed in serial monogamy—being faithful until it didn't work and then ending it and moving on. She just didn't end it before she played around. I don't know what's true. I haven't been in any relationship long enough to know, including us. We've been together longer than any previous relationship I've had, and nothing's changed the way I feel about you."

"Well, be sure to tell me if it does change and I start boring you, so I can at least try to fix that."

I laughed. "Are you trolling for compliments?"

"No, I'm serious."

"I will be surprised if either of us gets bored—frustrated, pissy, scared, pushed to the end of our ropes, but never bored. Although boring—maybe a better word would be *peaceful*—isn't all bad."

"True."

Relationships take a lot of work, and not everybody wants to work, but cheating seemed to me to be both harder to do and the death knell for a relationship. Sometimes it was a death knell for those involved. My friend Libby ended up totally derailing her life and those around her by taking two lovers, getting pregnant, and ending the affairs—earning her lover Ian Patterson's payback in the process and dying at his hands. All because she was bored and frustrated with her husband. I'd nearly died as well. To say it wasn't worth it was an understatement. I doubted Geoff Hudson had thought it was worth it as he lay dying.

"I don't see Mia killing Hudson, but his wife? She'd have a good reason to," I said, changing the subject a bit.

"Yeah, but according to what I've read in the police report, she has an alibi." He set the plates on the countertop. "I'm worried about the statement his resident made. He says when he exited the dressing room, he saw Mia kneeling over Hudson with the osteotome in her hand and saying something to him. He didn't hear everything she said, but he says he heard her say 'deserved it' and that she looked angry. She says she pulled the osteotome out from under him. He says she was holding it over him. She says she was telling Hudson that she'd try to help him and denies saying what Nichols says he heard. There were no other witnesses who could confirm what either of them did or didn't say."

"That is worrisome." As we tidied up the kitchen, I remembered Angel telling me once how millions of people cheat on their partners and don't end up hurting or killing them. *At least not physically*, I thought. I wasn't so sure about the emotional damage. I could still remember the devastated look on Libby's husband's face as he told me he'd always love her, even though she'd cheated on him.

I watched Angel and thought how lucky I was to have someone who loved me the way he did. I walked behind him, wrapped my arms around his waist, and rested my head on his back. "You're not boring, and I love you," I said.

He turned with a smile on his face and took me in his arms. "You're far from boring, *chica*, that's for sure, and I love you too."

And true to form, as things were heating up between us, we heard Teo call out to me from his bedroom.

"*¡Ay, mijo, ten piedad de tú padre*," he moaned, letting go of me.

I laughed as I walked toward Teo's bedroom. "Have mercy on you? Not likely, my love. He's never going to have mercy on either one of us."

"That's for sure," Angel replied with a laugh.

"Later. We'll pick this up later," I called over my shoulder.

"Yes, we will."

Our relationship had certainly changed in ways we never anticipated. But then, who does?

FIVE

"Y OU WERE ABLE TO GET BAIL FOR HER?" I asked, surprised.

"I'm pretty sure I didn't have a lot to do with it. Her father and her aunt are prominent lawyers here in town. Her aunt knows the judge personally and spoke to her before the hearing. I presented all my arguments—no previous record, a well-respected member of the health care community, not a flight risk, and not guilty—but I think Judge Kingsley had already made up her mind. To appease the prosecution, she set the bail at an astronomical level—one million dollars, which her father agreed to pay—and required Mia to surrender her passport and wear an ankle monitor. It's not what you know, it's who you know, clearly."

"A million dollars. Jes—uh … geez," I said, glancing over at our son, who had stopped playing in front of the TV and was watching both of us. I'd worked in the OR and with cops too long, and curbing my swearing in front of Teo was a work in progress. "What will that cost her father?"

"Fifteen percent, which he won't get back, and if she takes off, whatever he put up as an assurance is forfeit."

Angel scooped up Teo, who'd walked over and started tugging at Angel's slacks, and carried him over to the couch. Dropping down onto it, he asked, "*Que tal, mijo?*"

"*Bueno, Papi.*" Teo snuggled into his father's chest and launched into his unique two-year-old Spanglish to tell Angel about his day.

There were times when neither Angel nor I could decipher what he was saying, but most of the time he managed to get his point across. And whether Angel understood or not, *Papi* could do no wrong. He was a great dad, patient, playful, and totally besotted with his son. I was in love with him, too, just a little less talented in Teo's estimation. I figured it was the old "familiarity breeds contempt" principle—I was there most of the time because my work was sporadic and flexible. Angel was at work or in court forty plus hours a week. Therefore, in Teo's estimation, time with him was more valuable.

Angel took the glass of wine I held out to him and took a sip. "Regardless of why, Mia is at least out of jail and in the custody of her parents."

"Her parents? That's odd for an adult."

"She lives in the guest house at the back of their property. The judge ruled she could go to work or doctor appointments, meet with me, and go to anything urgent, but otherwise she's restricted to their property. She's been put on leave from the hospital, so work isn't an issue. She's happy, and so are her parents. That's one hurdle breached. Now I just have to get her acquitted."

Teo reached for the glass. "Want some."

"No, *mijo*, this is grown-up juice. *Mamá* will get you some of your own." Angel looked up at me and grinned.

"No! Want some."

"Okay, but you won't like it."

"Angel …" I said, frowning.

He just grinned and dipped his finger in the wine. "Open up," he said and dripped a couple drops into Teo's mouth.

"Uck."

"Told ya. How about a juice box?"

Teo nodded enthusiastically. "My juice."

"What d'you say to *Mamá*?"

"Pease."

Angel smiled and gave him a hug. I rolled my eyes. *Papi* seemed to have a knack for avoiding confrontations with a two-year-old. When I returned, juice box in hand, Angel said, "I'd like you to spend some time with Mia and get the full story about Hudson. I don't think she's being completely honest about her relationship with him, so see what you can get her to talk about. And I'm definitely going to want you to talk to his resident."

"I'm curious about the osteotome. It had to come out of an ortho set. The most likely source would be a used one, and then where would you conceal it? How would you keep Hudson from seeing it before you stabbed him with it? I mean, why not take a scalpel with a twenty blade on it and slit his throat or something?"

Angel raised his eyebrows and looked taken aback. "How about we talk about it when this one is asleep?"

Yeah, learning how and what to talk about in front of a toddler was a work in progress as well. I reached down and held my arms out to Teo. "Come on, little man, bath time."

Teo started to scowl, so Angel stood up and carried him toward the bathroom. "What's that duck of yours been up to, *mijo*?"

"Slit throat!" he declared.

"No, *mijo*, *Mamá* said sore throat." Quick thinking on Angel's part, I thought.

"Slit throat!" Teo replied.

I heard a sigh and an *¡Ay Dios!* from Angel. I let my head drop back on the couch in surrender. One more thing Angel's mother, Sophia, would hold against me after Teo repeated it in front of her. All I could hope for was that he'd forget it before he said it to anyone other than to Frost, who'd at least laugh before he admonished me for talking about that kind of stuff in front of a two-year-old.

❧

As we sat on the couch enjoying the quiet and our wine, Angel rubbed his forehead and yawned. "Back to what you mentioned, do you think the choice of weapon is important?"

I shrugged. "It could be. We need to find out where she was that day and whether she had access to any ortho sets. It could also rule her out as the killer if there were no ortho cases on the day he died, there weren't any missing osteotomes from the ortho sets, she wasn't circulating or scrubbing on any, or if someone involved in a similar case had a grudge against him."

I shifted toward him. "I don't see how it could be a spur-of-the-moment choice of weapon. Any weapon other than, say, a pen in your pocket, implies premeditation, but it'd be easy to get a knife and blade. They're easily concealed and can be pretty deadly in the right spot.

"For example, if his throat was cut from behind, that'd rule her out because he was a fair bit taller than she was, according to the autopsy. It'd be hard for her to manage that. Slicing his neck from the front would work, although there'd have been arterial spray all around and all over whoever killed him, but his fatal wound was in the abdomen. The osteotome was a direct stab from what I could see in the photos, and most of the blood was on him and the floor around him. I don't know, it just strikes me as an odd choice of weapon."

"Good to know. Get the names of people who're friends with her and those who may have witnessed or experienced Hudson's persistence. Maybe one of them saw something that night. See what you can find. Ask Frost to see what, if any, legal trouble the guy might have had—harassment, assault, restraining orders, that kind of stuff. I told Mia you'd be calling. Other than names and contact info, I'd prefer you didn't write up a report. Just tell me what she says."

I was used to this by now. If it was written down, then it became discoverable and would have to be turned over to the prosecution. All depositions would be, eventually, but Angel never liked to have to do it until he had to.

"I don't think it's going to be easy to access people who knew her or Hudson. You could formally take their depositions, but people are on guard during a deposition. Under normal circumstances, people are always willing to gossip, and that's where you often discover the important stuff. I could ask to be assigned to the OR where she works, you know, through the temp agency. That might help."

He frowned slightly. "I don't think that's a good idea. I want all the info we get to be unassailable. If you go in as a nurse and pick up gossip, it's hearsay. Better to get people to provide their information the usual way, then I can get a formal deposition from the ones with important information."

"Okay, it was just a thought. I'll set up an interview with Mia." I sipped my wine in silence for a moment. "So," I said at last. "Do you think Teo's going to repeat 'slit throat' to your mother?"

He grinned. "Oh probably, and at the worst possible time. If I'm there, I intend to be clear it was you who said it."

I punched him in the arm, and he laughed. "Traitor."

We sat in a glassed-in patio at the back of Mia's parents' house that was filled with plants in various artistic groupings of pots ranging from small to huge. The scent of damp earth and the perfume of a number of flowers that were flourishing in the slightly humid air made every muscle in my body relax. If heaven exists, I imagined it must smell like this room. The housekeeper had escorted me through the living room and into the patio, where Mia sat, a glass of something I couldn't identify sitting untouched next to her on a small end table.

She motioned to an unoccupied chair across from her. "Would you like something to drink?"

"A glass of water would be nice, thanks."

She nodded at the housekeeper, who disappeared and returned

a few minutes later with a heavy-bottomed crystal glass of sparkling water with a lemon slice in it. The whole tableau reminded me of my friend Libby's house and her housekeeper. Being here brought back the sense of being trapped by wealth and privilege, and it rattled me a bit. I hoped things turned out better for Mia than they had for my friend.

We spent some time on social niceties before I focused on her. "Mia, one thing that's important in a situation like this is being honest about what happened—"

"I have been."

"I don't think you've been completely honest." She glared at me, but I could see a faint blush creeping up her neck. "I think there was more to Geoff Hudson and his interactions with you than you've said so far."

"Does my lawyer know you're accusing me of lying?"

"I work for him, and my job is to find out the truth, which we hope will help him defend you. He can't effectively defend you if you don't tell us the entire story. And trust me, it's eye-opening what the prosecution can find out and smear you with at trial. That's their job, and our job is to be prepared and have a defense against it."

We sat silently for several minutes. "Was there something more serious going on between you and Hudson?"

She stood up abruptly and walked to the bank of windows that looked out onto the backyard. *I wonder what she'll tell me*, I thought.

She turned back toward me. "Nothing was going on other than he wanted me and I didn't want him. I knew he was married, and I wasn't interested. I got the sense no one had ever turned him down before. He didn't like being told no and never really gave up trying to get me interested. His constant overtures made being at work almost unbearable."

"So he pursued you right up until his death?"

She nodded.

"And it wasn't the other way around? He didn't rebuff your advances or end a relationship with you?"

Her face flushed, and her brows nearly met in the middle. "That's always how it goes isn't it? Blame the woman, make her the scorned lover who wanted revenge. No, he didn't dump me, I didn't pursue him, and I didn't kill him."

I didn't think that was the whole truth about her and Hudson, and I knew, somehow, Angel or I had to get her to tell us what that was. "Okay, let's go over what happened, starting with when he first approached you, right up until his death."

Frost and I sat across from each other at Cody's. Other than the office, it was this restaurant we had always met at to discuss cases.

"Frost, I've got a list of names, people Mia was friends with and others she thought might be helpful. I'm going to get the names of those the police interviewed from Angel and start contacting them. I want their take on what happened and what her relationship with Hudson really was. I don't think she's being honest about it."

"No surprise there. It's a rare person who's entirely honest under these circumstances. Your boy should have copies of the police interviews, but let me know if he doesn't. I can get them and the names of anyone they interviewed. Roberts can probably help me with that. I can use the family connection to put a little pressure on him if he objects."

Paul Roberts, a homicide detective who knew both of us, had married Angel's youngest sister. The family connection was useful, but even Paul had his limit for helping the defense regardless of his family ties.

"Can you see if there were any complaints filed with the state board against Hudson and try to interview the hospital administration folks? You're a little more intimidating than I am. They might tell you more than they would me. If you could find out whether there are any restraining orders or other legal actions against him, that'd be helpful."

"Yeah, I'll get started on that this afternoon."

"I think we'll be lucky if the hospital will comment on any issues with his behavior. They're not usually willing to discuss that. If there's any hint of official issues, then Angel can subpoena the chief of surgery and the hospital administrator. I'm going to talk to the people Mia identified and see what I can find out."

"You think she's innocent?" he asked.

"I think so, but I also think she's lying about not having a relationship with Hudson. She says there wasn't one, that he pursued her despite her rebuffing him. I don't believe it. I questioned her about it and told her the prosecution would dig through her entire life and crucify her with whatever she was hiding. But she stuck to her story. That's not a great start if she's lying."

"People never tell the whole truth, kid. If I learned nothing else as a cop, it's that there's always more to the story and there's usually an important reason for keeping it a secret. It never stays secret for long, though. Affairs or relationships can go sour, and people cheat on each other. Those are always good reasons to kill someone. Divorce by death is pretty appealing to some people. Hudson's wife is a viable suspect."

"Normally, I'd agree, but I don't see how she'd have access to the operating room or the instrument that was used. It's unlikely anyone outside the OR would know what it was, and it's not something you could easily find or carry around with you. The wife could have paid someone to do it for her, I suppose, someone who worked in the OR. Finding out if there are any rumors about her having an affair or financial issues that would make killing him worthwhile is a good idea."

"When it comes to dead husbands it's usually the wife, but according to the police reports I've read, she's alibied by a mutual friend. I'll dig into that and make sure it's a solid alibi. As for paying someone else to kill him? Getting someone else to do the dirty work is risky," Frost said. "Even if it's a lover, people can turn against each other when something serious is involved. The more serious the issue is, the more likely someone will get cold feet or get remorseful or pissed off or break when questioned and rat out the instigator. When things heat up, people self-destruct. Sometimes it's just a waiting game."

"Hard to know who's responsible right now. I can't see any reason for Mia to kill him. I suppose if he was trying to force himself on her, but according to her he never assaulted her, he just kept pursuing her. That's harassment but it's hardly a strong motive for killing him. Regardless of who did it, his death was premeditated. The osteotome had to have been lifted from a used set at some point. There'd be no other way to get one. If it had been taken from an open set sitting in an OR, its absence would have been discovered almost immediately. Plus, you don't carry osteotomes around in your pockets just in case you need to stab someone."

Frost laughed. "The wife's not a surgeon, is she?"

"No, I think she's a family law lawyer. You know, divorce, child custody issues."

"I don't know, kid. Unless there are some extenuating circumstances, that pretty much rules her out. No opportunity."

"Infidelity is a valid motive, but there are just too many 'I don't know how she would have managed to do it' issues. She wouldn't have known when his cases would finish or where he would be. He could have been in an OR, still working, in the ICU, or in the postanesthesia care unit—anywhere, really. And she'd have stuck out like a sore thumb. The OR's not easily accessed or familiar to anyone who doesn't work there. Regardless, we need to try to find out what was going on between her and Hudson, just in case," I said.

"It's never good to let someone off the suspect list until you're sure they weren't involved," Frost said, finishing his coffee.

SIX

I THINK MIA HAD DECIDED I WASN'T THE TYPE to be impressed by her parents' home or money, so at our second meeting we sat in her small carriage house apartment's living room. It was nicely decorated and furnished, separate from the main house, and if it had belonged to anyone other than her parents, it would have cost her a fortune to rent. There had been no offer of a drink on my arrival, and she was a little frosty with me.

Ignoring her cold demeanor, I perused the list she'd given me of women Hudson had been involved with. "He was a busy boy, it looks like." There were twelve names on the list, along with their contact information.

"Seems so," she replied. "This isn't info I know firsthand. I talked to a friend who gathered it. She knew two of the women personally, but the rest relies on gossip. It'd have to be confirmed somehow."

"And he slept with all of them?"

"According to my friend, he hit on all of them. The ones he hooked up with, she marked with an asterisk. But keep in mind, the ones without an asterisk could be lying about not getting involved with him."

You could be lying about it as well, I thought. Although I thought she was innocent, I found her hard to read. Challenging her hadn't gotten us off to a great start, and I wondered how long it would be before she told us the truth about Hudson.

"Still, seven—that's a lot of screwing around. There's bound to be at least a few who didn't like being one of a crowd, or maybe someone connected to them didn't like what he did." I read the names carefully and saw Alicia Harvey's name was not on it. "Who gave you the names?"

"The list was compiled by Janice Kramer. She overheard Kathy Johnson and Carol Rogers talking about how sad Hudson's death was and how he'd been coming on to women in the department. Janice joined the conversation, and Kathy admitted she'd gone for drinks with him at a nearby bar. According to her, it didn't lead to anything more involved, but she knew two others she was pretty sure had hooked up with him. Between the three of them, they put together this list."

"Thanks, Mia, this helps. It's interesting Alicia's name isn't mentioned, based on what you overheard in the dressing room. We can interview them and see what turns up. Maybe they know something that'd help. I really appreciate you getting this."

"If there's anything else I can help with, please let me know."

"Other than this list, it's probably best you stay out of it and let us do the investigating. But if you find out anything else or see or hear anything that might be related, let me know."

I stood in front of the portable AC unit I'd picked up last summer after discovering that our attic-level office was a furnace in hot weather. It was at least eighty degrees at the moment, and the cool air was a huge relief. There was a space heater in the tiny closet that came in handy in the winter when you could see your breath at times. We'd been spoiled by efficient heating and cooling; older generations must have been tougher. Tougher than me at any rate.

Frost stretched in the chair opposite my desk. "So, where are you at with the women on your list?"

I turned toward him, enjoying the cool air on my back. "It's one of those situations where determining who's telling the truth is going to be a full-time occupation. I talked to Alicia Harvey. Mia seemed to think she was involved with Hudson. She mentioned that Alicia was in tears the night of Hudson's death. When I pushed, Alicia denied being involved with him, which makes me wonder why. According to the gossip, people are pretty sure she got involved with Hudson. Maybe she fell for him," I said.

"She denies it and says she was upset that night because she liked him, not because she was involved with him. She said everyone was upset. According to Mia, though, no one else was crying about it. When I mentioned Alicia's denial to Mia, she told me Brent Perkins, an ICU nurse she knows, saw Alicia come out of a dictation room the day before Hudson's death. According to him, she was flushed, her lips were reddened, and seeing him surprised her. Hudson emerged a few minutes later and looked very satisfied but embarrassed when he noticed Perkins. If nothing else, he got a quick … some quick … oral gratification. That's involved in my book."

Frost laughed. "You fascinate me. You swear like a sailor at times, and yet you can't bring yourself to say 'blow job.'"

I felt heat flush my face as I walked over to my desk and sat down. "I can't say things like that to you. It'd be like saying it to my dad."

My dad would have been about Frost's age if he hadn't passed about ten years ago. My mom and I had never gotten along, and before she'd passed we had very little contact with one another. Frost had filled the gap my father's death left, and Angel's grandmother had stepped in as a mom replacement.

He just shook his head and chuckled, then frowned. "I didn't realize her friend saw it. That adds weight to the fact that Alicia's lying about whatever her involvement was."

"Yeah, she's lying about her involvement with him, and I can't figure out why. It's not like she's in the running for prime suspect. She was in a room with four other people when they heard Hudson had been killed. I talked to the nurse she relieved, and the nurse checked the surgical record for the procedure and gave me the time Alicia showed up. If she killed him, she had to have been pretty damn quick, and there are too many issues to make it feasible. The timeline doesn't work, in my opinion.

"Killing someone, especially if it's not something you've done before and you're not a psychopath, is pretty traumatic. She'd have to be damn cold to kill him and walk into an OR and relieve someone for a break. Aside from that, she would have had to change clothes 'cause they'd probably have blood on them. And more problematic is where the hell would she have gotten the osteotome or kept it until she decided to stab him? Confronting him would have been a gamble—she would have had no way to know exactly where he was. It's just one dead end after another." It was so frustrating. Every single time a possibility arose, it got shot down.

"I think you need to talk to Alicia again, see if you can push her about Hudson and her alibi enough to rattle her, see what she says," Frost said.

"Interestingly, Alicia is sure Mia was involved with Hudson, which is a new take on the story. It's the first I've heard anyone suggest that, and I've put a lot of pressure on Mia to admit her involvement, if there was any, and she won't budge. It's funny how Alicia and Mia both deny being involved with him and yet they each implicate the other."

"Sounds like they aren't real fond of each other. Maybe both of them were involved with him and knew it. Never known a woman who liked to share."

I nodded and absently picked up a pencil and tapped it on the desk. Then, realizing what I was doing, I stopped and grinned at Frost. "I've been around you too long. I'm picking up your bad habits. I still think the alibi provided by Geoff's wife is ... odd."

Frost had gone over the police reports and discovered Hudson's wife's alibi relied on Matt Finley, an orthopedic surgeon at the same hospital where Hudson had worked. According to her, she was planning a birthday party for Hudson with Finley, and he backed her up. "According to the police interview, they both claim to be just friends. I plan to interview both of them myself. Maybe something will turn up," he said.

"You could put pressure on this Finley. Maybe Bev Hudson means more to him than he indicated when the police interviewed him, and maybe the whole alibi is a cover for him. He's an orthopedic surgeon at the hospital, and he'd know how to get the instrument. He'd know Hudson's surgical schedule and would know where to wait for an opportunity to kill him."

"All reasons I want to talk to them personally."

"Have you talked to Hudson's partner, Jan Mykowski? In the days leading up to his death, Mia saw them arguing on a couple occasions, and she said he mentioned a confrontational meeting with Mykowski and his office manager. And that," I said, "makes me wonder why Hudson would have mentioned it to her when she says she kept rebuffing him."

"Yeah, Mia is a puzzle. I spoke with Mykowski and the office manager, and both have airtight alibis. Mykowski was in the middle of a procedure at another hospital, and the manager was celebrating her anniversary at a restaurant." He saw the look on my face. "Sorry, kid, I think your boy's gonna have his work cut out for him getting her off. Everything okay? You've been a little distracted the last couple days."

I waved my hand dismissively. "I'm fine. This case is just frustrating. I wish Angel had never been asked to handle it. Owen Cameron, his senior partner, has always kept a close eye on Angel's work for no reason that I can figure out. Angel's not someone who needs supervision. Cameron's been micromanaging this case since he turned it over to Angel."

"I wouldn't worry. It's probably because Mia's his niece."

"I think Angel's worried that if he loses it could cost him his job or at least cause problems for him."

"You win some, you lose some, kid. Angel knows that, and so does Cameron. If losing the case is going to jeopardize his job, he needs to know that and decide whether he wants to stay. He could easily lose the case. Neither of us has found anything to clear her."

SEVEN

CAROL ROGERS ESCORTED ME TO A SMALL, enclosed patio off the hospital cafeteria. It was a warm day, but the area had a tree, several benches, and some landscaping around the edge of the flagstone patio. It was quiet, and we had the place to ourselves as we sat on the bench in the shade of the tree.

"Thanks for agreeing to talk with me," I said. "I work for Mia's lawyer, and I'm trying to interview as many people as possible who knew her and were there the night of Hudson's death."

"I'm happy to help."

"I appreciate that. Tell me what you know about her relationship with Hudson and what happened."

"I don't think they had a relationship other than as coworkers. She told me he'd been pursuing her, but she'd been turning him down and trying to brush him off. I never heard any conversations to back that up, but Sam Woodley, one of the orderlies, saw a confrontation Mia and Dr. Hudson had in the cafeteria a few days before his death. It was late in the evening, they were sitting at a table talking, and it looked like they were arguing. According to Sam, it was pretty heated. Hudson stood up and started to leave, Mia stepped in front of him, he said something to her, and she slapped him—hard. Sam said Hudson said something else, then shoved past her and left.

"I spoke to her about it. I was worried about what Hudson had done." Carol continued, "All she would say is he said something offensive to her. I told her she should file a complaint, but she refused and said she just wanted it to go away. She wouldn't tell me what he'd said. The way he acted … he wouldn't take no for an answer. That's not harmless."

"No, it's not."

"It was all over the OR by the next day. I like Sam, but he gossips, and it was just too juicy of a story for him not to spread it around."

"So clearly there was something upsetting Mia or Hudson, maybe both of them. Do you think it had anything to do with his death?"

"I've worked with Mia a lot. We're friends, but I wouldn't say we're close. In spite of that, I can't imagine she'd do what she's accused of doing."

"Do you have any reason to doubt her about her involvement with Hudson?"

"There was speculation. They were seen talking on several occasions and then the incident Sam saw in the cafeteria. None of those seemed to be about professional issues, like cases or patients, but honestly? Mia isn't close to anyone in the OR. She was a curiosity because of that, and as I said, people gossip. No one overheard their conversations. I guess it's possible they were involved, but she's been adamant they weren't." She shrugged.

"So what was going on in the days leading up to his death?"

Carol paused and picked at a cuticle for a few seconds before she stopped, frowned at it, and shoved her hand into the cover jacket she wore over her scrubs. "Hudson was … stressed, Mia was stressed, and the tension around him was palpable. Normally, he was easy to work with—as long as you weren't his resident. The week or two before his death, he was short with everyone and rode Ted Nichols, his resident, unmercifully. I'd heard his partner was leaving, which is disruptive to patients and the docs involved and may have contributed to his mood. People were tiptoeing around him."

"Tell me what you saw."

"He had a major blowup with Nichols; he just lost it. Mia was scrubbed in on the case, and I was circulating. Unloading on Nichols wasn't unusual, really, but it seemed to me to hit a boiling point that day. He ended up throwing Nichols out of the room. Understandable, really. He thought Nichols might have cut the patient's facial nerve. He hadn't, thank God."

She hesitated. "I saw Hudson talking to Mia in the hallway several times the week of his death. The conversations always seemed … intimate but pressured, as if he didn't want to be having them. I guess—I don't have proof—he might have been involved with her."

All of which was good information, I thought as I left the hospital. But all Carol could testify to was the case she'd been involved in and the glimpses of Hudson talking to Mia. The confrontation and what was said then and during Hudson's conversations with her was Carol's opinion—hearsay. The more people I talked to, the more hopeless I felt about finding anything that would clear Mia—and the more worried I became about Angel and the repercussions of Mia being convicted.

Joanne Wilson was next on my to-do list. Mia had listed her name as one of the people we should talk to but said she wasn't a close friend. She didn't elaborate, but the subtle look on Mia's face, which she was probably unaware of, made me think she really didn't like Joanne.

In the OR, you learn—have to learn—how to read people whose faces are obscured by masks. You have to listen to the tone of their voice and watch their eyes, brows, and body positions or subtle changes in these to know what the unspoken subtext is. When you first come to work in the OR, it can feel like being in a foreign country and not knowing the language, whether verbal or physical. Based on Mia's body language, I wanted to see what Joanne had to say. There was always less of a "be nice" filter with those who weren't friends.

Wilson, a tall, dark-haired woman with a scowl on her face, arrived fifteen minutes late for our appointment at a local restaurant. She sat down across from me in the booth I had picked out and ordered a glass of wine from the hostess who'd escorted her to the table. When the hostess told her the server would be over to take her order, she snapped, "Just bring me a glass of cabernet and let the server know you did. I don't want to wait."

Ugh, not in a good mood, I thought, deciding to take a conciliatory approach in hopes of improving things. "I really appreciate you being willing to meet with me. We're interviewing people connected to Dr. Hudson and Mia Stewart to get a better picture of what happened to him," I said. "A while back, Mia says she overheard a conversation between you and Alicia Harvey in the locker room. Alicia seemed to be encouraging you to go along with an offer to hook up made by a married surgeon. According to Mia, you told Alicia you weren't going to and that, if she wanted to, she could have him. Was it Geoff Hudson?"

"Yes, as it happens, it was. Why?"

"Your name wasn't on the list of women he hit up. I wanted to confirm he was the one who approached you."

"What list?"

"We have a list of women he approached and those who would admit to hooking up with him." I decided not to tell her who had helped create the list or that Mia had supplied some of the names.

"Then I'm glad I'm not on the list."

The hostess arrived, plunked down the glass of wine, causing it to slosh dangerously close to the edge of the glass, turned, and left. I wondered if she'd spit in it as Joanne took a large mouthful.

"Mia said a friend of hers saw Alicia exiting a dictation room rather flushed and untidy, followed a few minutes later by Hudson. That would imply they had some sort of assignation, yet Alicia denies having any relationship with him other than as an employee in the department. I haven't talked to Mia's friend yet, but it sounds as if something pretty intimate happened between her and Hudson. Do you know if she acted on your suggestion to take him up on his offer?"

She watched me without commenting.

"If Alicia was involved with him, why won't she admit to it?" I asked.

"What would the point be now? He's dead. It hardly matters if he was cheating on his wife every chance he got. Why would it matter if she hooked up with him?"

"I'm trying to get a picture of what was happening in the weeks before his murder. It helps to understand what was going on, and it can reveal other avenues of investigation. She has an alibi for his time of death, which is why I can't figure out why she doesn't just admit to being involved with him. From what people have said, Alicia has a long history of indiscriminate liaisons. What difference would it make if he was just another conquest?"

She took a drink of her wine and looked around at the people in the restaurant, then stared at me. "People in the department gossip. About *everyone*. Gossiping about whether Mia killed Hudson gives them lots to feed on. They've always gossiped about Alicia. People don't really like either of them. They see Alicia's liaisons as slutty behavior, so they gossip about her, and it gives them a chance to feel superior. They see Mia as a snotty little rich girl who won't give most of us the time of day. Her getting caught kneeling next to Hudson covered in blood has caused a feeding frenzy of speculation."

I waited, and when she didn't continue, I said, "You haven't answered my question. Was Alicia involved with Hudson, and if she was, why wouldn't she admit to it?"

"She probably didn't say anything because she was in love with him. I'm guessing she didn't want people to know what her involvement with him was and then assume he was just another *indiscretion*."

Her comment stopped the conversation pretty effectively. When I finally wrapped my head around that, I said, "Alicia was in love with him? Are you sure?"

"She told me she'd hooked up with him thinking it'd be a one-off kind of thing—which was what she preferred—but he continued to see her. They'd been seeing each other for a month or so, and in the process, she fell head over heels. It was kind of sad, really. She's never been in love, as far as I know. She's always been the user—no connection, no regrets, no long-term relationships—and she seemed happy with that. Then she falls in love with a married man who's screwing women right and left and honestly expects he'll feel the same about her."

She sighed, turning her wineglass around by the stem. "He didn't, and he wasn't going to, but she couldn't see it. She knew he had been with other women, but she honestly thinks if he hadn't been killed, he'd have left his wife and married her, and he's no longer here to disprove that. I guess when you fall hard, you're willing to believe anything."

I sat back in the booth and let that sink in. "Do you think she'd have killed him if he'd told her he wasn't interested?"

She snorted a derisive laugh. "He wasn't going to ruin a good thing by telling her he wasn't interested. He was getting sex from her pretty much whenever he wanted it, even at work. Why would he cut that off?"

"If that's the case, why would he pester Mia so much? Apparently, she didn't want to take him up on his offers because he was married, and he wouldn't take no for an answer."

"Is that what Mia says?"

I nodded. "Do you think it's at all possible Mia was involved with him?"

"I've no idea what was going on between them, if anything."

"Do you think he perhaps led Alicia on with promises? You know, like 'I'll leave my wife, and we can be together'?" I asked.

"Alicia didn't need encouragement to keep seeing him. She was hooked regardless of what he'd promised her, and I think he knew it. There was no need to hold out a carrot about leaving his wife. Which makes me wonder why he would bother with Mia. Why pursue someone who isn't interested when you already have someone who is?"

Joanne continued to play with her wineglass and seemed more melancholy now. "Alicia told me she hadn't said anything to him about her feelings; she was afraid to say anything and mess up what they had. I tried to talk to her. I tried to convince her the connection they had was nothing but sex and would never become anything else. If he left his wife for her, which was highly unlikely, he couldn't be trusted to not cheat on her too. That's when she cut me off. I couldn't be happy for her and wouldn't share her fantasy, so she hasn't had anything to do with me since."

"I'm sorry."

"Well, that's how it goes when you try to talk sense to someone about a guy."

"I appreciate you telling me all this, being willing to speak to me."

"For the record, I think Mia is capable of killing Hudson," she said as she finished the last swallow of wine, stood up, and gathered her things. "There's a coldness to her I've never liked. I have no proof she was involved with him or that she killed him. But she was in the right place at the right time. If she didn't do it, then I don't know who did. Maybe your boss can find out."

"We're working on it," I replied as she turned and left.

EIGHT

ANGEL SIGHED AND SHOOK HIS HEAD. "You're not helping, *chica*. Their speculations are more damaging than helpful."

"I'm sorry. I'm not really coming up with anything that clears her. I'm discovering she wasn't well liked. Joanne's reasoning about Alicia is pretty solid. If you hadn't told a married lover you were in love with him or told him what you hoped for, then a confrontation or rebuff was unlikely. Her alibi—despite there being an extremely unlikely opportunity to have killed him—pretty much eliminates her." I could tell he was frustrated by what I'd found.

"I suppose his dalliances with others was a reason, but it sounded as if Alicia was living in her own fantasy world, and perhaps she really believed he would give up the other women and his wife once he realized how much she cared. But I didn't get that from Alicia. It was Joanne Wilson's take on things based on what Alicia told her. Alicia has denied any involvement with him to me."

"Keep digging. There's nothing that proves Mia didn't kill him, at least so far, and unless that changes, all I can do is create enough reasonable doubt that a jury won't convict her. In some ways, what you've found adds to that doubt. Although Joanne Wilson's information means Alicia might have had a reason to kill him, it looks like she didn't have an opportunity. Right now, she's a possible but highly unlikely suspect, unless you or Frost turn up something to change that."

He sipped his wine as we sat out on the back patio after dinner. "This OR sounds like a hotbed of sex and tempers and gossip. It's a wonder they get any surgery done."

I laughed. "All workplaces are like that. I remember some of the stories you told me about the DA's office. My guess is it's going on in your office too. Maybe a little less obviously than in this OR, but it's always there. Sex and gossip make the world go round, my love."

"I told you, I wasn't involved with him. I don't know why you think I was." Alicia had declined a cup of coffee when we met at a coffee shop near the hospital. She was pretty. Petite with blonde curls that ended several inches below her chin and big baby-blue eyes that would normally have given her an innocent, sweet appearance, but she was far from sweet at the moment.

"Because two people have said you were, one of whom saw you coming out of a dictation room Hudson was in. According to this person, you looked slightly disheveled and as if there'd been some intimate contact." I waited for a response. I'd learned from Frost how useful silence was for forcing someone to talk. It usually worked, but she said nothing.

"Why, if you were involved with him, would you deny it? It hardly matters now in terms of how he'd react to you admitting the relationship."

"Because it's no one's business."

"It became everyone's business when he was killed. You know investigators for the prosecution will talk to the same people I have, and then you'll be under their scrutiny. Especially if you've denied it to them as well."

She shook her head angrily. "Fine. I suppose you talked to Joanne Wilson and Brent Perkins. Everybody thinks they know what was going on, and they don't."

"Why not tell me then, set the record straight?"

"We had something special, something different from what I had with other men, and we were in love."

"He told you that?"

"We didn't talk about it, but I could tell, and I was in love with him. If he'd lived, we would have been together once he left his wife."

"What about Mia Stewart?"

"What about her? She killed him. I hope she rots in prison."

"Was he pursuing her?"

"No. He assured me he had no feelings for her; his conversations with her were work related."

"Did you believe him?"

"Of course. He wouldn't lie to me. He loved me." She stood up and shouldered her purse strap, and I watched her leave the coffee shop.

The lies we tell ourselves, I thought as the door closed behind her.

"I wanted to let you know what I found out from the women I talked to on the list," I said. Frost and I had met for lunch.

"Let me guess, they all have rock-solid alibis and no real reason to have killed him, right?"

"Yeah, pretty much. I talked to Alicia after what Joanne told me, and I pushed her pretty hard. I got her to admit she'd been involved with Hudson, and she'd convinced herself that if he'd lived, he would have left his wife, and they'd be together. Of course, by her own admission, they never talked about it. She just 'knew' that was how he felt. She'd have a motive if she found out he was involved with Mia as well, which is good, but we have nothing to connect her with the murder. The time frame makes it virtually impossible. I'm not sure her admission helps, other than to throw doubt on anything else she might say in the future."

"And Mia is sticking to her story?"

"Yeah. She continues to say he pursued her but she refused him because he was married. I'm not sure I believe her about that."

"You think she was more involved than that?"

"I think she was involved with him. Maybe not for long, but it wasn't just him trying to get her to go out with him. I think it was more involved than that. If they were an item, I'm not convinced she was the one who ended things. This guy had his choice of women who were willing to get involved with him—Alicia was more than willing. Maybe, unlike Alicia, Mia pressured him for a commitment, and he dumped her. If he dumped her, the fact that he took up with Alicia would be motive enough, I suppose."

"Yeah, but if they were involved, and he broke up with her, there would be no reason for him to pursue her," Frost said. "So we need to find out what the truth about her and Hudson is. Either way, she has a reason to kill him, whether she wanted him to leave her alone or wanted him to pay for dumping her."

"Exactly," I said. "We only have her word that she refused his attempts to hook up and that he continued to pursue her. If they were involved and he broke up with her, maybe she was the one who wouldn't give up."

Frost ran a napkin over his mouth. "Stabbing him makes more sense if she was the obsessed one, although I'm sure your boy doesn't want to hear that. Keep the pressure on Mia and see if you can get her to tell you what was really going on between them. She's unlikely to tell you or Angel she was obsessed with Hudson, but if they were involved and he dumped her, Angel needs to know that. See what others have to say. Maybe we just haven't talked to the right person yet. Somebody has to have seen something."

"I feel like we're working for the prosecution." Nothing we had found would help defend her.

"No, we're gathering information. Where it leads is out of our hands. If it points to her or something shows up that's evidence against her, Angel needs to know, or he'll get blindsided by the prosecution. And I need to know if that evidence turns up."

I'd never asked him before, but I was worried. "If there was something, some hard evidence that proved she did it, would you tell the DA?"

He sat back and took a long drink of his coffee. "I'd have a moral obligation to. It wouldn't stop Angel from defending her, but I can't keep quiet if it's hard evidence. If it's not but it's damning, then I just won't work on the case."

I nodded. I'd expected his answer, but if she was guilty, it put both me and Angel in an awkward situation. He'd have to defend her regardless of her guilt. I wasn't sure what I'd do, and it bothered me. Frost tended to be pretty black and white; I'd always seen the gray areas. I was living in one at the moment. Frost and Angel were standing on opposite sides of the question of her guilt, and I wanted to please both of them. On top of that, I didn't like her, and the thought that perhaps she was guilty kept rearing its ugly head more and more often.

"I paid a visit to Finley at his office," Frost said at last, breaking the silence. "He admitted he had been involved with Hudson's wife for about six months. He swears the two of them were at her house that night. They knew Hudson was working late, Finley's wife was sick, and the Hudsons' daughter was at a sleepover, so it seemed like a perfect opportunity for a little cuddle in the comfort of her home. Then I met with Beverly Hudson at her office to see what she had to say. I didn't mention that Finley had told me they were involved, but she finally admitted to the ongoing affair and verified his story."

I shook my head in exasperation. "God, does everybody cheat on their spouse? This job—this case—it's beginning to feel that way."

"No, not everybody, but if people didn't cheat, we'd lose a ton of clients."

"Yeah, that's true. Sad but true." I took a bite of my sandwich, but the subject matter was getting to me, so I changed the subject. "Why go to their offices?"

He leaned his forearms on the booth's table and grinned at me. "People don't like investigators or cops showing up at their workplaces—especially docs and lawyers. It alerts the staff, clients, and partners that something's up. They often talk just to get rid of us and be able to tell everyone it was nothing."

"Clever. I'll have to remember that."

"They verified each other's story. It doesn't mean they didn't figure at some point they'd be asked about the affair. They could have worked this all out before anyone ever talked to them. That's what I'd have done. There's no one who can confirm what they say happened."

Frost continued. "I've been talking to Hudson's neighbors to see if anyone noticed Finley arriving or leaving that night, and I'm doing the same in Finley's neighborhood. So far, I'm coming up with nothing. It's as bad as a high-crime area after something happens—nobody saw anything, nobody knows anything."

"If Finley's plan was to kill Geoff, I'd make sure someone other than his wife, the woman I was cheating with, could back my story up."

"Maybe, but sometimes this kind of alibi looks more likely than a totally sewn-up one. I mean, how many of us think about alibis? How many people ever need one?"

"If I was going to kill someone, though, I'd make sure I had an airtight alibi," I said.

"Look, we have time. The trial isn't until the end of June, so we've got time to keep digging. We'll find something."

"I don't know what to think. There's nothing to back up Mia's claim that she didn't do it or that anyone else who makes a likely suspect did it. Angel can't do much with a defense like that."

"Stuff turns up. It always—or almost always—does."

"Fingers crossed."

NINE

A FEW DAYS LATER, I TALKED WITH MIA AGAIN. I didn't think she'd killed Hudson. I hadn't found anything to prove or disprove her involvement, but the entitled, somewhat condescending way she spoke to me reinforced what her coworkers had said about her. My antipathy wasn't serious enough to refuse to talk to her; it just made doing so a chore. She'd been cool toward me since our first meeting at her parent's house, but she'd answered my questions. Perhaps my standing up to her after our last conversation had put her in her place. At least I hoped so.

"I've heard Hudson didn't have a great relationship with his resident. Can you tell me what your take on that was?"

"Residents are assigned to a service for a year, and things usually go smoothly. But Hudson and Nichols never hit it off. At first, it was just annoyance, but that changed over time. Geoff rode him mercilessly. The guy wasn't all that good, and I always wondered how he'd gotten a surgical residency with Geoff. He was a nice guy but a quiet, passive person and he took his lumps from Geoff without comment.

"I tried to soften Geoff's relentless badgering by being kind to Nichols and helping him when I could. After one particularly bad case, I suggested he ask the chief of surgical services to intervene. He refused and seemed resigned to how he was being treated.

"He said he respected Geoff because he was so talented, and he knew he had a lot of work to do to prove himself. I'm not sure he'd have ever been able to do that or that Geoff would have toned his criticisms down.

"I wasn't the only staff member who hoped the conflict wouldn't come to a head before Nichols finished his rotation. Despite all his charm, Geoff had a vicious, critical side, which was never more obvious than when he worked with Nichols.

"I've wondered if they didn't have some fatal confrontation that night. They'd just finished a complex neck dissection, and I heard Geoff rode Nichols the entire time. Maybe something he said flipped a switch for Nichols. He's totally passive, but even passive people have triggers. I could see Geoff pushing him over the edge."

And despite the possibility of Nichols being a suspect, I wondered if Mia wasn't using Ted as a scapegoat for her own benefit. He said he'd seen her holding the osteotome and telling Geoff he "deserved" something, presumably getting stabbed. I could certainly understand her wanting everyone to consider him a possible suspect. If so, she was good at alluding to it under the guise of feeling sorry for him. Regardless of Mia's intent, Nichols was someone who had to be interviewed.

"He's strayed in the past, but he'd always been subtle about it. Recently, though, it was obvious he was hunting. So something changed," Brent Perkins said as we drank coffee in the cafeteria on his break. "From what I've heard, he hit up a couple of the nurses in the ICU where I work. He issued his invitations so they were casual, easy to decline, and wouldn't make working with him uncomfortable, but it was clear what he was suggesting."

"So once they turned him down, he didn't pursue them further?"

"Not that I know of. I can give you a couple names of women he approached."

"That would help." I waited while he wrote down two names and handed me the napkin. "What do you know about him and Alicia Harvey?"

"I try not to be too judgmental about people. As long as what they do isn't hurting anyone, it's none of my business. But Alicia made a name for herself and seemed to enjoy the notoriety. She was pretty open about her sex life—more power to her, in my opinion—but attitudes are very different when it's a woman. People talked and judged her for it. Based on what I saw, she was involved with Hudson. I don't know how seriously. Her dalliances—they really couldn't be called affairs—never lasted long."

"I understand you witnessed her leaving a dictation room and Hudson exiting a short while later. Is that what makes you think she was involved with him?"

He snorted a laugh. "Yeah. I was coming to the OR to pick up a cutdown tray—we didn't have any on hand—and I saw him go into a dictation room. She followed him into it. It took me a few minutes to get the tray from the front desk, and on my way back to the ICU, she popped out of the room. Her hair cover was off, and her hair was messed up. She was running her hand through her hair to smooth it, and her lips were reddened. She saw me and frowned. Hudson left shortly after she did. I'd put money on the fact that he got a quick blow job."

"What d'you make of her demeanor when she exited the room?"

"That she wasn't happy I'd seen her. He looked a little disconcerted when he saw me. Regardless of who he slept with, he was always somewhat circumspect at work. I mean, he had a reputation, but he didn't talk about his conquests or, as far as I know, have any sex at the hospital. It was obvious he was trolling, but it was the first time I'd ever witnessed anything compromising at work. I think it was Alicia's idea and she surprised him."

"If he didn't want their affair public, why would he go along with that?"

"The dictation rooms are small, and they've got doors with frosted windows that can be locked." He paused and shrugged. "Do you know any guys who'd turn down a blow job offered like that? I don't."

"No, probably not," I said, embarrassed. I could ask all sorts of questions in the OR that many would consider embarrassing, but hearing about blow jobs from people I didn't know made me uncomfortable. *The things you learn about yourself*, I thought.

Changing the subject, I asked, "What do you know about his resident, Ted Nichols?"

"He's a nice guy, but as my grandmother used to say, Ted wouldn't say suey if the hogs were eating him. I don't know him well, other than working with him when he comes to the ICU with a patient. You might talk to Chris Johannson, Finley's ortho resident, and Mark Gutierrez, the anesthesia tech. They're both friends with him. They could probably tell you more than I can."

The two nurses Brent indicated Hudson had hit on said he'd made some subtle approaches a few weeks back, and both had declined. He'd been pleasant about it and had said nothing further to either nurse. Again, I wondered why, if he was involved with Alicia, he would pursue Mia. Some men truly can't deal with rejection, but he was turned down by others and hadn't pursued or harassed them, so why Mia?

TEN

THE MORE I KNEW ABOUT HUDSON, his wife, and Finley, the more the issue of infidelity—and all the reasons it would give someone to justify killing a spouse or a lover—kept circling my brain. Love and hate were two sides to an extremely thin coin, and it often didn't take much to flip from one side to the other.

I stopped at a friend's parents' house to pick up Teo on my way home. Allen Elliott, my friend Chip Elliott's dad, made a sad face when he answered the door holding Teo in his arms. Allen had always reminded me of David Sedaris. He had short light-brown hair and wore a pair of round glasses. He wasn't tall, topping out at about five foot seven, compared to his husband Phil, a tall, lean, scholarly-looking attorney. In lighter moments, he had a wicked sense of humor.

"So soon? I'm not ready to hand him back."

Teo eyed me as he sat in Allen's arms, one arm wrapped around Allen's neck, the other holding an obviously new stuffed toy. Allen, Phil, and my mother-in-law spoiled him rotten. "Be careful, I might just leave him with you."

"Stay here!" Teo shouted, clearly not wanting to leave. Who would?

"Baby, we need to get home. Your daddy will be home soon." I watched as he drew his eyebrows together and glared at me. "You spoil him rotten, Allen, and he doesn't need help with that."

"What's a favorite uncle supposed to do?"

He opened the door further and invited me in. Allen and Phil's normally immaculate living room looked as if a hurricane had hit it. Toys—and there were many—were scattered across the floor, and remnants of a snack sat on the coffee table. I had to smile. Allen had tried to keep the living room clean by putting the snack on a large place mat, and the floor around the coffee table was covered in a plastic sheet with bears on it.

"Come in for a bit," he said. I sat down on the couch as Allen deposited Teo on the floor next to several of his toys. "You look annoyed. What's up?"

"Frost and I are helping Angel with a new case. A cheating surgeon was supposedly killed by a nurse he was trying to hit on. She wasn't the only one he was hitting on, and I've confirmed that at least one of the women took him up on the offer. Apparently, cheating was his side hustle. It baffles me. I know it happens all the time. God knows Frost and I follow all sorts of partners around, trying to discover whether they're cheating or not, but if you're married and want to cheat, why get not just get divorced?"

"It doesn't always work that way, sweetie, you know that. Divorce isn't an easy decision or process, and it can get ugly fast. Sometimes, it's easier to go with the flow and get your jollies elsewhere."

"You and Phil have been together for quite a while, right?"

"Forty-three years."

"Have things been good for you?"

"For the most part, yes." He sat back and scrutinized me. "Are you and Angel doing okay?"

"We're fine. This case makes me wonder what keeps people together. I think my parents loved each other, but kids don't always know what goes on in a marriage unless it's out in the open. Angel's parents seem to love each other, but they're Catholic, and Catholic or not, that generation, as far as I can tell, rarely considers divorce unless there is abuse or something equally serious going on."

He was quiet for a bit and then said, "It's hard to say what keeps people together. Some people stay together out of obligation or fear of being alone, some figure the alternatives are no better than what they currently have, and some stay together because in the end they love each other." I heard him sigh. "With Phil and me, it's because we love each other, but we went through a period a year or so into our relationship where it wasn't clear to either of us. We nearly broke up over it."

"Did either of you cheat?" It was quiet for a moment. "I'm sorry, I shouldn't have asked that."

"No, I don't mind," he said finally. "We didn't cheat on each other, but we separated for a time with the understanding that we were both free to … I guess free to experiment with other people to try to figure out what we wanted and whether we wanted to be in a relationship with each other."

I sat without responding. I wished I hadn't asked him about this intimate, personal part of his life. Sometimes I just didn't know when to shut up.

"It was eye-opening. I discovered that what was out there wasn't what I wanted. I wanted Phil, and thank God he felt the same way. We got back together six months later and made a commitment to each other. When we could, we made it legal, and it wasn't long after that we adopted Chip. It felt as if our lives were complete then."

He tilted his head and furrowed his brows. "One thing we promised each other was we would be honest. I think all you can ask of anyone is for them to be honest with you. Love is fickle—sometimes it lasts and sometimes it doesn't. All you can do is promise not to lie to your partner, to not deceive them. If there's trust, that's all you need."

My eyes blurred with tears. I nodded. "I didn't mean to stir up unpleasant memories."

"You haven't. Talking to you has reminded me of the commitment Phil and I made, which is always a good thing. It's easy to become complacent and take your partner for granted. You need to work to see it doesn't happen. If you don't, that's when trouble starts." He grinned at me. "I'm glad you brought it up, actually. I need to do something special for Phil tonight."

That made me smile.

He got serious again. "Parenting can have a huge effect on a couple," he said, tipping his head in Teo's direction. "That's when you really have to work at it, to remember your child isn't the only important person in the house. I think when couples only see themselves as parents, and forget they're also friends and lovers, that causes problems." He reached out and squeezed my hand. "Phil and I are always here for both of you if you need us. Plus, we love babysitting."

I smiled. "I know. I'm so lucky in my choice of friends—and not just because of the babysitting services."

Now for the fun part, I thought as I stood up and Allen collected Teo's travel bag. Dragging him away from a day of indulgence was never fun. "Okay, little man, time to head home."

And the temper tantrum began. *I love my son, I love my son, I do not want to go to prison, I do not look good in orange*, I kept repeating to myself as I buckled him into his car seat and headed home with him screaming his lungs out all the way, despite his favorite Raffi songs playing.

Personally, I had begun to hate the song, *"Baby Beluga."* There were times that song and other kids' songs ran on an endless loop in my head. I'd even caught myself humming them in the shower. Maybe I should introduce Teo to Taylor Swift or Bruce Springsteen or Bonnie Raitt and throw in some Maná, Enrique Iglesias, and Ricky Martin for the Spanish. At least if I sang those in the shower, it'd be worth it.

ELEVEN

FINE!" MIA ALL BUT SHOUTED AT ME. "I was briefly involved with him—briefly—and cared about him, but I broke it off when I found out he was married. I hadn't made any friends who could have taken me aside and told me about him. He never talked about his wife or being married at work, and he never wore a ring. And I didn't ask, which was stupid. It only lasted a few weeks before I broke it off. No one knew about it, so I can't give you the names of anyone who might have. *I didn't talk to anyone about it*." She paced in front of me frowning. "All anyone knew about was the episode in the cafeteria, and they drew their own conclusions from that. I don't know what else to tell you, and I don't appreciate you badgering me."

I was losing patience with her. Mia acted as if we had no right to ask about anything, and I hadn't been able to convince her it was in her best interest to talk more openly to me or Angel about it.

"Do you *want* to go to prison?"

She looked surprised. "I'm not going to prison."

That surprised me. If I were her, I'd have been seriously worried about the possibility. "There's a damn good chance you could, and you need to take this seriously. You had motive and opportunity, and you have no alibi. Why do you think you were arrested? You're the prime suspect. You were there. You say you were in the sterile supply room doing an inventory, but no one, Mia, *no one* can verify that you were still there when he was stabbed. You had access to instruments, and you had a good reason to want to get rid of him.

"Most incriminating of all, you were kneeling next to his body, covered in blood, and had handled the osteotome. Ted Nichols says you were holding the osteotome over Hudson, looked angry, and were telling Hudson he deserved something. So far, you haven't given us anything to work with that could at least cast reasonable doubt about you murdering him. And you've lied to us about your involvement with him. You should think about that and start cooperating."

She frowned and then relented. "I didn't tell you we were involved because it was embarrassing. He didn't like it when I called it off. He claimed he loved me and would leave his wife for me if I'd give him time to file for divorce. But that's what they all say, and they never follow through."

"It sounds like that's happened to you before."

Her face twisted into a mask of annoyance. "No, it hasn't. I've known women it's happened to. All men lie. You just have to figure out which lies are worth ignoring."

That was more cynicism than I'd expected. "And you didn't believe him, I take it."

"Of course not. A week after I broke up with him, he took up with Alicia. That says it all."

"So what happened in the cafeteria that night? All anyone knows is that you ended up slapping him. What was said?"

"He was impossible to deal with after the breakup. Not just with me, with everyone. Frustration radiated off him, and it didn't take much to set him off. He rode Ted Nichols unmercifully. Honestly, I don't know why Ted didn't report him or quit. Ted had more reason to kill him than I did.

"After we finished a case one night, I finally asked him what was wrong, why was he being so hateful. He said he was getting ragged on by his wife, his partner was leaving to move to another state because her husband had been transferred, and the fact that his partner was leaving had upset his office manager. Apparently, some staff would have to be let go. And of course there was Nichols. That wasn't new, but on top of everything else, he … wasn't handling things well at all.

"He asked if I would get a cup of coffee with him. He said he missed talking to me. Like an idiot, I figured there was little harm in doing that. I thought maybe he'd finally let go if we could talk. But it was a mistake."

"What happened?"

"He said he was having a difficult time dealing with things. Losing me had been hard. His wife was giving him grief about everything, he claimed. He said his wife fired the nanny because she thought he was screwing her. He says he wasn't, but who knows? I mean, he was screwing Alicia at that point, so why not the nanny?

"I felt like a complete idiot. I didn't know he even had a child until he said that. He said he'd never mentioned it because he thought it would affect our relationship. He never mentioned a lot of things.

"He kept going on about his wife, and I lost it. I told him I didn't want to hear any more, that he should either divorce her or shut up and stop whining. I got up to leave. He stood up and asked me to stay and talk. I told him no, that I was done listening to his whining … He called me a bitch, and I slapped him. That's what the orderly saw, and that was the start of more problems.

"My supervisor asked me to take a couple days off. I wasn't going to file a complaint, although she urged me to. I just wanted it to go away. I thought the time off would help. When I got back, he stopped me in the parking lot that evening and apologized. He said … he told me—again—he'd have left his wife for me and that he loved me. I think he meant it, but the absurdity of him telling me that while he was screwing Alicia was so like him. It was all about him."

"And this case is all about you, Mia. You need to stop concealing things. You told the police you weren't involved with Hudson, and it turns out you were. If the prosecution somehow finds out, they'll parade it all in front of the jury, who will nail you for the murder. Your aunt may have pulled strings that got you bail, but neither your aunt, your parents, nor your uncle has any say in what happens during the trial. Withholding information from us does, and it's not smart."

I got up and began walking to the door of her apartment when I heard her say, "Why wasn't I told you and Angel were married and have a son?"

I turned around and blinked several times. Her question caught me by surprise. It made me uneasy, and I really didn't like her addressing Angel by his nickname. Professionally, he used Angelo. Angel was a family nickname. And it really bothered me that she knew about Teo. "Excuse me?"

"I want to know why you weren't up front with that. You keep badgering me about telling you the truth. Seems like neither of you did."

"Our personal life isn't up for discussion, and we don't owe you an explanation. We're not accused of murder, and you're a client."

"I read his bio on the website, and it was vague. It only says how long he's practiced, his job history, and that he's a native Coloradan and married. I knew he was married. The ring's hard to miss. But I wanted to know more about who was representing me. So I asked my uncle, and he filled me in. I guess he figured I was family, so he gave me more info than if I was a regular client. Businesses investigate their employees. You two are my employees." She shrugged, as if what she had done was normal.

"That can be remedied easily enough."

"Not if your husband wants to keep his job."

I stared hard at her, tamping down my immediate urge to assault her. "Stay out of our personal lives if you want him to continue to represent you. There are some lines you don't cross."

All the way home, I debated whether to tell Angel or Frost what she'd said. I was angry and unsettled, but telling Angel or Frost would infuriate them. Angel had to represent her, and knowing what she'd done would complicate an already complicated situation. Frost would go into full protective police mode and try to get me off the case. I huffed out a breath and wondered what possible reason would have made her investigate us or mention it to me.

Hudson had been right. She was a bitch, and I felt some sympathy for him.

TWELVE

"WHAT HAPPENED WHEN YOU TALKED TO MIA TODAY?" Angel asked as we got ready for bed.

I hadn't mentioned Mia's threat. Regardless of what I'd said to her, Angel couldn't get out of representing her easily. If he tried to, it'd create problems between him and Owen Cameron. If I told him, either he wouldn't see her invasion of privacy as an issue serious enough to back out of the case or it would add to his worry. If it made him as angry as it had me, he might do something rash. Things were touchy enough with this case; I didn't want to throw more fuel on the fire.

I focused on finding my sleep shirt in the bureau drawer to give myself time to collect my thoughts. "After I pushed her pretty hard, she finally admitted to having an affair with Hudson. She says it was brief and she called it off after learning he was married. She talked me through the last month and her encounters with him. She says the slap was because he called her a bitch when she told him to quit complaining to her about his wife, and a few days later when he apologized to her, he told her he loved her and would have left his wife for her. But that's Mia's version. Whether he said any of that is anybody's guess. It's not really consistent with him screwing Alicia, and what I've heard so far gives her a decent motive, in my opinion."

"Jesus, don't say that to anyone but me," he said as he stripped and put his clothes away. Angel had never worn pajamas in all the time we'd been together, and the sight of him made me rethink the sleep shirt. He sat down on his side of the bed and watched as I undressed.

"It sounds like he was as entitled as Mia seems to be. He wanted what he wanted and wasn't used to hearing no," I said. "It probably never occurred to him how ridiculous he sounded when he told her he loved her, all the while screwing Alicia Harvey—but that assumes she's telling the truth about what they talked about and what he said later. She's lied since we connected with her, so I don't know if she's telling the truth this time or not. Regardless of what was said, Mia had cause to hate him at the very least. Maybe he said something to her the night of his death and pushed her over the edge."

Angel groaned. "You're not reassuring me at all."

"She's infuriating. I have to drag everything out of her. I finally told her if she didn't start talking, you'd have a hard time keeping her out of prison."

"You don't tread lightly, do you?" He stood, pulled the covers down, and got into bed.

"Somebody needed to rattle her cage. If I'm the bad guy, then you can be her knight in shining armor." He gave me a look as if I'd just confirmed something for him, and I wondered if Mia had complained about me. "I think she just assumes that because Owen and her aunt are lawyers, she's going to walk. They managed to finagle bail for her, so in her mind, she may think she won't be convicted, that they'll step in and fix everything. I don't think she's even considered how serious her situation is and that everything points to her. What she has told me makes some sense, if it's true, but I never come away feeling like she's telling me the whole truth.

"It doesn't make sense that he'd pursue her like that and carry on with another woman. I don't know, I think there's something more to it. She's sticking to her story that she ended the relationship, and he wasn't happy about it." I slipped into bed next to him, minus my sleep shirt, and cuddled up.

"All I can say is I wouldn't be fine with him telling me he loved me and taking up with another woman right in front of me. I'd be hurt and pissed. And continuing to pester her if he dumped her and took up with someone else makes no sense at all." I paused, then continued. "I know this is irrelevant, but I don't like her."

"Apparently, she doesn't like you either. She called this afternoon and said she didn't want to talk to you again. That if there were further questions, I could ask her."

"Good. You can have her or let her deal with Frost. If she doesn't like me, let him make her life miserable. Maybe she'll fire us all, including you, and we can be done with this clusterfuck."

"Okay," he said, drawing the word out as if he didn't want a fight. "If that's all that happened, why doesn't she want to talk to you?"

It was now or never to say something to him about what she'd said, but I didn't. "She's just an entitled little bitch who seems to think she doesn't have to cooperate, and I push her. She's not used to being pushed or confronted when she's acting like a twat."

"A twat? When did you become British?"

"All those British shows we've watched lately have rubbed off, I guess. Twat's a great word, and it's better than the c-word, but both apply."

I started to turn over, away from him, and he stopped me. "I shouldn't have brought this up in our bedroom. Don't turn away. Come here, *Corazón.*"

I was glad the sleep shirt lay abandoned on the dresser.

"He's got no complaints on file with the state regulatory agency and no recent lawsuits," Frost said to Angel and me as he sat holding Teo, who was contentedly playing with his car keys, on his lap. Frost had certainly earned the honorary grandfather title. He trumped even Angel—much to Angel's annoyance.

"Story, Grampa," Teo demanded.

"Not tonight, buddy. I need to talk to your mom and dad about business."

When Angel wasn't around, Frost was still telling Teo cop stories. He left out the gory details, but they weren't Disney stories. Or maybe they were—it just wasn't Bambi's mother getting killed. Frost usually ended his stories with an injunction to Teo not to do whatever crime Frost had been describing because it was wrong and he'd end up in jail. Frost always added that jail was a "bad place filled with bad people." Teo would nod solemnly and ask for another story. It was anyone's guess how much of it Teo understood.

After the "slit throat" episode, which of course Teo repeated in front of his horrified grandmother, resulting in a lecture for me, I'd complained about Frost's stories a few days later.

"Frost, he's old enough now to understand at least some of what you're telling him, and he's just two. Can't you find other stories to tell him, maybe read him one of his books?"

"You only have so long to talk to your kids before they get to an age where they think you're an idiot and stop listening, so you've got to get the lessons in early. Teo will know the consequences of being stupid, and you won't have to bail him out later. 'Sides, it never hurt my boys."

A plus, I guessed, if it worked. I had to admit his two boys had never been delinquents, so maybe it was a good thing.

Tonight he told Teo no, and surprisingly there was no tantrum. Teo just wiggled off his lap and wandered off, jangling Frost's keys in time to some unrecognizable song he was singing.

"You might want to reclaim your keys before he loses them."

"He's fine. We do this a lot at my house." Frost continued, "Hudson had a lawsuit probably ten years ago. No judgment against him and nothing since. He's got a clean record with the state. No one unhappy enough with him to file a complaint, anyway. I spoke with the chief of surgery, and she wasn't terribly helpful. All she would say was he was an excellent surgeon and known for his top-notch care of patients. She said the hospital had never had a reason to temporarily suspend or consider permanently ending his surgical privileges, and they were all shocked by his murder."

Frost rolled his eyes. "I tried to push her about his behavior with Mia and other women in the department, but she clammed up. His behavior is a touchy subject, and while it never ended as badly as this episode did, I think there have been other problems. I just couldn't get her to talk about it."

"Mia told me she refused to file a complaint, which is unfortunate, so it's her word against the official line. Maybe the other women didn't pursue it either, but from your point of view," I said to Angel, "that might or might not be a good thing. There's nothing on record as far as we know, but that also doesn't ID any other women he may have harassed who could be considered suspects."

I continued. "In my experience, it takes something pretty serious for a hospital to suspend or revoke privileges. She's unlikely to discuss any close calls or warnings he was given. Hospitals don't air their dirty linen."

"I'll have to subpoena her and the head of HR for a deposition anyway. I'll get copies of their files on him and copies of any complaints or incident reports," Angel said, entering his to-do list on his phone. "Any other legal issues?"

"According to what I could find out, he's had a few speeding tickets and one domestic disturbance," Frost said. "I cajoled Roberts into digging out the report. The next-door neighbor's wife called the cops about six weeks ago after hearing a loud argument—loud enough to be heard by the next-door neighbor, and those houses aren't close together—accompanied by breaking glass and shrieking coming from a woman, who they presumed was Hudson's wife.

"When the cops arrived, neither of them appeared injured, and both claimed it was just an argument that had gotten a little out of control and resulted in some decorative ceramic pieces being smashed. Their daughter was at a friend's house, and both Hudson and his wife said they weren't injured and apologized for the trouble, so the cops left, and no further incidents were reported. Sounds like both of them have a temper."

Angel had been listening with a frown on his face, not unusual when he was thinking about a case. "Annie, Mia told you his behavior was erratic in the weeks leading up to his death. A disturbance like that backs up that he was under some stress, unless those kinds of arguments were a norm for him. Frost, you talked to the neighbors. Had they heard other arguments lately? What did they think of the couple?"

"Nobody was talking when I canvassed the neighborhood about Finley, and at that point I wasn't aware the incident had taken place. I can go back and talk to the neighbor who called 911 and see what else she knows."

"Annie, would you do that? She might be more open to talking to a woman. I think we need to find out if this was a regular thing with them." He glanced up from his phone at me. "What did Mia and her coworkers think about his state of mind?"

I sighed. "A number of the people I've talked to so far said he was stressed for some reason. Mia said he was irritable and seemed under pressure of some sort in the last few weeks. She saw an argument—or at least a heated discussion—with his partner. Apparently, the partner was leaving the practice because her husband had been transferred.

"That's stressful. The remaining partner has to pick up the patient load of the departing one, and depending on how busy the practice is, that could be a fair number of patients. It's also a busy surgical practice, so it's not like they see patients every couple months for routine issues. Their patients usually require surgery, and Hudson was already one of the busiest surgeons at the hospital. Then there's the issue with his resident, which, from what Mia and others have said, had been going on since the guy arrived. Added to that, there was tension and unhappiness at home.

"He had plenty of reasons to be unpredictable," I said as Teo plopped his stuffed dog on my lap and handed Frost his keys.

"Thanks, buddy," Frost said, ruffling his hair as he slipped his keys into his jacket pocket.

"Welcome." Teo toddled off back to his room, and once again I was surprised at the ease Frost had with my son. I was going to have to find out what the secret was. I'd have been looking for my keys for days if I'd given them to Teo.

"I'm not sure the issue with his wife was a norm for him. I'll set up an appointment to talk to her and see what I can find out, and I can see what the neighbor who called 911 has to say when I contact her. I'm going to arrange an interview with Ted Nichols, his resident, to find out what was at the bottom of their conflict. I'm also going to connect with two people who've been identified as friends of Nichols to get their take on the conflict." I hesitated, then said, "The other factor in the stress might be Mia harassing him, not the other way around."

Angel scowled at me. "You're not working for the prosecution, Annie."

"No, but if that was the case, then you need to know and figure out a way to defend her against a situation that would make her even more likely to kill him."

"She's got a point," Frost said.

"You two make me nuts." Angel sighed. "Okay, see what you can find out. I'll need to depose the wife and the resident, so try not to piss them off." I scowled back at him, and he waved his hand in surrender. "Find out as much as you can about his behavior with other women in the department and what happened the night Hudson was killed and let me know. I can depose them if what they know is helpful."

THIRTEEN

I SAT IN ANGEL'S OFFICE, LISTENING TO WHAT HE'D HEARD from Mia. I was always a bit stunned by his office on the seventeenth floor in a downtown Denver skyscraper with a great view of the Front Range. He'd certainly moved up in the world since his assistant DA days.

"What all did she have to say?" I asked.

"Not really anything more than what she's told you." He frowned and looked a bit puzzled. His exhaustion was clear; dark circles lived under his eyes, and as it was nearing six in the evening, a dark five o'clock shadow made his face look even more weary. "I don't know why she arranged the meeting, to be honest. Everything she talked about was what she'd told you. I … I got the impression it was more of an excuse to hang out. It was weird."

"She's weird," I replied. I was probably being paranoid, but it seemed in character that she'd want an excuse to be alone with him.

"This whole case is weird. And we're no closer to figuring out who, other than Mia, might be the killer or finding any way to clear her. It keeps me up at night."

"I know. I'm worried about you. You're not sleeping or eating well. I wish to hell you could walk away from this case."

"I wish I could, too, but I can't."

I reached across his desk and gave his hand a squeeze. "Well then,

Frost and I will just keep looking for something that would help prove she didn't do it. There are plenty of people who had a reason to want to see Hudson dead, but they all have alibis. Nichols doesn't really have an alibi—it's like Mia's. He says he was in the locker room, but no one can vouch for him being there or when he was there. No one can vouch for what he says Mia said to Hudson either."

"No, but he was an eyewitness. That carries a lot of weight. Both of them had a strong motive to kill him, but I can probably use Nichols's relationship with Hudson and the fact that his alibi isn't ironclad to throw some reasonable doubt at the jury."

"He certainly had an opportunity. The locker rooms have doors exiting into the main hallway leading to the OR and the ICU. He could have slipped out, waited for Hudson to come back from talking to the family, stabbed him, and returned to the dressing room without anyone seeing him. If blood had gotten on his scrubs, he could have easily changed into new scrubs. It was late, and people had either gone home or were working in rooms, as far as I can determine, so he'd have had time to do it unnoticed."

"That's good information. I can't imagine wading through this case without your help. Your OR expertise is invaluable." He leaned back in his chair and scrubbed his hands over his face.

I smiled. "Then again, if he stabbed Hudson and quickly walked off, which would be a great way to avoid being seen, maybe there wasn't anything on them."

I stood up and walked over to him, motioning for him to stand up. "Like this," I said.

I stepped in close, wrapped my left arm around Angel's waist, jerked him into me, and made a stabbing motion with my right hand. I grinned when he jumped in surprise.

"If you did it like that, you'd get blood on you. But if he stepped up to Hudson and stabbed him, then immediately walked away, there wouldn't have been enough contact for any blood to get on him."

Angel sat back down and frowned. "That's not a comforting thought, since Mia had blood on her scrub top."

"In the photos, it looked to me like it could have been transferred from her hands to her top. Hard to say, and she hasn't said anything about it. I can ask her but I'm not really her favorite person right now."

"Let's give her some cool down time before you broach it."

"His catting around had probably created a lot of ill will. I haven't talked to Hudson's wife to see what she'll tell me from her end, but I think his behavior was his attempt to self-soothe with women, and it wasn't working. Maybe that's why it had ramped up in the week or so leading up to his death."

I walked over to the window and stared out. "If we believe that Mia cut things off and he wouldn't let go, then the confrontation in the cafeteria may have been the last straw for both of them. If he tried something more, she could have killed him. But you don't just carry an osteotome around in your back pocket. They're generally inside ortho spine instrument sets, not rolling around free. Whoever lifted the osteotome had to take it from a used set after it left the OR where the set was used. It couldn't have been taken during a case. Its absence would be noticed once the instruments were counted. And they're big, hard to conceal. That's not easy, and lifting one from a set implies premeditation."

"Thank you, Counselor," he said, heavy on the sarcasm. "So far, she hasn't talked to you about his death, right?"

"Not in any great detail, no."

"I want to keep making her repeat the story to make sure it stays consistent. You keep saying you don't think she's telling the whole truth. Maybe if I keep pushing, she will. I'm going to arrange for her to come in. I know she doesn't like you, but that may work to our advantage if you're there. It could make her uncomfortable, and we might get something helpful out of her. Once we have the whole story from her, then I'll know what direction to go."

He looked worried, and I watched as he ran his hand through his hair distractedly. Frost tapped pencils when he was anxious or agitated; Angel ran his hands through his hair. It was all but standing on end at the moment.

I walked over and smoothed it down with my hand. "Are you just tired, or is there something else going on?"

"I'm worried. Nothing you or Frost have found helps clear her, and all I'm left with is trying to convince a jury there were plenty of people who *could* have killed him and hope I create enough doubt that they acquit." He let his head fall back against the headrest of his leather desk chair and scrubbed both hands over his face again. "I could lose my job over this clusterfuck."

"Owen wouldn't fire you … would he?" The threat from Mia echoed through my head.

"Mia is his niece, he and his sister are lawyers, and they expect a positive outcome. Owen's checking in almost daily to see how it's going, and he's diverting new cases to Rick Edwards. It's driving me nuts. At the very least, Owen could keep me in a holding pattern for years. I haven't made full partner yet. I don't know if he'd do that, but then I don't know that he wouldn't. The only sure thing is no one will be happy if I lose the case."

"We'll figure something out."

I stroked his hair as I stood behind his office chair and looked down at him. I let my eyes wander over his face as he rested his head on the back of his chair, his eyes closed, lashes resting on his cheeks, full mouth relaxed. I remember thinking the first time he introduced himself to me that his nickname was very appropriate—he looked like an angel. When his eyes were open and he was in a playful mood, he looked like a very naughty angel. I hadn't seen the playfulness in weeks.

"I hope you're right, *chica*. Where are you at with setting up an interview with Hudson's wife?"

"After the last few days of her avoiding me—in court or with clients, per her admin, or playing telephone tag with her—I finally connected, and I'm going to talk to her tomorrow afternoon. Unless she cancels on me. I get the sense she doesn't want to talk to me. Not sure why. Despite having good reason to off him, she'd have no access to an osteotome, wouldn't know where she could get one, and wouldn't know how to get into and out of the OR without being seen. She has nothing to worry about, but maybe the reason she keeps blowing me off is she's embarrassed by all of it coming to light." I shrugged. "Assuming I get to talk to her, I'll let you know what I find out. I plan to pop over to the neighbor who called 911 and see what she has to say. She wasn't at home when Frost was canvassing the neighbors, so I'll see if I can connect with her."

Angel nodded. "I'm deposing the chief of surgery and the head of HR tomorrow, and I've subpoenaed copies of Hudson's personnel files and any files kept by the chief of surgery on him. I need to find out if his behavior was an established pattern or something more recent. I'm going to be tied up all day. It may run late."

I was early for the meeting with Beverly Hudson, so I pulled out the note I had written the neighbor's address on and walked up the side-walk to her door with my business card ready.

The woman who answered the door was probably in her sixties, had a pleasant round face, and was nicely dressed. I held out my card. "Mrs. Clayborne? I'm Annie Collins. I work for the attorney repre-senting Mia Stewart regarding the death of Dr. Hudson. I wondered if I could talk to you for a few minutes?"

"Sure. Is this about the 911 call I made?"

I nodded as she stepped aside and invited me into the house. "Tell me what happened. What did you notice that made you call 911?" I asked as she offered me a chair in the living room.

"It was, oh, probably about nine in the evening, and my husband and I were in the family room. It's on the side of the house, and you can see into the Hudson's living room from our window." She smiled hurriedly. "Not that we do that. I was just trying to explain how I heard what was going on."

I smiled. She probably did check them out through her windows, but that wasn't why I was here. "And you heard them fighting?"

"Well, I heard a lot of yelling. I have no idea what they were yelling about. I wasn't close enough to hear the actual conversation. A man and a woman were yelling, so I assumed it was them. The blinds on the windows facing us were closed. I ignored it at first, but it kept getting louder, and then I heard the smashing sounds and her scream. I called 911 because I didn't know if she was in danger." She shrugged. "The police came and talked to them, then got my statement, and I assume everything was okay. The police never got back to me."

"Was that kind of thing normal for them?"

"No, not at all, which is why it alarmed me. I mean, I've heard some arguments, especially if they're out in the backyard or the driveway, but nothing like that one."

"What were the arguments that you were able to hear about?"

"I don't like to tell tales …"

"He's been murdered, Mrs. Clayborne. Anything you can tell me might help."

She smoothed her pant legs nervously. "They weren't a happy couple. From the arguments I overheard, he wasn't faithful, you know, not … well, apparently he strayed … a lot, and they argued about it frequently." Her face flamed with color.

"But the argument you called the police about—smashing pottery and her screaming—was a first?"

"Yes."

"Nothing since?"

"No, nothing like that. It's been quiet."

Well, that didn't add anything to what I already knew. Their arguments were frequent, they weren't happy, and this one argument had escalated. It did make me wonder if others had escalated that Mrs. Clayborne knew nothing about.

"Thank you, Mrs. Clayborne. I appreciate your time. If you think of anything else, please give me a call. The number's on my card."

FOURTEEN

BEVERLY HUDSON WAS AN ATTRACTIVE WOMAN in her mid-forties, athletic looking and well cared for. Her dark-brown hair was only faintly threaded with silver. Her choice not to dye it made me think she was pretty comfortable with herself and not trying to maintain a younger appearance. As far as I could tell, she'd had no Botox or fillers, unless it had been done subtly. *A wife clearly in her forties, married to a philanderer, might have a hard time competing against younger women,* I thought. *Maybe she's decided not to try, or maybe she doesn't care to compete.*

"I work for Mr. Cisneros, Mia Stewart's lawyer, and I wanted to ask you a few questions. I appreciate you agreeing to meet with me." I handed her my card and Angel's as we sat down in a comfortable upscale living room.

"You're persistent. I've already spoken to the retired detective at the office, but I finally decided to meet with you just to put a stop to the calls."

"Why didn't you want to talk to me?"

"It's embarrassing to know all this is out in the open. Besides, I don't see the point in rehashing it. They arrested and charged the nurse who killed him."

"So you're convinced she killed your husband?"

"Based on what I've heard, I'm not sure who else it could be."

"You're not aware of any enemies he had who might have wanted him dead?"

"Don't be ridiculous. There were people who didn't *like* him, but not enough to kill him. Snipe at him, politically sabotage him, but not kill him."

"Did his cheating upset you?"

She glared at me. "Of course it did, early on, but my husband's been cheating on me for some time. Our marriage hasn't been a love match in years. Geoff was incapable of being faithful. Our marriage now is, was," she corrected herself, "more one of convenience. But you're barking up the wrong tree if you think I had anything to do with his death. I've had ample reason and opportunity to kill him for a long time, and I haven't. Furthermore, I have no access to the OR, I wouldn't know one instrument from another, and I wouldn't have had a clue where to find him."

"I understand Matt Finley was here, and you were planning a birthday party for your husband."

"We were. Geoff's birthday is next month. He'll be … would have been forty-six."

I saw a glitter of tears in her eyes. That was a first. Up to this point, other than being angry, she'd acted emotionally disconnected. It seemed to me that no matter how you tried to shield yourself from a partner's betrayal, there was always a part of you that hurt.

"You said your husband had been cheating on you for some time, yet you were planning a birthday party for him?"

"That strikes you as odd?"

"Yeah, it does."

"Appearances are important, Ms. Collins. We have a young daughter, and the trouble between me and my husband is not something I want her to worry about. She is the only reason we were still together, and she's young enough to worship her father. That wouldn't have lasted. Children are more perceptive than people give them credit for.

"He was a lousy husband, but he was a good father, and fathers are important to girls. I wanted to present a united front so she could have a normal relationship with him as long as possible. While his death is a huge trauma for her, at least she'll remember him as a good man."

For a while, I thought, *until she's old enough to hear the gossip or discover why he was murdered. That will be a wound she might never forgive him for.*

"Can you tell me what the fight between you and your husband was about—the one that prompted your neighbor to call 911?"

"I don't even remember what started it. We argued about a lot of things."

"But you don't remember what caused an argument resulting in a visit from the cops?"

She rolled her eyes at me, and when I didn't move on, she said, "I fired our nanny. I should never have hired her. She was too young and too attractive, and he couldn't keep his hands off her. But at the time, I needed a nanny, and she seemed quite capable. I accused him of screwing her and told him I fired her. He wasn't happy."

"He told someone he hadn't been intimate with the nanny—"

"I'm sure he did. He would never have admitted it. He denied it to my face, and the argument went downhill from there. It made me so angry I threw a nearby vase at him."

"Had that type of argument happened before?"

"We argued," she said with a shrug. "You wear a ring, so I assume you're married. If you've been married any length of time, I'm sure you argue with your spouse regularly. We were no different. It was certainly the first and only time a neighbor called the police about it, but as I said, it had gotten a little out of hand. I have no control over what he did, but I certainly wasn't going to tolerate him screwing her under my nose, in our home."

I decided to take another tack. "A number of people have said he was stressed about something in the week or so before his death. Other than the nanny issue, any idea what was bothering him?"

"There was a lot going on for him. His partner was leaving, and we were not getting along. Any number of issues were weighing on him, I imagine."

"Issues? Like money problems or legal problems?"

"No. Are we done here?" she asked, standing up. Apparently, she was done.

"What issues were bothering—"

She cut me off. "I have no intention of answering that. If your employer feels the need, he can contact my lawyer and arrange for a formal deposition. Here's his card."

She retrieved a card from her jacket pocket and thrust it at me.

I took the card. "I appreciate your time. I'll see myself out." *Lawyers,* I thought as I headed across the street from the Hudsons' residence to my car. *Total pains in the ass.* Even my lawyer could be one at times.

I thought about what Beverly Hudson had said about arguing. Maybe I was lucky. Angel and I argued, but not regularly, and it never ended up with the police being called. The lack of arguing was probably more due to the fact that he was an easygoing guy and not much got him fired up. When something did, though, it was impressive, and there tended to be a lot of shouting on both our parts. Nothing had ever been damaged during one of our arguments, and thankfully, none of our neighbors had ever felt the need to call the police.

Angel took the card I held out to him. "She said for you to call her lawyer and set up a deposition. Otherwise, she isn't going to talk about it further."

"Lawyers are always a pain to deal with," Frost said with a laugh, looking pointedly at Angel. He liked Angel, always had, but he never missed a chance to needle him since Angel had gone over to the defense side of the courtroom.

"I spoke with the next-door neighbor who called 911. She said she and her husband heard the couple arguing now and then. But what they'd heard before was when the couple was out in the open—in the backyard or the driveway. The argument that prompted the 911 call was the only one that alarming, and nothing similar has happened before or since."

"I reviewed Roberts's interview with Hudson's wife," Frost said. "Matt Finley's her alibi. She gave Roberts his name, but in her interview she denied they were having an affair. She was evasive with Roberts—both of them were. Neither admitted the affair to him or anyone else until I cornered them in their offices the other day."

"She answered my questions pretty openly, until she decided not to." I said.

"They corroborated each other's alibi when I talked to them. Unfortunately, there's no one else who can confirm any of it. But they backed each other up, so it holds unless something comes up that breaks the alibi."

Frost ran his hand over his face, as if to wipe the tiredness off it. The scruff of his beard, which was predominantly gray now, sounded like sandpaper under his hands. The tiredness stayed put. "If I could find a way to break their alibi, it'd at least bump Finley up on the suspect list. He'd have had the opportunity to get the osteotome, and his motive could be the wife. They'd at least have to be eliminated as suspects."

"But you can't," Angel said.

"Neither of us can at the moment," I said. "She told me what she told Frost, but in far less detail. She made no mention of having an affair with Finley, and I didn't get a chance to ask. She said they met to discuss a surprise party for Hudson. I find that a little hard to believe. If he was cheating on her, and she was cheating on him, why would she care about planning a party for him? I confronted her about it, and she said it was about keeping up appearances for their daughter. Seems to me if that was all it was, she and her daughter could have just taken him out for dinner or something."

"Finley backed up the wife and said it was for Hudson's upcoming birthday." Frost flipped through the small notebook he carried around with him. "Next month. And people like to keep up appearances."

"Frost, where was Finley's wife?" Angel asked.

"She'd been ill and was laid up at home—flu, I guess. Roberts talked to her, and apparently she knew about the get-together. Bev Hudson was supposed to meet with them at Finley's house, but the wife told him to go somewhere else to meet. I don't think she has a clue her husband is carrying on with Bev Hudson."

"A birthday party that requires three people meeting to plan it for a man who'd been cheating on you for quite a while? That just doesn't fly in my opinion," I said.

"I agree it's odd, but I can't break their alibi at the moment," Frost said. "They met at Hudson's house, supposedly after the help had left for the night. So no solid witnesses, just Finley's wife backing up the fact that they were supposed to meet. Being an orthopedic surgeon, he'd have easy access to the instrument."

"Yeah, but it doesn't matter what he is if their alibi holds. It's a shaky alibi, as far as I'm concerned. There are no witnesses to confirm they were at the house." I rubbed the back of my neck in frustration. "According to you, Finley's wife says that's what he and Beverly Hudson were doing, but she really has no idea where he went, just that he went out."

"They all gave me the same time frame for when they supposedly got together and when Finley left as they told Roberts," Frost said. "If they're not lying, it takes him out of the running. If he wasn't at Hudson's house with the wife, there was plenty of time to get to the hospital and kill Hudson. If he was with her, then the timeline doesn't work, so unless we can break their alibi, they're both off the list. I'm going to talk with their housekeeper and the neighbors to see if anyone actually saw him arriving or leaving."

"Give me the times, and I'll check with the ICU and the ortho floor to see if Finley made an appearance that night. I still have a number of people on my list to interview."

"This is good information. It opens up the possibility that Finley could have been the killer," Angel said. "I can use it to cast some doubt on it being Mia. I almost hope you can't find anyone to confirm he was there the entire time, but keep looking. I need to know one way or the other."

Frost crossed his arms over his chest. "It's a good idea to check with the ICU and the ortho floor staff. If we can't find anyone to back up their story, we need to keep on them. Both their stories are identical. Sometimes if you ask people to tell the story backward, the holes show up. People who're telling the truth rarely have trouble doing that." Frost stood up and headed to the door of Angel's office. "Just so you know, I'm having to put some pressure on Roberts to get him to cooperate. You know how it is—cops do all the work to get a suspect arrested and charged, and defense attorneys do everything they can to get the suspect acquitted. So there's only so far he's willing to go."

"All right," Angel said. "Don't put him in a compromising position."

"You two have a good night. Kid," he said to me, "let's talk in the morning and figure out what we need to do."

FIFTEEN

WHAT IS SHE DOING HERE? I told you I didn't want to talk to her."

"Mia, she's here at my request. She has OR experience and can bring up issues I might not be aware of."

She stared at me for several moments, crossed her arms over her chest, then said, "Fine."

"Talk to me about the night Hudson died and be as specific and detailed as possible. If inconsistencies arise between what you tell me and what other witnesses report, I can focus on those," Angel said.

I sat across from Mia and kept quiet. My job was to listen and watch for any discrepancies or help Angel by asking questions pertinent to the OR. She wouldn't like it, so I hoped I could just sit and listen. I had reminded Angel of Frost's comment about asking her to tell her side of things backward and see what happened. He said he'd go over the police interview and see what he thought. He said if the cops thought she was lying, then the DA would, and he needed to know what made them think she was.

"Where should I start?"

"Talk about the shift. What were you doing, where were you, what caught your attention, what did you do, and what happened afterward?"

She closed her eyes for a moment and began talking.

"It was late, nearly the end of my last shift of the week. I had finished my last case earlier in the evening. I went to dinner, and when I returned, there were no cases for me to help with, so I was working in the sterile supply room, checking expiration dates on instruments and supplies. I'd been in there for about an hour and a half when I saw the time—my shift was over in fifteen minutes—"

"What time was that?" Angel asked, interrupting her.

"About seven fifteen."

He nodded for her to continue.

"I finished what I was doing and headed for the dressing room. I heard the automatic door to the OR near the dressing room opening and closing, like it was blocked by something. As I rounded the corner to investigate, I saw a person's legs dressed in scrubs blocking the doors. A bright-orange Croc had fallen off one foot. I guess I knew at that point who it was. Geoff was the only one who wore bright-orange Crocs."

I saw a sheen of tears that she quickly wiped away.

"I ran to the door and pushed it open toward the locking mechanism. Geoff was lying on his back in the middle of a large pool of blood, smears of it spread on the floor, as if he—or someone—had slipped or struggled in it before he fell, and the door had smeared blood in a fan as it opened and closed."

Mia reached for the bottle of water sitting next to her on the conference table and drank half of it in several gulps. "I dropped down next to him, in the blood, which saturated the knees of my scrubs. My shoe covers picked some up as well. He was barely conscious, and I could see he was half lying on a large osteotome. I-I pulled it out …"

Mia stopped talking and rested her forehead in her hand. As if talking to herself, she said, "I grasped the handle and pulled it out from under him. It left blood on my hands. I left it on the floor next to him, and I put pressure on his abdominal wound. Seeing the extent of the bleeding, I doubted anything I did would help." She squeezed her eyes closed and fought back tears. "But I had to try."

Angel reached for a box of tissues and handed it to her. "Ted Nichols says you had the osteotome in your hand and he heard you say something about 'deserved it'—"

"Ted Nichols is lying! I didn't have it in my hand when he showed up. I pulled it out from under Geoff and left it on the floor, and I never said anything about Geoff deserving what had happened to him. I-I told him he *hadn't* deserved it."

"Okay, then what?"

"He … His eyes fluttered open … He reached up and touched my face and said, 'Sorry.' His arm fell to the floor and … and he was gone."

"That's how the blood got on your face?" Angel asked.

"Yes."

"How did it get on the front of your scrub top?"

It seemed to stop her in her tracks. "I … I don't remember … Maybe I wiped my hands on it. There was blood … everywhere."

Angel nodded. "What do you think he meant when he said he was sorry?"

"Sorry for what had happened between us, I guess."

"It's hard for me to believe someone who you say told you he'd leave his wife for you, someone you broke up with, who took up with someone else almost immediately afterward, would still pursue you."

I watched Mia. She frowned and began to play with a loose thread holding a button on her sweater. *She never tells the whole truth and nothing but*, I thought, waiting to hear what she said.

Mia continued to fuss with the thread until the button began to dangle precariously, and she stopped. "I don't think any of the women he'd had affairs with had ever broken up with him. I think he was the one who always called things off. I think he thought his involvement with Alicia would make me jealous and make me reconsider."

I slid a look at Angel and saw him take a deep breath. "Were you jealous?"

"Angry, I guess. It embarrassed me and showed me how right I had been to break it off. But that just gives me another reason to have killed him, doesn't it? I didn't want him, and I didn't want anyone else to have him either. Isn't that what they'll say?"

"It doesn't matter what they say. I need to know the truth. These things never stay secret. Someone may have overheard a conversation between the two of you or heard something he said to someone else. I can't defend you if I don't know. You have to trust me and tell me everything, even if it's embarrassing or you think it will cause problems. Let me be the one to sort that out."

She rubbed her neck tiredly. "I moved back here a year or so ago, and I had just started at the hospital. I didn't know Geoff well or that he was married. He was a busy, well-liked surgeon, but that was about all I knew. As I said before, I hadn't made any friends—I don't make friends easily—and was out of the gossip loop. I might have known about his marriage otherwise, and I didn't ask anyone about him. I should have.

"We did a lot of cases together over the next few months, and eventually he asked me to get a drink. I accepted, we hit it off, and I made the mistake of going out with him several times after that. Things between us became serious pretty quickly … and I slept with him. I should have known that he was married when he asked me to keep our relationship private."

"Why'd he ask you to do that?" Angel asked.

"He said it was because of all the gossip it'd cause, that we wouldn't be able to enjoy a normal relationship because we'd be the subject of everyone's speculations." She scowled and shook her head irritably. "I know what you're thinking, that I must have been incredibly naive not to see the red flag. I suppose I was, but he'd been wonderful, attentive, considerate—everything you look for in a man."

"I wasn't thinking anything of the kind. I'm not here to judge, Mia. I'm here to listen and try to figure out how to defend you."

"I'm sorry. It's embarrassing to have to talk about this." She paused and took a sip of water. "We'd been seeing each other for about six weeks when, quite by accident, I discovered he was married. I overheard a conversation about him. I confronted him, and he admitted he was married, so I ended the affair and refused to see him again."

She shrugged. "He wasn't happy. When I confronted him, he told me he was in love with me and planned to leave his wife and begged me not to cut him off. I told him when he was divorced to let me know, but I wasn't going to continue to help him cheat on his wife. He kept trying to get me to change my mind. It's been difficult. He's a surgeon and used to getting his way."

"And he pursued you right up until his death?"

"Yes. You know about the confrontation we had."

Angel frowned as he scribbled on his legal pad. "The prosecution will use that as motive, say he provoked you in the hallway in some way that resulted in you killing him. Your incident in the cafeteria adds weight to that. The osteotome is a huge stumbling block. As Ms. Collins has pointed out to me, it's not something a person would carry around and use on impulse. It would have to be removed from a used set, so it looks like premeditation."

"Don't you mean your wife?" Mia gave him a sly smile. She pulled the dangling button off her sweater and played with it, turning it over and over between her fingers.

"My wife?"

She rolled her eyes. "Yes, your wife. As I told *your wife*, both of you keep hounding me about the truth, and neither of you mentioned that."

"It's irrelevant whether we're married," Angel said brusquely.

"Hardly irrelevant. She doesn't like me, and I don't think either of you believe me. I'm pretty sure she thinks I did it. She says the osteotome reeks of premeditation. She's clearly not helping me, is she? My freedom rests on the job you do to represent me. I don't trust her, so it does matter whether you're married. Who're you going to believe? Me or her?"

I could see the snap in his eyes, and I thought Mia didn't know who she was up against. "And you have, on repeated occasions, failed to tell either of us the whole truth. Your freedom doesn't rest on whether *my wife* likes you or not, it rests on you not lying to either of us. I don't have to prove your innocence—the prosecution has to prove your guilt—but I have to be able to refute whatever they say and defend you so the jury doesn't decide you're the killer. If they surprise me with something at trial that you haven't mentioned, then we—you—are screwed."

I stood up and began to collect my things. "Where are you going?" Angel snapped.

"I think it would be best if I left."

"It would not. Sit down."

I had to bite my tongue. Angel had never talked to me that way, but I sat down.

There were several moments of silence before he spoke again, his voice clipped and angry. "If you don't like or trust us, me in particular, then I'll speak to your uncle and have him reassign your case to someone else, either in this firm or another one. I need to know, now, what you want to do."

She looked taken aback, then suddenly there were tears in her eyes. "I-I'm sorry. I don't want to make any changes. I'm scared. I'm innocent but they're going to send me to prison, aren't they?"

It was all I could do not to roll *my* eyes. She was quick to flip from entitled bitch to poor, scared little Mia and produce convincing heart-tugging tears.

Angel frowned. "Not if I can help it. From now on, no more lies or half-truths." She nodded. "And I only intend to say this once: My personal life and that of my wife is *none of your business*. Our relationship with you is strictly professional. Are we clear?"

She nodded.

"Let's take a break. I'll be back in a few minutes." Angel stepped out of the office and closed the door.

I sat for a moment, then stood. "I'm going to make a phone call. There's a restroom down the hall to the right if you need to use it."

I walked down the hall in the opposite direction, toward the staff lounge at the rear of the office suite, and found Angel there, a bottle of water in his hand and a deep frown on his face. He turned on me when I walked in the small room.

"Did she pull that shit on you?"

"Yes. I basically told her the same thing you did. She knows about Teo. Owen filled her in on our entire lives, apparently."

He slammed his hand on the countertop and muttered something in Spanish. "And you didn't tell me."

"I didn't want to put you in a difficult situation. I thought telling you would make representing her harder. I'm sorry, I should have told you."

"If she pulls anything else like this, tell me." I nodded. "This case! Jesus, the more I struggle with it, the deeper I get sucked in."

I walked over, ran my hand down his arm, and took his hand. "Rumor has it if you find yourself in quicksand, don't struggle, just float till help shows up."

"There's no help coming, *chica*. I'm it."

"Then we'll go down together."

SIXTEEN

YOU DIDN'T SPEAK TO HIM PUBLICLY the day he was killed or have an interaction that someone in the department might have witnessed?" Angel asked when we reconvened.

"No! I didn't work with him that day, and the last hour or two of my shift, I was working in the sterile supply room. I didn't kill him!"

"Is there any way you could have accessed an osteotome in the supply room? Before the time of his death?"

"No, those are in the ortho sets, they're not wrapped individually. Whoever stabbed him had to have taken one from a used set."

"Where are they stored?"

"They're not really stored in the department. The sets come up from sterile processing on the case carts. After a case, staff take the used instrument sets on the case carts to the room where they're returned to the sterile processing department."

"Is it near the sterile supply room?"

"It's not far from it."

"Easy to access?"

"No. Staff have to access it with their badges to return the case carts. They also use their badges to access the elevator to return the instruments for cleaning and sterilization. We all have badges that allow access to areas like this."

"So anyone, including surgeons or anesthesia personnel, could access the area?"

"I suppose."

"Could you have accessed it from the sterile supply room where you were working without being seen?"

"Yes."

"Did you work on any cases that used ortho instruments that day?"

"I scrubbed on one earlier in the day."

Angel sighed. "That's unfortunate. It means you had an opportunity to take the instrument."

"How is this helping me? I didn't take the instrument. It sounds like you're working for the prosecution."

"Mia, if I ask the question, you can be sure the prosecution will have asked it and gotten an answer. I have to ask, and I have to find a way to defend against it. I've told you this before. I'm trying to find a way to diffuse things like this."

She nodded. The sullen look on her face made me think she'd rarely been crossed or confronted or been in a situation that forced her to trust someone as completely as she had to trust Angel. This was not a situation she had any control over, other than to tell the truth, which seemed like a constant struggle for her.

"What happened after you found him?"

"I heard someone shout and looked up to see Nichols standing in the hallway by the men's changing room door. He looked horrified and asked me, 'What have you done?' I was shocked that he would think I was responsible for Geoff's death. I told him I hadn't done anything, that I had found Geoff like that. He turned and disappeared. In a few seconds, people surrounded me. Nichols reappeared and pulled me away from Geoff.

"While Nichols held on to me, a surgeon and an anesthesiologist examined Geoff. I strained away from Nichols to see what was happening, and he pulled me back, causing me to step on his foot. It felt as if he had no shoes on under his shoe covers. The surgeon declared Geoff dead and told everyone to stand back. I think someone, maybe the anesthesiologist, had called security, and I guess they called the cops."

She was breathing rapidly, and it looked as if she was beginning to panic. "I didn't kill him, but no one believes me, not even you, Mr. Cisneros, and you're my lawyer."

So she doesn't have the nerve to call him Angel to his face, I thought. *Maybe what he said made an impression. Her use of "Angel" when she talked to me had to be to unsettle me.*

"You're in good hands," I said, wanting to support him. "I would trust him with my life. You can too." Angel gave me a crooked smile.

Mia glanced at me and frowned, as if she had forgotten I was there or wished I wasn't. She took a drink from her bottle of water and began again. "Two detectives arrived and cleared everyone away but told them not to leave, that they'd want to interview each of them. The late shift was arriving, and it was pretty chaotic for a bit. Staff who had been relieved by the late shift personnel were slowly congregating around us as well.

"One of the detectives asked if there was an office he could take me to, while the other stayed by Geoff and made a couple phone calls. Nichols let go of me so the detective could take over, but he continued to stand near where Geoff's body lay. He seemed unable to look away from it, but then, none of the people who'd gathered could. Alicia stood by the front desk, sobbing in her friend Joanne's arms.

"The detective escorted me to Barb Davis's office. She's the OR supervisor. He asked me what happened. The accusations Nichols had made and the way the detective detained me worried me, then he isolated me in the office. It scared me, and I told him I wanted to call a lawyer. He left, and I called my dad, who sent Uncle Owen. Dad told me on the phone not to say anything to the detective."

"I'm glad you listened to him."

"When Uncle Owen arrived, he insisted on talking to me privately and asked me about what happened. After the detective took my statement, he told us he needed their forensic tech to get photos and some samples. The tech took photos of everything. She took my scrubs and took my fingerprints. She did a DNA swab and took swabs of the blood on my face. One of the other nurses brought me a clean pair of scrubs so I could go back to the changing room."

"Did you see or hear anyone near Hudson or leaving the area when you first found him or while you were trying to help him?"

"I wasn't really paying attention. I was so shocked at seeing him and so focused on him, I don't remember hearing anything or seeing anything until Nichols showed up. At least, nothing that distracted me from trying to help him. The detective said he didn't have any further questions at the moment. He told me not to return to work until he could get my involvement sorted out, and he allowed us to leave. I was arrested the next day. My uncle said not to talk to anybody, not even friends or family, about what had happened."

"Have you talked to anyone since then?"

"My father, my mother, Uncle Owen, and you two. No one else."

"Do you believe her?" I asked after seeing Mia sent home via a car service.

"Annie, it doesn't matter whether I do or not. I have to figure out how to get her acquitted. But between us, yes, I believe her. The problem is, she had history with him, and she lied to the police about it. If the prosecution has discovered it, and they will when we exchange files during discovery, they might try to call her as a witness. She can't be forced to testify, but if they try to call her and she exercises the right not to testify, or claims the fifth amendment when questioned on the stand, it can look bad. Juries aren't supposed to draw negative inferences about that, but they often do. Having a defendant on the stand is a really bad idea, and she's not likable."

"Does that matter?"

"Juries are always a gamble, and they can be swayed by things unrelated to facts. A defendant who agrees to testify and comes across the way Mia does at times isn't all that sympathetic. It could do more harm than good, especially if the reason she's testifying is because of her lie about their relationship. She never revealed their relationship to the cops and has steadfastly denied one even to us until just now, so I don't want her testifying unless, somehow, it would work to our advantage."

He looked exhausted, and the frown that had set up residence on his face when Mia commented on our marriage was still firmly in place. I hated this case, and if I was honest, I hated her.

"Then there's the ongoing tension between her and Hudson and her reaction to his remark in the cafeteria," he continued. "Without anyone to corroborate what they were talking about or what he said that triggered her, it's exactly what the prosecution will use against her. It shows she was angry with him and aggressive in her reaction to whatever he said to her. She was found kneeling over him with his bloody handprint on her face. The prosecution will probably say it was the result of him trying to defend himself against her."

Angel rotated his chair so he was gazing out his office window. "All of it's a problem, but the worst problem is the damn osteotome. She finally admitted she'd scrubbed a case that gave her access to one. It's infuriating that she keeps withholding information. I can't figure her out."

He swung his chair to face me. "It's fortunate that the osteotome handle is rough and there were no identifiable fingerprints on it ... but the handprint perfectly matches her hand in size, and she admitted to handling it, so it'll be hell convincing a jury she didn't use it on him."

"The question to raise if the prosecution says she planned it is, did she get the osteotome out of a set, and where'd she keep it until she used it?" I said. "It wouldn't be easy to conceal, not like a scalpel or something similar. I suppose she could have slipped it up the sleeve of her cover jacket and taken it to her locker, but if that's the case, when did she retrieve it, and where did she keep it until she confronted Hudson? If it's from a set, we need to know when it went missing. The SPD will have a record of it."

"What's an SPD?"

"Sorry, it's the surgical processing department. If the osteotome went missing the day of Hudson's death, the day she scrubbed the ortho case, then it's pretty incriminating."

I watched as Angel rubbed his forehead. I knew that nothing that Frost or I had found out helped him. There was a slump to his shoulders that I rarely saw, and I wanted to tug him out of his chair and take him home, but his day was far from over.

"Frost is running a background check on Nichols and will do the same for anyone involved in the two ortho cases that day. I want to talk to the anesthesia tech and to Finley's ortho resident. According to the ICU nurse who saw Alicia coming out of the dictation room, they're both friends of Nichols," I said, hoping to ease his worry.

"I especially want to talk to Nichols. By all accounts, Hudson put him through hell. Who knows? He may have snapped and killed him." I rubbed my temples to relieve the headache that was building. "It seems like an overreaction to being harassed by a surgeon you're working for, especially when you don't have much longer to have to work with him. But then, killing someone who keeps asking you for a second chance seems far-fetched to me as well."

"It's not, really. Love, hate, bullying, and frustration with someone standing in the way of something you want are all prime reasons. That kind of anger tends to build until something triggers it," Angel said.

He'd turned his chair around and stared out the office window again. Storm clouds hung over the Front Range in the distance west of downtown, and rain was predicted. "Hudson's wife and Nichols both had motive. The wife might have gotten fed up with his philandering and decided to kill him so she didn't have to split their assets. If so, she had to get someone else to do it, and she's covered herself pretty well. Something Hudson said or did could have pushed Nichols over the edge. And Hudson could have said something that triggered Mia."

"Yeah, all true. Unfortunately, so far, nothing clears Mia," I said. Angel shrugged. Storm clouds of his own seemed to hang over him. "What will you do if the majority of the information we gather implicates her as the murderer?"

"If the evidence against a client is overwhelming, I tell them that and try to get them to agree to me broaching the possibility of a plea with the DA's office."

He scratched the edge of his jaw as he stared off in the distance. "If you or Frost find anything that seriously implicates her or proves she did it, though, I need to know immediately and start talking plea deal with her. And that won't make Mia, her parents, or Owen happy."

"I just can't square Mia killing him because he wouldn't quit asking her to resume their affair," I said. "If it continued, and she felt harassed, she could have filed a formal complaint. They would have had to address it. That doesn't warrant killing him. I can relate to his resident wanting to kill him, but by all reports he's so passive, he just endured Hudson's abuse. I suppose even passive people have triggers."

Turning to me, he said, "Everyone has triggers, *chica.*"

"True." I grinned. "I can totally relate to the wife having motive. If you were cheating on me, you'd be history."

Angel raised his eyebrows. "I'll keep that in mind. Just so you know, I feel the same way."

"Good to know," I said, then turned serious. "Does her invasion of our privacy bother you like it does me?"

"I don't like it, but I think I nipped it in the bud."

I raised my eyebrows. "You nipped me in the bud as well. I know you were upset with her, but I don't appreciate you telling me to sit down the way you did."

"I'm sorry. I was so angry with her and annoyed that you thought you should leave. I didn't want you to leave and give her the satisfaction of getting her way, but I shouldn't have done that."

I laughed a little. "It sort of felt like being reprimanded by my first-grade teacher for talking in class, but I forgive you."

He smiled and pulled me onto his lap. "Thanks. You said she did the same thing to you." I nodded. "What'd she say?"

"Thanks to Owen—and you need to talk to him about it—she knows almost everything about us. She went out of her way to find out. She even called you Angel when she brought it up to me. Owen obviously called you that when he told her about you. She didn't use it today in front of you, but I think she could see you were pretty pissed about what she'd already said. She knows about Teo, and it freaked me out. Why would any normal client want to know our personal details?"

Angel shook his head. "Owen's my boss, her mother is his sister, and her aunt is a lawyer. Mia probably thinks she has a right to the information. She's scared, and maybe it makes her feel better to know. It's intrusive and annoying, but I don't think there's anything to worry about."

"You're way too forgiving. When she said you were her lawyer and she had a right to know, I told her that could be remedied. She said not if you wanted to keep your job. That's a threat. If she's capable of killing Hudson, what else is she capable of doing?" I waited, and when he didn't respond, I said, "Is there any way you can hand her off to someone else?"

"No, I can't."

SEVENTEEN

TED NICHOLS WAS TALL—SEVERAL INCHES OVER six feet, by my guess. He was a thin guy with washed-out blond hair that had begun receding and blue eyes so pale they were almost colorless. He was stooped, which I suspected was the result of a lifelong effort to not tower over people. I didn't know him, but I wondered if stooping, like his paleness, was a way to make himself less visible.

We sat at a table in the cafeteria. It had turned into the easiest place to connect with staff members I needed to talk to, and there was usually a quiet corner where we could sit unobserved and not be overheard.

"It would be helpful if you'd tell me about the night Geoff Hudson was killed—what you remember, what you saw, anything that jumps out at you."

"I've spoken to the police."

"I realize that, but Mia's attorney likes to have us interview the people involved as well. If you wouldn't mind?"

He nodded resignedly. There was a depressed air about him, as if any spark of life had gone out a long time ago. I felt sorry for him. He was like an abused dog, cowed yet still wanting the approval of his abuser and just as unlikely to get it.

"If you ask anybody in the department, they'll tell you he didn't like me. Or maybe it wasn't that personal, maybe he just didn't think I was good at surgery, maybe that's what he didn't like. I'm passable, but

I wasn't up to his standards. He was incredibly talented. I just hoped I could hang on until the end of the rotation with him. I guess I don't have to worry about that anymore."

He stopped abruptly, anxiety written all over his face. "I … I didn't kill him. I didn't mean that the way it sounds."

"I get it. It must be a relief, though, to know you don't have to work with him now. I understand he was pretty hard on you. Where were you when he was killed?'

"We'd finished a big case, and Hudson told me to go home. He said he'd talk to the family. It had been a long day, and I don't think he wanted to be around me anymore. I went to change. I sat down and took my shoes off and just sat there … I was exhausted, physically and mentally. You can't imagine what it's like to be on alert every minute, worried you'll screw up somehow and suffer the consequences or cause a problem for a patient."

His shoulders drooped when he let out a heavy sigh. "So I ended up sitting there for, I don't know, maybe ten or fifteen minutes, enjoying the quiet. When I went to undress, I discovered I'd left my phone in the OR we'd been working in. I slipped some shoe covers over my socks and went to get it. Hudson would've reamed me if the answering service or someone on the patient units wasn't able to get in touch with me during the night and they had to call him. He never wanted to be called unless it was something seriously urgent. Once he left for the day, it was all my responsibility."

He paused, and his eyes drifted off. "When I stepped out of the changing room, I saw Hudson on the floor. Blood … Blood was everywhere—on him, around him—and Mia was kneeling over him, holding the osteotome. I-I heard her say something about 'deserve it' or 'deserved it.' She looked angry or maybe just concentrating or shocked, it was hard to tell. I asked her what she'd done. She had blood on her face and hands."

"You told the police she was holding the osteotome over him. She says it was lying on the floor—"

He cut me off. "I know what I saw. She was holding it."

"Okay, then what?"

"I was so shocked, all I could do was ask her what she'd done. I finally snapped out of it and ran to get help. When I returned with help, I pulled her away from him and held on to her until the police arrived."

"Why'd you hold on to her? She wasn't going to disappear."

He shrugged and didn't reply immediately. "I don't know. It was all I could think to do."

"Why didn't you go to him when you first saw him and try to help? You went to get help instead, without checking to see if he was alive. Why?"

He scowled at me. "Nobody loses that much blood and survives. I didn't think I could help."

"It's interesting to me that you immediately asked what she'd done rather than what happened. Did you think she'd killed him?"

"I don't know."

"It sounds like you did. What made you think she'd killed him instead of thinking she might have been trying to save him?"

"There'd been several incidents between the two of them lately. As I said, she looked angry to me, and she was saying something to him. I've told you and the police what I heard. Based on that and her demeanor, I just assumed."

I took a different tack. "You had a difficult relationship with him. Could he have affected your future rotations or progression in the specialty?"

He lowered his head and massaged the back of his neck with his hand. "Yes," he said, raising his head and looking at me. "I don't know whether he would have, but assessments and recommendations are important. A lack of one is just as damning as a poor one. I don't know what he would have said about me, if asked."

"Why didn't you talk to the chief of surgery or your program director about his behavior? Surgeons can be a pain, but his behavior seems particularly abusive. Maybe they could have reassigned you or spoken to him."

"I thought about it, but it would have made things worse." He huffed out a humorless laugh. "You don't do that if you're a resident. You just keep slogging away until the rotation is over and then hope that a better assignment will follow. If I'd said anything, I'd have been labeled a whiner, not man enough to just deal with things, and Hudson would have been furious. How would reporting him have helped?"

"I see your point." I thought for a minute or two. "Why do you think he disliked you? It seems particularly personal from what I've gathered."

"You didn't know him. He was brilliant. Surgery was a part of him, almost like … I don't really know how to describe it. He didn't hesitate, didn't have to think things over. He simply knew what to do and did it. And I don't. Even you questioned my reaction to seeing him that night. You think I should have assessed him to see if he could have been saved. My first thought was to find someone who could help him. I guess that says it all."

He pinched his temples between his thumb and middle finger, and his brows drew together in distress. "I'd never measure up as far as he was concerned."

"You don't seem happy here. Are you?"

"Not particularly."

"Why go into a surgical residency if you're only passable, as you called it?"

"It was expected."

"By whom?"

"I don't think that's relevant or any of your business." He stood up abruptly. "I have work to do," he said before he turned and strode off.

The next evening, Angel didn't get home until late and slumped onto the couch after dropping his briefcase in its usual spot near the door. "Have we got any beer?" he asked, letting his head rest against the back of the couch.

"Bad day?" I asked, opening a bottle of beer and bringing it to him.

"I got the forensic reports today. The only fingerprints found at the scene were Mia's. That is easily explained by the fact that she discovered him and handled the osteotome, but it doesn't help clear her," he said after taking a long pull on the bottle. "They weren't able to find any bloody scrubs in the changing rooms or in any of the laundry collection areas or trash receptacles, other than the ones she was wearing."

I sat down next to him. "Doesn't sound good."

He took another pull on the bottle. "That's the understatement of the year. Unless you and Frost can find something the cops or forensics haven't, I'm not sure I can get her off. If she's convicted, there goes my job."

"I know you're worried, but surely Owen wouldn't fire you."

"Let's hope not, but there are plenty of ways to encourage someone to quit besides firing them." He took a couple more long pulls of beer and said, "You've got no real control over what a jury will decide. You can put on the best defense possible, and they'll convict for some obscure reason. Maybe they don't like the defendant or the lawyer. It's anybody's guess. You can never predict what they'll do. Owen knows that, but in this case, he may not accept it." He tried to take another sip of beer. Getting nothing, he looked at the beer bottle and seemed surprised it was empty. "Did you save anything from dinner? I'm starving."

"Your mom sent food home when I picked up Teo and, as usual, included a dash of guilt about my parenting skills. I'll heat it up."

He got up and walked to the fridge, pulled another bottle of beer out, and opened it. "I'm sorry she does that to you. Maybe we should consider cutting down her time with Teo until she gets the hint to back off."

I laughed. "You poor hopeful fool, Sophia never backs off." I had been thinking about the osteotome all day. "Can you get a look at the murder weapon? Are there detailed photos of it?" He nodded as I put his plate of food in the microwave. "There should be a serial number on it and a manufacturer's name. I could call them and find out who purchased it—you know, what facility. I don't know if it will help, but if it wasn't one of the hospital's, then somebody brought it with them."

He was silent, then said, "Huh. I figured it belonged there. Didn't think it might have come from somewhere else."

"Look at it carefully and tell me what it looks like."

"What would I be looking for?"

"It's basically a chisel. Osteotomes are either straight tipped to slice and shave, or they have tips like tiny ice cream scoops or slight U-shaped tips, you know, so you can make a curved groove with one. Look at the cutting edge. Look for damage or a bent shaft or something."

"Why?"

"'Cause if it was damaged in some way, then it's an instrument they'd take out of service. Sometimes docs and other people like to take those home. They're not supposed to, but ..." I shrugged.

"You think Hudson might have?"

"I'm not saying it was Hudson who took it, but if he did, then his wife would have had access to it, and she had plenty of reasons to be pissed at him. She could have given it to Finley, and he could have used it on her behalf. But it could be anybody in the department. A lot of the docs have hobbies they could use it for, like woodworking. Some people just like collecting things. I once saw a piece of art made entirely of old abdominal retractors. If an osteotome can't be used in surgery because of damage, it could still be used maybe in woodworking or carpentry or something similar."

"Okay, but how would we find out whether someone took it?"

"Once you figure out if it belonged to the hospital, I'll talk to the sterile processing department supervisor. Can you get the manufacturer and the serial number for me?"

"I have photos in the file at the office. My morning's free, but I have to be in court at two, so come by before lunch, and we can look at the photos. You know what to look for better than I would."

"It could be Nichols. He had reason to hate Hudson and could get his hands on an osteotome. The question is whether he'd do that. Hudson's been married close to fifteen years. Seems like if his wife wanted to kill him, she'd have done it by now. There's no indication that Finley had any serious issues with Hudson. Bev Hudson might have persuaded him to carry out the murder for her. I guess it would depend on how serious his relationship with her is. The affair was only about six months along from what I understand. Seems unlikely that he'd kill for her, but who knows? I asked around, and I haven't found anyone who saw Finley that night. If I were on a jury, though, Mia would look pretty guilty to me."

"I know. She scrubbed on an ortho case earlier in the day, was at his side, admitted to handling the osteotome, and was covered in blood." He took a drink of his new beer. I had never seen Angel drunk, but if he continued at this rate, he would be. "That's what I have to work with right now, so I'm hoping you or Frost comes up with something that points to someone else—more than just theorizing."

The microwave dinged, and I took the plate out and set it on the table. "If Mia's telling the truth about the osteotome lying on the floor, maybe the killer pulled the osteotome out of Hudson and dropped it or walked away from him and it fell out. You're not supposed to remove a knife because it's likely to make the bleeding worse. In this case, that would help ensure Hudson bled out. No way to tell, I guess." I heaved a sigh and handed Angel a knife and fork. "And she wasn't covered in blood. Don't make it sound worse than it is."

"Blood on her scrubs and her hands and a palm print on her face. I don't work in surgery, but that's pretty covered in blood as far as I can tell."

That's probably the conclusion the jury would come to as well after seeing the photos.

EIGHTEEN

T DOESN'T LOOK DAMAGED TO ME," I said, staring at the photos of the osteotome. "The cutting edge isn't chipped, and the shaft isn't bent. This isn't one they would take out of service. It had to be lifted from a used instrument set that was on its way back to sterile processing." I returned the photo to Angel's desk.

"They don't normally package osteotomes individually, but an ortho set would have a complete set of them in a rack. The missing osteotome should have been noticed when the set arrived in the sterile processing department. There should be a record of it. It would have the date, what was missing, and what case it was used on. Did you get the information from the manufacturer?"

"I have the serial number and the name of the company that makes them. I called, and I'm waiting for them to call back. Do you need that before you talk to the SPD supervisor?"

"No, I'll just ask about any irregularities with instrument sets or missing instruments and get the day and set it went missing from."

"Good. It would be ideal if it originated somewhere else. It would rule out Mia being the one who killed him. How would she get an instrument from a hospital she doesn't work at?"

"Are you going to give the information to the cops?"

"If it turns out the osteotome was from another hospital, then that clears Mia entirely and basically puts an end to the case. The court would have to dismiss the charges, and that would be a gift from heaven, so keep your fingers crossed.

"If it's from her hospital and, God forbid, from the set used on the case she scrubbed on, then we're screwed. I'll have to give the information to the DA during discovery. They have to give me all their information as well. There's no reason to give anything to the cops. The DA can share what I give him with the detectives on the case if they want, but other than testifying at trial, they're out of the loop at this point."

"Well, let's hope it came from another hospital. What will you do if it didn't?"

Angel slumped back into his desk chair. "Hope to God you or Frost finds something that clears her." He looked up at me and quirked the corner of his mouth. "It's funny how old habits sneak up on you at times like this. They say there are no atheists in foxholes. I guess it's true. I suddenly feel like going to church and lighting a candle. Not sure it'd help."

"It might help you."

"No, it'd just demonstrate how desperate I am."

"I'm trying to find out if any osteotomes went missing in the days leading up to Dr. Hudson's death. I'm hoping you'd be willing to discuss that with me."

"I've spoken to management, and they said to give you the information you need. I've also spoken with the two instrument techs who were handling those sets and checked our records." Jonelle Bates perused several sheets of paper on her desk and continued. "The hospital's instrument tracking system shows that a spinal instrument set returned without an osteotome the day of Dr. Hudson's death. The techs had been trying to track its whereabouts with no luck and assumed it had been lost in the trash or somehow misplaced until they heard about his death. The case the set was assigned to started at 7:30 that morning and finished at 12:30 that afternoon."

"So at some point after that case, someone could have had access to the osteotome. How would they get to it without being noticed?"

"Sets that are ready to come to the SPD for cleaning and sterilization are returned to the case carts, which are taken to the holding area and put on an elevator that brings them down to our department. The area where the carts are taken requires a badge to get in and to open the elevator, so I suppose it could have been taken then."

She offered me the sheets of paper with the tracking information, and I left. It was entirely possible for someone to lift an osteotome—or any other instrument in the case cart area—without being observed. Mia had scrubbed that ortho case and had been the one to return the cart to the transport room. Angel was not going to be happy when I told him.

Maybe I should find a church and light a candle.

I stopped by Angel's office on the way home and gave him the information. "Sorry, it looks like the osteotome belonged to the hospital. She gave me the serial number for it, so check that against the one in the photo." I shrugged. "At least we know when it disappeared. We can track people's movements and find some potential suspects, but Mia scrubbed on that ortho case, and she'd be the one to transport the cart to the pickup room."

Angel scratched at the top of his head, ruffling his curls, then slapped both hands on his desktop in frustration. "Nothing about this case is easy. I guess having it belong to another hospital was too much to ask for."

"I talked to the head nurse before I came here and asked her if she remembered who else was working the other ortho cases. She says there were two cases but only one spine case on the schedule that day, and

Matt Finley was the surgeon. That's the set the osteotome went missing from. His resident, Chris Johansson, was scrubbed in with him. Glen Paulson was circulating, and Mia scrubbed on it. The anesthesiologist was Bob MacPhearson. She gave me the names of the staff involved with the other case as well, and I have them on my list to talk to."

"That seems pretty specific. How'd she remember that?"

"She didn't actually remember them. I asked her to check the schedule for that day to confirm who was assigned to the case. She wasn't authorized to give me a printout of it—too much confidential patient info on it—so it'd be a good idea to subpoena the schedule of cases for that day if you think you'll need it. They can redact the patient's names. All we'd need to know was who was assigned to the cases that day."

Angel had been writing down the names of the staff involved in both cases. "They'll all need to be interviewed. If anything important pops up, I'll get depositions. So Mia was scrubbed in on the case that's missing the osteotome?"

"Yes. The other case, a knee replacement, started later that morning and finished at the same time."

"That's good news. It throws doubt on whether she was the one who took the osteotome. Someone else could have accessed the case cart and taken it."

I sighed. "Not really. She was the scrub person. It's her responsibility to take the case cart to the pickup room and send it down to the SPD. Those carts don't sit around unattended. The scrub takes them to the pickup room and puts them on the elevator."

Angel looked at me as if I had lost my mind. "Whose side are you on, Annie? We just found something to raise at least some reasonable doubt, and you're blowing holes in it."

"I'm always on your side, you know that. I'm trying to play devil's advocate. Do you want me to tell you what you want to hear or what you need to hear? You know the ADA prosecuting the case will get all this information, and they'll come to the same conclusions."

Angel sighed and nodded. "Yeah, they will. Sorry, I'm just frustrated as hell. Still, this is helpful. It raises questions, and if I can find things to plant doubt in the jurors' minds, then I'm halfway home. Right now, that's about all I have."

Trying to lighten his worry, I said, "It's possible—but not likely—someone else could have taken it. The only hope is maybe someone else was there when she got to the pickup room and offered to take care of her cart for her, or she had someone else transport the cart. If that's the case, then that person had an opportunity to take the instrument. I can check to see what happened."

Angel closed his notebook and sat back in his chair. "That's good. A large part of her defense is going to rest on Mia's character, and that'll give the jury an opportunity to question whether she'd actually do something like this."

I rolled my eyes. "I've not seen much character that'd convince me if I was a juror."

"Then I'm glad you're not. Their only exposure to her will be in the courtroom, so all I have to do is convince her to behave herself."

"Did you get anything more concrete from that forensic expert you consulted?"

"Not enough. He reviewed the crime scene photos, the autopsy report, the evidence photos, and the photos of Mia in her scrubs and of her hands and face. He's of the opinion that, if she killed Hudson, the blood on the front of her scrubs would depend on how close she was when the stabbing took place, the way you showed me. And he also says there would have been extensive blood coverage on the hands of whoever killed him. Her hands were covered in it. She says it was because she was trying to stem the flow of blood. He says that's entirely possible.

"According to him, based on the level of the stab wound, she could have done it. I asked if it could have been someone taller, and he said sure, if the person held the osteotome at their side and stabbed from that level. That approach might also have concealed the osteotome until it was too late for Hudson to avoid it, regardless of who was using it. The caveat is the wound didn't have an upward trajectory, which he says it might have had if the killer was taller and used an underhand motion. So it makes it more likely that someone her height stabbed him."

"Of course, if the person was significantly taller than Hudson, like Nichols and Johansson are, then the wound wouldn't need an upward trajectory," I said. "Nichols has got to be at least six foot three. I haven't seen Johansson yet, but ortho residents are often big guys. Hudson was five foot ten. You should talk to your expert about that, see what he says."

Angel rubbed his eyes tiredly and yawned. "The evidence, he says, is consistent with her story of finding Hudson and trying to help, but it doesn't definitively let her off the hook. I can talk to him about the height issue and see what he'd be willing to testify to, so thanks for that. The prosecution will no doubt have their own experts who will be happy to point out all the reasons she fits as the killer. But the more doubt I can throw on her being the killer, the better." He laughed. "Nurses are well respected by the public, certainly more respected than lawyers. So we need to convince a jury that, personally and professionally, Mia wouldn't have done anything like this."

"Carrie Saunders was the scrub, and Rick Daniels circulated on the other ortho case. She wasn't on the list Mia gave me of women Hudson hit up, and Rick Daniels's girlfriend doesn't work at the hospital, so I don't see a connection there. As far as the case Mia was involved with, I can't think why Finley's resident would have any reason to even hang out with Hudson, but he was Nichols's friend—that might have given him a motive. I haven't been able to talk to him yet. MacPhearson, the anesthesiologist, works—worked—with Hudson pretty regularly, but according to Mia, they got on really well. It's much the same for the other case's staff. No real connection or motive, but Frost and I will interview all of them."

"The sooner you two can do that, the better."

NINETEEN

ALL THE INSTRUMENTS WERE THERE WHEN MIA and I did the final instrument count, and all the spots in the osteotome rack had an osteotome in them. None were missing at that point. You can double-check with Mia. She took the case cart to the pickup area," Glen Paulson insisted.

"Do you know if any of the team you worked with that day had a bone to pick with Hudson?"

"No. Finley was friends with Hudson and his wife, but obviously they didn't work together on cases. And Chris Johansson—Finley's resident—is friends with Ted Nichols, but again, other than that he had no contact with Hudson. General surgery and ortho rarely cross paths."

"And you? Did you get along with him?"

"Barely knew the man. I mostly work ortho, not general surgery. I've done a few cases with him, and he's an easy surgeon to work with. I've never had any problems with him."

"Mia and possibly Alicia Harvey have been identified as having issues with him. Do you know of anyone else who might have?"

"No, he kept his extracurricular activities pretty quiet. I try to stay out of the gossip, but it's hard not to hear it. I never witnessed anything between him and Mia or Alicia. I heard the speculation going around about the confrontation in the cafeteria that Mia had with him, and I heard the rumors about Alicia hooking up with him. Other than that, I couldn't say."

"And Mia was in the room when you returned from the postanesthesia care unit?"

"Yeah, she was helping get the room ready for the next case."

I thought for a few moments. "How long were you in the PACU? Do you remember?"

"I think it was probably twenty minutes or so. I can't be sure. The patient's surgery was extensive, and he wasn't in the best of health, so it took a little longer than usual to do the handover."

I couldn't verify where Mia had been before she returned to set up for the next case. She'd have had an opportunity to take an osteotome from the used set before she sent it to the SPD and put it somewhere out of sight. Assuming she had taken it. She was in the room cleaning when Glen Paulson returned from taking the patient to the PACU. He couldn't really say when she'd returned to their room, just that she was there when he returned. That was a plus, I guessed, but the length of the handover in the PACU would have given her some extra time to take and hide the osteotome.

The set missing the osteotome was from Mia's case, but to be thorough, I spoke with Carrie Saunders, the scrub on the other case, and the circulator, Susan Evans.

"We did a count, and everything was there. Susan took the patient to the PACU, and she'd have to pass the front desk. Cheryl Johnson was there that day and should be able to verify that. I took the case cart to the pickup area, sent it down, and returned to our room to get ready for the next case. I didn't see anyone else or any unattended carts in the pickup area."

"You didn't see Mia? Your cases ended approximately the same time."

"Nope, didn't even pass her in the hall. Just so you know, I barely knew Hudson. I rarely worked with him. Probably three times in the last year. He wasn't even on my radar."

"Meaning what?" I asked.

"He had a rep for hitting on women in the department. He never hit on me, and I was fine with that. Can't say that about all the women in the department, though."

"Anyone in particular stand out to you as having a problem with him?"

"Well, Mia certainly did, based on the cafeteria incident I heard about. Maybe Alicia had issues. Pretty sure she hooked up with him. I can't see why she'd kill him. She's never been into exclusive relationships from what I know. I don't remember anyone else being obviously pissed at him."

"What about Finley and Johannson?"

"What about them?"

"Any problems with Hudson that you know of?"

"They're orthopods. They pretty much hang out with the orthopedic crowd. I know that Johansson is friends with Ted Nichols, Hudson's resident, and I've heard Hudson hounded Nichols unmercifully. Whether that's cause for Johansson to kill him because he's friends with Nichols? I doubt it. He's a nice guy, easygoing, hard to rile."

"What about Finley?"

She shrugged. "I know he and Hudson were friends. I like working with Finley, but other than that, we don't have any social contact."

"And MacPhearson? Any thoughts about him?"

"He works with most of the surgeons here. I've never heard anyone complain about him. He's good at what he does and seems to get along with pretty much everybody."

Interviewing Susan Evans had been pointless. She backed up Carrie's story and left me once again with nothing that cleared Mia. Glen Paulson couldn't confirm when Mia returned to their room. He'd been in the PACU long enough that he couldn't vouch for her nor could any of the other people assigned to the room, and that was worrying.

Bob MacPhearson was a pleasant balding fifty-something guy with a paunch that strained his scrub top. He'd lost most of the hair on the top of his head and what remained of his hair ran around the back of his head in an ear to ear fringe.

"Geoff was a good surgeon. I never had to worry about him doing something stupid that would make keeping the patient alive difficult. Cases for the most part ran smoothly, and we got along well. Can't say that about his resident. Having him here for his rotation has been wearing."

"Wearing? How d'you mean?"

"I'm not defending Geoff's treatment of him, but Ted Nichols was not cut out to be a surgeon, and I think working with Geoff made all his insecurities explode. Geoff got increasingly frustrated with him, which degenerated into verbal abuse, and that made everyone uncomfortable and on edge. The last few months, cases have become increasingly tense. That's not a great environment in which to perform surgery.

"I'm pretty easygoing, but the guy made me nuts. It turned Geoff vicious. Nichols couldn't make a decision under pressure if his life depended on it. Making decisions under those conditions is what makes or breaks a surgeon. He never should have gotten as far as he has. I don't know why he chose to specialize in surgery or why no one has tried to talk him out of it."

"Sounds like a disaster waiting to happen."

"It's already happened, it just took a while. I'm terribly sorry it ended in Geoff's death. For all his personal deficits, he was a gifted surgeon."

The whole case was a disaster, and talking to the crew who had worked with Mia hadn't improved things for her. No one involved with the case had issues with Hudson, the instrument count was correct when the cart left the room, and Mia was the one who returned the cart to the pickup area—unsupervised and easily able to remove an osteotome without a witness and with plenty of time to find a place to hide it until later that night.

I'd been thinking about how she'd get an osteotome from the set to her locker. I couldn't think of any other place she'd have stored it. As I had suggested to Angel, she could have slipped it up the sleeve of her warm-up jacket and taken it to her locker unseen. To stab Hudson, though, meant she wasn't in the instrument room like she claimed. If so, she'd have been able to leave the room, retrieve the osteotome, and wait for him. Angel wasn't going to be happy, and I suspected Owen wasn't either. Things were not looking good. I hoped Mia liked orange.

TWENTY

I KEPT THINKING THAT MIA MIGHT REMEMBER something, anything, that would help if she was pushed, so I went to talk to her again. I wasn't looking forward to it because of the nonsense in Angel's office, but I had no intention of backing away. She looked taken aback when I showed up at her door.

"What're you doing here? I was pretty clear with your husband that I didn't want to talk to you."

"And I think he was pretty clear with you that if you don't like how he's handling your case, he'll ask your uncle to find another lawyer to represent you."

She stood in the doorway and eyed me for a few seconds. "I'm curious, do you let him talk to you the way he did in the office when we last met? I sort of figured you were the one who wore the pants in the family based on our interactions. I guess I was wrong."

"I'm not here to discuss my marriage with you. Now, can we quit dancing around your obsession with me and get some work done? If not, I'll go, and you can deal with the former homicide detective we use."

Her eyes narrowed, and she gave me a tight-lipped smile. Stepping aside, she said, "By all means, let's talk."

I followed her into her small living room and sat across from her. Frost's comment about getting a person to tell their story backward popped into my head. "I want to try something different. I want you to tell me about the day Hudson died but tell it backward, from finding him back to the start of the day."

"Why?"

I sighed. "Mia, you were scrubbed in on the ortho case the day of Hudson's death that turned up missing an osteotome, you found him, and you are the prime suspect. So far, we haven't been able to find anything to dispute that. Sometimes telling the story backward helps people remember things. Just cooperate, please?" I had no intention of telling her it also made it easier to spot gaps and lies.

She threw her hands up in the air in frustration. "This is so pointless! I've talked and thought about this till I could recite it in my sleep— if I were getting any."

"Well, go over it again for me from when you found Hudson to when the ortho case ended earlier in the day instead of sitting there whining."

"This is why I told your husband I didn't want to talk to you. You're rude."

"I think, if nothing else, this case is proving you don't always get what you want, and trust me, they're a lot ruder in prison, so walk me through it—again."

"Fine." Clearly it wasn't, but at last she knit her brows and thought for a moment. "My shift ended at 7:30. I left the supply room at about seven fifteen to head to the changing room and go home. I heard that clicking and swooshing the automatic doors make when they open and close, and I smelled blood. I mean, I didn't realize what it was initially, but it was blood. I turned the corner and saw him lying there with the doors opening and closing on him. I ran over and pushed the doors open and forced them back to the wall so the locking mechanism would engage. Geoff was lying in a pool of blood. His scrubs were covered in it, and there were several smears leading away from him, like he'd maybe struggled and slipped before going down. And of course, the doors had smeared the blood in an arc as they opened and closed. He was partially lying on the osteotome, and I pulled it out from under him, which is why my handprint was on it."

"Nichols has told the police he saw you holding the osteotome—"

"I wasn't, or maybe he saw me with my hand on it when I pulled it out, I don't know, but he's wrong."

I wasn't going to argue, so I asked, "You didn't call for help. Why?"

"I guess I was too shocked at seeing him lying there. I probably would have if Nichols hadn't shown up."

"All the issues you'd had with him, the trouble he'd caused, yet you tried to help him—"

She cut me off. "For God's sake, I was angry with him, but I would never have left him to die. You really must have a low opinion of me."

"I'm asking questions the prosecution will wonder about as well. Maybe it'd help to think of me as the prosecution."

"That won't be difficult, but I don't appreciate your attitude."

I shrugged and waited to hear her begin again. At last, getting no further reaction or response from me, she resumed her story.

"I remember thinking it was odd he'd be lying on it—the stab wound was in his abdomen. Maybe whoever stabbed him pulled it out and dropped it, and he fell on it. I was panicked. I wasn't sure if anything could be done for him, but I pulled the osteotome out from under him so he'd be flat on the floor, and I put pressure on his abdomen."

She took a deep breath and swiped at her eyes. "I told him I was there and would try to help. He looked up at me, reached out and touched my face, and said he was sorry. Then his arm fell, and he was gone. The next thing I remember is Nichols asking me what I'd done and taking off to get help. It looked like he'd come from the dressing room."

"Why would he be in the dressing room instead of with Hudson?" I knew what Nichols had told me, but I wondered what Mia's take on it would be.

"The last month, Geoff had refused to let him talk to families. I think that's what Geoff was returning from or maybe on his way to do when he was stabbed," she said in frustration. "It was the end of the day for Geoff; according to the surgery schedule I'd seen earlier, he'd have been finished with his last case. He despised Nichols, so maybe he told him to go home to be rid of him."

"That's pretty strong language. Why'd he despise him?"

I had begun to feel sorry for Nichols. No one seemed at all hesitant to criticize him. He had to know about people's opinions; he certainly knew how Hudson felt. Why he hadn't switched specialties was puzzling. Why would you continue a job you knew you weren't good at and that made you unhappy? Then Angel popped into my head. I wasn't entirely sure he was happy on the defense side of the courtroom. He was good at it, but I wasn't sure he'd admit that it didn't suit him. I don't think he believed me when I told him to do what made him happy. His salary made life pretty easy, and Teo and I were probably two of the main reasons for him to stay put. *A discussion for another day*, I thought as I turned my attention back to Mia.

"He had no confidence at all, and he never seemed to catch on. Unless it was simple, straightforward surgery, he waited for Geoff to tell him what to do. You know how some people are naturals for a job? It makes sense to them, they understand what's needed, the work flows well, and they're good at what they do … and some just never catch on. He never caught on, and Geoff was a fanatic about surgery. He was an excellent surgeon, fast, sometimes frighteningly smart, and Nichols couldn't keep up. Geoff said *resident* was a good word for him because he was just residing until his rotation was up."

"Did Nichols rely on Hudson to move him to the next level or give him a good recommendation so he could take the next steps in his career?"

"I don't know for sure, but my guess is his opinion would count. I don't know how heavily. I don't know whether Geoff would have let his personal feelings interfere with a review. Of course, he wouldn't mince words if he thought the guy wasn't measuring up. If he just didn't like him, then I doubt he'd let that interfere." There was a pause. "But I think it was more than personal dislike. I think he felt that Nichols wasn't good enough to be a surgeon. In that case, he might have said something. An evaluation like that could have put an end to Nichols's career, in surgery at least."

She stared off into space, as if reviewing something in her head. "I never saw Nichols push back; he took Geoff's rebuffs and criticisms without any reaction. He never stood up for himself. And the weird thing is, Carol told me he's going to speak at Geoff's memorial at the hospital on Friday. That kinda surprised me, but it's probably politics. A resident can't bad-mouth his deceased mentor or refuse to say anything at his memorial service.

"Might be something for you to look into a little more closely. Threatening your career is something that's worth killing someone for, under the right circumstances," Mia said, then hastily backpedaled. "Although, Nichols doesn't strike me as being gutsy enough to do that. He really is a passive kind of guy. I'm not sure how he's made it this far or why he'd want to be a surgeon. He'd do much better in the path lab or research, someplace that doesn't require thinking on your feet."

Not the first time you've given Nichols a good motive for killing Hudson and then backed off, I thought. "That's all good. It gives me something else to look into."

"Oh, and I noticed Alicia standing in the crowd that collected. She was crying—a lot. Everyone else just seemed stunned. When Detective Carlson escorted me to Barb's office, Joanne Wilson was holding her and letting her cry. It surprised me. I think they'd had a recent falling-out. They'd stopped hanging out or chatting with each other. Maybe it was over Geoff. I don't know if that's important."

"No, that's good." That fit with what Joanne had told me about Alicia.

"It's weird, not sure why I'd remember it, but when Nichols pulled me away from Geoff, I stepped on his foot. He didn't have shoes on under his shoe covers." She had a faraway look, as if she were back in the hallway, standing near Hudson's body. "Why would he have shoe covers and no shoes? Where we were wasn't a restricted area, so he didn't need shoe covers. Hell, he could have come out in his stocking feet … It doesn't make sense."

"It may not now, but you never know if it will eventually. Okay, so back to the story. What happened before you found Hudson?"

"It was a slow night. The early part of the day had been busy, and I was tired. I'd scrubbed two more cases after the ortho case finished. I skipped lunch and then took an early dinner at four thirty. I got back from dinner at five and volunteered to work in the supply room. It was quiet, and I could work at my own pace.

"I had been in there for about an hour, checking supplies for outdates, making sure everything was stocked. I was frustrated because a lot of the packages and supplies had been misplaced or were out of order by date. People get in a hurry and just grab stuff, or they return it and put it in the wrong place.

"But it's quiet in there; all you hear is the hum of the ventilation system. That noise and the door being closed makes it so you can't really hear anything going on outside the room unless it's incredibly loud. I chatted with a few people who came in at various points to get something, but no one had been in there for about half an hour." She paused.

"Who was the last person to come in the supply room?"

"Brian Davies. He needed another lap pack for his next case. The exterior packaging on the pack that had come on the case cart was damaged."

"What time was that?"

"I don't know. I didn't look at the wall clock or my phone. I didn't know I needed to."

There it was again—that snark in her voice—as if I were inconveniencing her rather than trying to find something that'd keep her entitled ass out of prison. She baffled me. I wondered again if she was a snot all the time or simply unable or unwilling to comprehend the trouble she was in. I was convinced she assumed because her uncle and aunt were high-priced, well-connected lawyers, it was a given she'd get off. She was lucky they'd been able to sway the judge into giving her bail and an ankle monitor when others in her situation would be sitting in jail awaiting trial. If the case continued the way it was going, she was going to find out the hard way that the system didn't always work that way, despite it being heavily weighted in favor of rich white people.

"Well, take a guess."

It was like pulling teeth to get her to help herself, and there was something about her that made my hackles rise every time I talked to her. I tried to give people the benefit of the doubt, at least for a while, but if I didn't like her, the jury probably wouldn't either. I wondered if she had enough self-awareness to realize how she came across to people. More than likely, Angel would have his work cut out for him trying to coach her successfully enough that the jury wouldn't see this side of her, whether she testified in her defense or not. Her attitude and body language did not work in her favor. Her voice brought me out of my mental wanderings.

"Six-thirty or so, maybe."

"So when did you get to the supply room?"

"About five fifteen, I think."

"What had you been doing before you went to dinner?"

"I'd finished up my last assigned case and helped terminally clean the room."

"Those two smaller cases weren't ortho?"

"No, they were general surgery cases."

"Okay, tell me about the ortho case."

"It began about seven thirty that morning. I scrubbed. It went well despite the patient having a lot of medical issues. The case ran over a bit, by about fifteen minutes."

"All the counts were correct?"

So much of working in the OR was trying to prevent mistakes or harm to patients, rightfully so. One unbendable practice was counting instruments, as well as needles, sponges, and knife blades, at the beginning of a procedure. Any additions of supplies that figured into the counts were tallied by the circulator as the case progressed. The scrub person and the circulator then counted all these items as the case was finishing. Any discrepancies or missing items had to be resolved before the patient was taken to the PACU to avoid leaving anything in the surgical wound. It was a rare occurrence that anything was left behind, but counting helped ensure nothing was. In this case, it would also help nail down when the osteotome went missing.

She shot me an annoyed look. "Yes, of course they were. When Glen took the patient to the PACU, I broke the back table down and returned the instrument set to the case cart. Then I took it to the pickup area to put it on the elevator to the SPD."

I watched her for a moment. "Was there anyone else in the pickup area?"

"No."

"And you put the cart in the elevator and sent it to the SPD yourself?"

"I ..." She started to respond, then she paused. "No. I'd forgotten about that. Like I said, the case had run over, and we were pressed for time to get the next case started. I knew Glen would be tied up in the PACU longer than usual, so I wanted to get back to the room. The elevator was taking longer to arrive than it normally did, so I waited for a few minutes, then left and asked one of the techs at the desk to wait and send it for me."

"Who was the tech?"

"Betsy Aronson."

Memory is fluid—it morphs as time passes, which is why eyewitness reports can be so unreliable. Her suddenly remembering asking another person to load her case cart on the SPD elevator made me wonder if she was really remembering what had happened or whether her mind was manufacturing information because everyone seemed to think there was something more to remember. At least she'd given me a name. I could interview the tech and confirm what she'd remembered just now.

"About how long were you in the pickup area before you asked her to take care of the cart for you?"

She shrugged. "I … I don't know for sure. Maybe three or four minutes."

"And the room is enclosed, with a door?"

"Yes."

That wasn't great; she could have taken the osteotome while she waited, and no one would have seen her. Or Betsy could have taken it. If so, it was unlikely she'd admit it. I was going to have to track Betsy Aronson down and interview her.

"Okay, that's new information and might prove to be helpful. I appreciate you going over this again. I know it's tedious." I was trying my best to be pleasant. I didn't want any blowback hitting Angel.

As she walked me to the door, out of the blue, she said, "I'm not sure if you realize just how horrible Geoff was to Nichols. I could understand him killing Geoff as a result, but I don't think he had the courage to do it."

"Never underestimate anyone," I said. "We all have it in us to kill, given the right provocation."

"I guess you'd know that better than anyone," Mia said, giving me a thin-lipped smile.

"*What?*" My hand dropped from the door handle in shock.

"I was curious about you. I know you don't like me. I Googled you, and there was a ton of reporting on you shooting your former lover. I was surprised. I wouldn't have thought you'd be that … gutsy."

I stared hard at her, and she took a step back. "You'd be surprised what can happen when someone is pushed too far. You should remember that."

TWENTY-ONE

BRIAN DAVIES WASN'T MUCH HELP fixing a time frame for Mia being in the sterile supply room. I hoped he'd been in there closer to the time she said her shift was over. I'd asked the OR desk assistant to have him call me when he was able, and the call came about fifteen minutes later.

"Mia says you were the last person she saw in the sterile supply room the night of Hudson's death. Can you tell me what time that was?"

I heard him blow out a breath, and the line was silent for a moment. "No, not accurately. Maybe six? I was in a hurry—I wasn't paying attention to the time. We were opening up for our next case, and the lap pack had a small tear in it, so I went to get a replacement. I was only in there for a couple minutes."

"And Mia was there?"

"Yeah," he said, sounding puzzled.

"No one else?"

"No."

"You're sure it wasn't later, like closer to six-thirty?"

"No, it wasn't. Our case was supposed to start at six fifteen."

"Okay, thanks for contacting me."

We just couldn't catch a break. Even her time estimates didn't coincide with Brian's. She might be as innocent as the day is long, but there was nothing to confirm her movements or her side of things.

The memorial service was held in one of the large rooms the hospital used for conferences and receptions. It was a good turnout and included Hudson's wife and daughter. Some were at the do in scrubs and others in suits and business attire. There were a number of OR people I recognized from my interviews. I wasn't sure how many were there because they liked Hudson or if they had been drawn by the drama of his murder. I found Carol Rogers and asked if Betsy Aronson was there. She pointed to a young woman dressed in scrubs standing a few people over. *I must be getting old*, I thought. *She looks like she just graduated from high school.* I moved closer to her so I could catch her and ask her a few questions when the service was over.

Several fellow surgeons spoke, all mentioning his talent and skill, and it seemed they liked him. I'd discovered, though, that no one spoke ill of the dead at a funeral or memorial service. Unless you knew the speakers personally, it was impossible to tell whether their tributes were sincere. *It must be comforting to his daughter to hear the compliments,* I thought. *I wonder what his wife thinks about them.* Looking at Bev Hudson's face, it was hard to tell if she was even listening.

I held my breath when Ted Nichols stepped up to the podium. His hand shook as he pulled a folded piece of paper from his jacket pocket and cleared his throat. He looked around the room nervously and unfolded it. After taking a deep breath, he began.

"Geoff Hudson was an amazing surgeon. He mentored me, and I've learned a lot from him. I only hope one day to be half the surgeon he was." He fiddled with the paper in his hands and looked anxiously around the room before a frown briefly drew his brows together. He took another deep breath and, it seemed to me, forcibly relaxed his face. "As all of you know, he was hard on me. But I believe that was to help me be a better surgeon, and there was no malice in it."

I saw several people near me raise their eyebrows or tip their head close to a companion and whisper something. Nichols's comment surprised me. If what I'd been told by others in the department—and by Ted himself—was true, malice had indeed been intended. It surprised me that he'd brought the subject up, but I supposed it was better to address the elephant in the room than try to ignore it.

"I won't be able to take advantage of his knowledge or skills now nor will others, and that's a great loss. I won't forget what he did or how it affected me." I watched his face and saw the barest flicker of anger pass over it. I took the opportunity to slip out of the crowd, but his statement sent a chill down my spine.

As I reached the door, I heard him say, "He will be missed. Thank you."

His statement could be taken two ways—he appreciated what Hudson had taught him, or he would never forget how Hudson had terrorized him. As much as I disliked Mia Stewart, she was right: Ted Nichols had a viable motive to want Geoff Hudson dead.

I waited at the door to the conference room and watched as people filed out. At last, I spotted Betsy Aronson and fell into step next to her.

"Betsy?"

She turned and gave me a questioning look, obviously trying to place me. "Yes?"

"I'm Annie Collins. I work with Mia Stewart's lawyer, and I wondered if I could talk with you for a few minutes?" I saw her hesitate and quickly added, "I won't keep you long, just a few questions."

"Okay."

Clearly, she was uncomfortable, but I maneuvered her out of the exodus of people and toward the door of a vacant conference room. "You were on duty the day Geoff Hudson was killed, correct?" She nodded. "I was told that Mia asked you to send her case cart to the

SPD for her. Apparently, her case had run over, and she'd been waiting for the elevator to the SPD to arrive. I guess she needed to get back to her room and get set up for the next procedure. Did you take care of that for her?"

"Yeah. I don't know why she asked. The elevator was open and waiting for the cart when I walked into the pickup room. She could have easily taken care of it herself."

"So you didn't touch anything on the cart or open the instrument set?"

She frowned and gave me a puzzled look. "God no. The instruments were dirty, contaminated by that case. I wouldn't handle instruments from a case I'd worked on without gloves and a damn good reason to do that."

"And it didn't look interfered with?"

"How do you mean?"

"I don't know—was the instrument case's lid ajar, was it not on the shelf straight, was there any indication that it had been opened?" I was running out of ideas.

"No, the set was closed and undisturbed. There'd be no reason to open it. None of the instruments could be used without being processed by the SPD." It was as if a light went on. "I wondered why she asked me to do that. As I said, the elevator was open and waiting when I walked in the room. It wouldn't have held her up for more than a couple minutes at that point to push the cart in and hit the down button."

"Did you see where she went after she asked you to take care of the case cart?"

"She headed in the direction of the women's dressing room. I guess she needed to use the facilities before she went back to her room."

"Did Hudson ever hit you up for a hookup?"

"No, he didn't, and I rarely worked with him." She stuck her finger out at me. "Let's get something straight. I didn't do anything other than push the cart onto the elevator and send it down to the SPD. I didn't take anything, including an osteotome, from that set, and I had no grudges against Hudson, so don't you try to pin this on me."

"I'm not trying to. I just wanted to verify her story."

She tipped her chin up at me. "Yeah, well, you'd be smart to take anything she tells you with a pound of salt. And you tell her lawyer, if they want to talk further, I'll bring a lawyer and it'll be a formal deposition. Now I have work to do."

She pushed past me and disappeared down the hallway. *Well, okay then*, I thought as I turned to leave. I'd probably caused more problems than I'd solved.

TWENTY-TWO

I SAT IN ANGEL'S OFFICE WITH FROST, relating what I'd learned in my interviews. "The only new info is that Mia remembered she'd asked Betsy Aronson to send the case cart down to the SPD. I talked to Aronson and didn't make a friend."

Frost laughed. "We rarely do, kid."

"She confirmed that Mia told her she had to get back to her room and the elevator was taking too long, so she asked Betsy to take care of the case cart. That's what Mia told me as well. Aronson, however, says Mia could have taken care of it herself because when she went into the room, the elevator was open and waiting for the cart. She says the instrument case was closed, she denies opening it, and it didn't look tampered with. She also said Mia headed for the women's dressing room, not the OR where her case was scheduled." I sighed. "Aronson was not happy about my questions. She won't talk to you unless it's a formal deposition and her lawyer is present. Sorry."

Angel shrugged. "Well, that's a minor inconvenience for me. I think a deposition is warranted. I'll probably call her as a witness, as her handling the cart creates the possibility that Mia wasn't the one who took the osteotome."

"I don't know. There was no lengthy time lapse between Mia leaving the transport room and approaching Betsy and Betsy taking care of the cart. No one else was in the room. And ..." I said, knowing what the response would be, "Mia headed toward the dressing room, not the OR." I saw the look on Angel's face and shrugged. "Best to know that ahead of time, don't you think? The only person you could implicate is Betsy Aronson, and she's got no motive."

"So she says. Alicia lied about her relationship with Hudson, and so did Mia. Maybe Betsy is lying as well."

I shrugged. I didn't think Betsy was lying. "As far as Alicia being a possible suspect, I talked to the crew that was in the OR when Hudson's death was discovered. They all said Alicia had been in the room for about ten minutes. She was giving the RN in the room a break. But she hadn't been there for the whole case. She was assigned to give breaks. She could have gone anywhere in between going from one room to the next, so that calls into question her whereabouts and gives her a small—very small—window of opportunity to have killed him," I said.

I hadn't told either of them about what Mia had said to me when we last talked. I was still trying to decide how to handle it. More than just dislike, she worried me. Her fixation on me made me extremely uncomfortable. Angel's confrontation with her about our personal lives being off limits clearly hadn't had much effect. Of course, what happened between me and Ian Patterson was in the public record, so it wasn't as if she'd found some deep dark secret. It felt as if she had, though. I was going to have to at least mention it to Angel; keeping things from him hadn't helped.

"You might have to subpoena copies of the surgical records for all the cases for the hour before Hudson was discovered, then we could check the recorded break times," I said. "The RN circulator would record Alicia's name, when she arrived, and when the circulator returned from break on the operative record, and we could follow her movements."

"Why do they do that?" Frost asked.

"Because, legally, a record of who was in the room has to be on the operative record. If something goes wrong or there's a question about something, then you know who was there."

"Huh, the things you learn."

"But generally, for a circulator relieving coworkers for a break or a meal, it's a small window of time exiting one room and entering the next. The time frame just doesn't work. She'd have to be fast and cold enough to stab Hudson and then go give someone a break. It'd take time to get an osteotome—and mind you, she was giving breaks quite some time after the last ortho set had been sent to the SPD, which was around one. Then she'd have had to store it somewhere until she needed it, retrieve it, find him, stab him, change clothes, and get to the room to relieve the circulator. And it would have been a gamble that she'd catch Hudson in a spot or at a time where she could stab him. I can't make all that fit with the timeline."

"The ME knows when he died because Mia witnessed it, but providing an estimate of when he was first injured is really guesswork," Frost commented. "What you've just described makes it pretty unlikely it was Alicia, don't you think?"

"I'd say it eliminates her, unless the time between her previous relief and when she arrived in the next room was long enough and coincided with his time of death. But it's all reliant on a lot of things happening at the perfect time. And then how do you explain how she got the osteotome in the first place?"

"Yeah, it's pretty far-fetched that she did it." Angel dug out the autopsy report and perused it. "The ME said the osteotome hit the right renal artery, and he estimates it could have taken from six to eight minutes for him to bleed out. The death wasn't announced until after Nichols spotted Mia, and that was probably closer to ten minutes after Hudson was stabbed. Based on how long it might have taken him to bleed out and Nichols's statement of the time he found them, we can be somewhat sure of the time Mia discovered him, but we have no idea if whoever killed him engaged in some sort of verbal confrontation before stabbing him. So, the time frame for their confrontation is anybody's guess."

"True, but we know when Hudson's case ended, which helps," I pointed out. "I might be able to find out who he operated on and contact the family to find out when he came out to talk to them and how long he stayed. I don't know if the hospital would give me that info, though."

"See if they will. If you think it's worth it, I can subpoena the records and depose the family."

"Nichols gave me an approximate account of the time he sat in the dressing room before he remembered to go get his pager. If there was enough time between Hudson returning to the OR and getting stabbed, it opens up the time frame that someone other than Mia interacted with him. And Nichols was there and knew where Hudson was and when he'd most likely return. The stumbling block is the osteotome—how'd he get it?"

"You mentioned his friend is an ortho resident ... Johansson?" Angel asked.

"He is, and I suppose he could have gotten the osteotome and given it to Nichols. Or he could have been the one to stab Hudson for Nichols."

"Annie, have you talked to Nichols?" Frost asked.

"Yeah." I told them about my initial conversation. "He spoke well of him at the memorial service they had at the hospital, which is weird considering his relationship with Hudson. But then again, it would probably have looked odd if he hadn't or if he'd said something negative. Politics. He'd have to be seen as supporting Hudson, or he'd look bad.

"His statement about not forgetting what Hudson had done or how it affected him was curious. It was just ambiguous enough to make it hard to tell if he was commenting on the harassment or what Hudson had taught him about surgery. But it makes me wonder. Lord knows he had every reason to want Hudson dead. I plan to talk to him again and question him a little further about whether Hudson was going to give him a poor evaluation. If so, that'd add to his motive."

"What did he say about Hudson when you first talked to him?" Angel asked.

"He said he liked and respected Hudson and that he knew Hudson wasn't especially happy with him, but he hoped he could alter his opinion before his rotation was over. But he'd been with Hudson for almost a year, and that hadn't happened."

Angel was skeptical. "That doesn't make sense to me. Listening to you talk about the interviews you both did, Hudson wasn't just unhappy with him, he could barely tolerate him and rode him mercilessly. How can you claim to like someone who does that to you or talk at his memorial?"

"He probably didn't like him," I said. "But people are reluctant to diss the dead. Makes them look like shits if they do. And as far as the memorial service, it would have looked odd if he didn't say something that addressed the issue, but he had to be careful, or he'd cause himself more trouble. Nichols probably knew he couldn't change Hudson's mind in the short time he had left, but he had a fine line to tread. You suck up to people who hold power over you—we all do."

"Still, it seems odd to me. I'm grasping at straws, I guess."

"Well, one good straw could save the day."

"We just haven't found it yet," Frost said.

I sighed. "I'll talk to him again and see what prompted him to speak at the service."

TWENTY-THREE

IT WAS ONE OF THOSE DAYS. I had planned on interviewing Nichols again and talking to a few other people, but the interviews had to be put on hold because Teo woke up with a cold and a slight fever. It threw a huge monkey wrench in my day and possibly the next few days. I tried to keep the frustration at bay—it wasn't the little guy's fault—but the trial was getting closer, and neither Frost nor I had found anything helpful. It was not a good day for either of us.

He'd turned into an easy baby eventually, but he was a strong-willed two-year-old, a charming little con artist who didn't like being told no. He liked saying it, though. We weren't at the point of locking him in the basement, but there were days when it seemed like a viable option. His grandmother didn't help. She spoiled him rotten, just like she had Angel.

Angel's grandmother, Maria Sandoval, had kept him on the straight and narrow as much as possible. It had apparently taken some effort on her part, though. There had always been a touch of the entitled golden boy about him, but all in all, Angel had turned out well, thanks to Maria. Teo had Frost. I just hoped he turned out like Angel and not Mia. Most of the time, I felt like the bad guy. Dealing with Teo after a day with *Abuelita* was exhausting. Today, dealing with a sick, miserable two-year-old was exhausting for both of us.

After breakfast, one which my son thoroughly rejected, I thought of the women on the list I had been given while trying to interest Teo in some juice and TV. I hoped the sugar would improve his mood and the TV offer some entertainment, but he refused both. Was one of those women a killer? If so, why? You'd have to know going into a liaison with Hudson that the chances of him being serious about you or being committed in any way were next to zero. But love and sex were dangerous latitudes to wander in. Sex could unexpectedly turn into love—like it had with Alicia Harvey—and then, if unrequited or spurned, turn into hate.

People killed for a lot of reasons. All it took was one push to go over the edge. And that reminded me of Mia's comment. I wasn't going to gratify her curiosity by explaining what Ian Patterson had done or that I had killed him in self-defense, but I had to force myself not to respond to that need all of us have to defend ourselves. She had an agenda. I hadn't figured out what it was yet, and it made me uneasy.

Putting my concern about Mia out of my mind, I called Angel. "Can you get Nichols's OR shoes and those of Finley, Johansson, and Harvey analyzed for traces of Hudson's blood on them? There might be at least traces of it, if one of them killed him. I'm not hopeful, but it's something to check out."

"Yeah, I can do that. How's Teo?"

"Crabby. So am I." I heard him chuckle. "Not a good response."

"Sorry, *chica*. I hope things improve."

"Me too," I said and disconnected.

Enough time had passed since the murder that testing any of the shoes of the people who had a motive was likely a waste of time, but we were running out of time and ideas. If one of them was the killer, there had been more than enough opportunity to clean the shoes and pour some bleach on them to effectively destroy the evidence or just throw them away. I'd have cleaned them and then tossed them in a dumpster as far from the hospital as possible, and I'd have gone some-where private and burned the scrubs. But I had learned to think like a criminal working with Frost. Often, people who killed didn't think clearly enough to cover their tracks—or they thought they had and forgot something crucial.

Forensics these days made it so much harder to get away with murder, although sometimes it required luck to catch a killer. A number of famous killers had been caught by sheer accident. Ted Bundy was caught because of a traffic stop, Dennis Rader because of a floppy disk, and David Berkowitz because of a parking ticket.

Maybe Nichols, Finley, Johansson, or Harvey had forgotten about their shoes—or not. The truth was neither Frost nor I had found anything that definitively offered up another suspect, other than the possibility of Nichols. And he had discovered Mia kneeling by Hudson, hands and scrubs covered in blood, which made him an unlikely or at least a clever suspect. There was the faint possibility that Johansson had done it, but that seemed remote to me. At the rate we were going, Mia would probably be convicted.

I had to call Frost and let him know I was out of commission. He could hear the fussing as I held the phone in one hand and Teo on my hip with the other. "Take care of my grandson, kid, and if for some reason you decide to kill him, give me a call, and I'll come over and spell you."

"Who could resist that offer?"

Frost laughed. "Give me the names of the people you had on your to-do list, and I'll touch base with them. Do you think Angel will get access to the shoes for testing?"

"I don't know, but I'm guessing he will. I'll ask when he gets home."

"I had a thought. Nichols had a lot to lose if Hudson trashed him in his review. If you have time today or tomorrow, do a little online digging on Nichols. See what his family is like and see if you can get any dirt on him. I didn't find anything on the criminal background search I did—no priors, not even a traffic ticket."

"Okay," I said, swaying from side to side with Teo in my arms, his head resting in the crook of my neck, and bouncing a little in that age-old mom behavior.

"Angel's gonna depose Dr. Swain, the chief of surgery, tomorrow, so maybe we'll find out more about Hudson's behavior. Angel deposed the head of HR so that's off my list."

I rattled off the people in Hudson's office that I'd planned on talking to. "Calling his office to arrange a time might be best. With Hudson dead, they're probably overwhelmed. If they put you off, then do what you did with Finley. Show up at the reception desk and tell the person why you're there loud enough for patients in the waiting room to hear. That should get you in rather quickly."

Frost laughed. "Okay, I'll keep you posted. Take care of my grandson and don't worry about anything today. Seriously, if you get the urge to strangle him, give me a call. You're not Mother Teresa." I began to sputter and protest, and he just chuckled and disconnected.

Teo was crabby, snot-nosed, and hell to deal with all day. Whiny and irritable, he was uninterested in any of the usual things that normally entertained him. Hot, sweaty, and limp with exhaustion, he insisted on being carried around the entire day. I wasn't Mother Teresa, and there were many days, like today, when I wondered whether I was even competent, let alone a good mother. From what I'd heard, most mothers felt this way—except my mother-in-law, who seemed to think she was perfect. While it was somewhat reassuring that I wasn't alone in my insecurities, it didn't ease the worry that I would be the reason he spent his adult life in a therapist's office.

Carrying nearly twenty-eight pounds of tired, irritable two-year-old wasn't easy, and when I had to set him on the floor temporarily, he cried and immediately begged to be picked up. Nothing seemed to soothe him. It broke my heart that he was so uncomfortable, and it frustrated me that I couldn't find a way to help.

He didn't want to watch TV, he didn't want to play with his toys, and he absolutely didn't want the children's ibuprofen despite the fact that he felt better after he got it. He pretty much didn't want anything I had to offer other than riding around on my hip. The only peace was a brief nap in our bed in the afternoon; he refused to lie down in his own bed. The nap didn't do much to improve his disposition or mine, but his fever broke, and he seemed to feel a bit better upon waking.

I seriously considered calling Frost at one point and taking him up on his offer. Teo and I were both exhausted. It was not the first time I had wished Angel's grandmother was still with us. Maria had had a way with people, especially children, and I could have used her common sense and guidance, but … I would have to walk this path without her. All I really wanted was for someone else to take over so I could lie down and go to sleep.

Angel checked in about an hour before coming home and could hear the exhaustion in my voice. He quickly offered to bring something home for dinner and said he'd take care of Teo once he got home.

Tonight, however, not even *Papi* could manage to make things right. Teo sat at the kitchen table in his booster seat as Angel and I tried to have a conversation. He put plates and food on the table as I prepared a plate for Teo. Angel had brought home mac and cheese for him along with some grown-up food for us.

"I had two people lined up to talk to, but this kind of put an end to that. Were you able to get the shoes looked at?"

Angel nodded. "Yeah, the judge agreed. The DA isn't happy, but …" He shrugged. "We can talk about it once Teo's asleep."

I nodded but was momentarily distracted by Teo's fussing. I put his dinner on the table in front of him. Mac and cheese was normally a big hit, but I saw the frown on my son's face.

"I've been running around like a chicken with my head cut off today. It's good to be home," Angel replied, serving himself some of the food he'd brought home.

Teo swept his plate away and nearly off the table. "No!"

"Teo, it's your favorite. It's mac and cheese, baby, try it." He gave me what we had begun calling "the look." He frowned and looked up at me from beneath his scrunched together eyebrows, his lips pouting, and reached a hand out toward the dish.

"*No gusta!* No want!" he shouted and fired a handful of mac and cheese at my face.

Before I could wipe it off, Angel had lunged up from his chair. "TEO!" he shouted, which made both Teo and me stop in amazement. Angel had never raised his voice with his son, something I couldn't lay claim to.

"You tell *Mamá* you're sorry right now."

Teo stared at his father, and you could almost see him wondering how far he could push this. "No! No like. No want. No want *Mamá!*" he shouted and pushed the bowl off the table onto the floor.

Angel came around to the chair, and I heard him mutter, "*mierda pequeña,*" as he extracted his "little shit" of a son out of his booster seat. He took him into Teo's bedroom and closed the door, which didn't do much to mute the temper tantrum that ensued.

I cleaned the mac and cheese off my face and shirt, put Teo's dish in the kitchen, and cleaned up the mess on the floor. After changing my shirt, I returned to the kitchen table and waited, picking at my food. Short of a tranquilizer, I wasn't sure even Angel could calm his son down.

I took a long sip of my wine. *There's a reason so many pregnancies are accidents*, I thought. *If people knew what they were in for, no one would have kids*. It had taken Angel and me some time to adjust to the idea of a baby. In his practical, easygoing way, Angel had adjusted much quicker than I had. There were days, like today, when I wasn't sure if I'd ever adjust. The last two years had convinced both of us that one kid was plenty.

Half an hour later, Angel emerged leading Teo by the hand. He'd stopped crying, although his face was red and wet with tears as Angel let go and gave him a small encouraging nudge toward me.

Teo walked over and looked up at me. "*Lo siento, Mamá,*" he said in a subdued voice.

I reached down and picked him up. "*Gracias, bebe.*" At which point he snuggled in, wrapped an arm around my neck, and began to suck on his thumb. That's when all the love came surging back. *Mierda pequeña* or not, I wouldn't trade him for the world.

"Remember to behave yourself, *mijo*," Angel said sternly from across the table, and Teo nodded. I had to stop myself from chuckling. It was a side of Angel I'd never seen before, nor had Teo, but people being cross-examined by him probably had.

After finishing dinner and having a bath, an antihistamine cold med, and a cuddle in the rocker for a half hour or so, Teo dropped off to sleep.

"So what did you talk to him about earlier? He seemed pretty subdued when you two came out of the bedroom," I asked as I picked up my glass of wine and joined Angel on the couch in the living room.

"It was a far-ranging conversation."

"With a two-year-old?"

He thought for a moment. "I guess it was more of a monologue delivered to a two-year-old under threat of death if he didn't listen."

I laughed. "That sounds more likely."

Angel was silent for a while, sipping his wine, then reached over and pulled me to him. "I told him he only had one mother and that no matter how upset he was, a man never took it out on his mother."

Before I could interrupt, he said, "I know. I don't need to be reminded that I don't get along with my mother and told her to fuck off once, nor does Teo need to know. I told him he was being a monster and needed to stop."

"That worked?"

"Well, not right away. I finally told him he had a choice: He could apologize to you and mean it, or he could stay in his room the rest of the night, no dinner, no dessert. I think the threat of no dessert convinced him."

I snorted a laugh. "Yeah, no doubt. I know you, though—you wouldn't have denied him dinner or dessert. With Teo, I've discovered that threats without follow-through are dangerous. I feel sorry for the little guy. He's had a rough day. But then, we all have. You look as exhausted as I feel."

He nodded. "I am. I've got the deposition with the head of surgery tomorrow, but honestly, I'm not entirely sure he'll have anything important to add. Right now, all I'm left with is convincing the jury there are a number of other people who could have killed Hudson. That's not good."

"Put it away for tonight."

I sat up and put my wine and his down on the coffee table. Turning to him, I straddled him and sat on his lap. I let my gaze travel over his face, taking in his large dark eyes, and saw him begin to smile. I leaned toward him and ran my fingers through his hair as I kissed him. I could feel him suddenly hard, pressing against me, and ground against him. I felt that familiar urgent need to have him inside me.

"I miss this. We've been so busy with work, with Teo ..." I said, rubbing against him, kissing him deeply, exploring his mouth, feeling the softness of his lips as he kissed me back. He gripped my head, holding me against his mouth, plundering it rather than giving me the quick, fast kisses of late.

Pulling away, he whispered, "Tell me what you miss, *chica*."

"I miss us—the 'before the baby' us," I said as I pulled his T-shirt off and dropped it on the couch beside us. "I miss making love here on the couch if it appealed," I said, kissing the hollow above his collarbone, feeling him shiver. "Or pressed up against the wall if it was urgent, or in the showers we don't take together much anymore." I placed another kiss on his chest, giving him a little nip and hearing his sharp intake of breath. "I miss making love without worrying about Teo walking in on us, interrupting us, having to wait until he's asleep, or having to confine it to our bedroom. I miss lying in bed on Sunday mornings, enjoying each other."

I reached down and undid his jeans, then rose up and undid mine. I stood up and dropped them and my panties to the floor and shrugged out of my top and bra as he scooted out of his jeans and boxer briefs. I knelt back on the couch and settled on him. He sighed and dropped his head back against the couch.

Closing his eyes, he whispered, "*Te sientes muy bien.*"

"This is what I miss." I moved slowly, rocking against him as he reached up and caressed my breasts, pulling me to him so he could take them in his mouth, each in turn, spearing a jolt of arousal with each tug on them. "God, I miss this."

"I'm always here. All you have to do is ask or let me know you want me."

His voice was tight with control. His eyes had become nearly black, his pupils dilated as they did when he was aroused. I knew as he pulled me hard against him, taking my hips in his hands and moving me faster and faster, that he was close. I felt my own orgasm building as he closed his eyes and moaned low and guttural, raising his hips, pushing deep into me, and I came with him, collapsing onto him as I shuddered and pulsed around him.

No matter what happened in our lives, this had always been perfect—a comfort, a release, love in its most elemental form.

"I love you," I whispered into his ear, my breath beginning to slow.

"*Te amo para siempre, Corazón.*"

We lay with eyes closed, breath and heart rates slowing, enjoying the aftermath. Angel fumbled for the couch throw blanket and pulled it over us. It was quiet for a moment or two, and then he said, "You're not on any antibiotics, are you?"

I laughed. "No, we're safe."

"*Mamá?*" we heard Teo say. "I thirsty."

I jolted against Angel, and he tightened his arms around me. "Now what do we do?" I whispered, knowing I was naked as a jaybird under the blanket, and he wasn't in any better condition.

Angel laughed softly, raised his voice, and said, "Go back to your room, *mijo*. I'll bring you a drink in a minute. *Mamá* and I are tired. Give us a minute to wake up."

I heard footsteps. "Me seep wif you."

"NO!" we both said at once.

"Go back to your room, baby. We'll bring you a drink in a minute," I said. I heard him hesitate and then heard his footie-pajama-clad footsteps as he returned to his room, and Angel and I collapsed in muffled laughter.

I pried myself away from him and pulled his T-shirt off the couch, using it to tidy myself up.

"Lucky T-shirt," Angel said with a wicked grin.

I laughed and tossed his T-shirt at him. He held it to his nose and took a deep breath as I pulled my undies, jeans, and top back on. He reached for my hand and pulled me to him for a final kiss. "I hungry. Maybe *Mamá* could bring me something to eat later, in our bedroom, with the door locked."

"Maybe I could, but don't call me *Mamá* when I do."

TWENTY-FOUR

OUR DAYS LATER, FORENSICS HAD COLLECTED all the shoes and their initial report was that all had traces of dried blood on them. The owners all used shoe covers, but shoe covers got torn during the course of a day and didn't offer foolproof protection. While not a surprise considering they were shoes worn in the OR, it was a little gross. I'd read somewhere that lab coats were pointless to wear outside the OR to keep your scrubs clean because they were so rarely washed. I supposed that pertained to shoes as well. Finding the blood traces gave me some hope that something would be found to exonerate Mia. It also allowed Angel to get a trial date continuance until the end of July.

The traces were minute, but as Frost said, it was pretty hard to get rid of blood. If the killer had stepped in Hudson's blood, they had probably cleaned their shoes off or never imagined the police would look. Now that their shoes had been confiscated, I wondered whether Finley, Johansson, Nichols, and Harvey were worried and what they might do.

As I sat at my laptop in our tiny office, I wondered whether examining the shoes would result in anything that would take the spotlight off Mia. The problem was, because they were shoes worn in the OR, they might have blood traces from multiple sources. If so, I doubted DNA analysis would be helpful. Frost said the samples would be considered contaminated if there was more than one source of blood. I didn't know whether that meant that no DNA could be identified at all or whether testing would yield gibberish in terms of information. Neither result would point the finger at anyone, but it needed pursuing.

Confiscating the shoes had tipped off the owners that they were under suspicion. If one of them had killed Hudson and had any other incriminating evidence in their possession, they had plenty of time now to dispose of it. And I suppose they also had time to disappear, if that's what they decided was the only option.

But then again, why would you keep a pair of shoes that you'd walked through your victim's blood in? These were medical people who knew about DNA testing—I mean, who didn't, with all the crime shows on TV? If one of them was guilty, there was most likely nothing to find, and that left Mia hanging. Angel didn't discuss it much, but the closer the trial got, the more he worried that he wasn't going to get an acquittal, and I knew he was getting pressure and micromanaging from Owen Cameron to see that Mia was acquitted.

I hadn't had a chance to investigate Ted Nichols' life while caring for Teo and Frost had been busy with other investigations. As a result I'd been trolling social media and the internet all afternoon trying to catch up. He didn't have any social media accounts, but in Googling his name, I discovered he was a California native who was the eldest of five kids. He'd graduated from Stanford medical school, a top ranked school. That couldn't have been cheap for his parents, especially if you were one of five kids. He'd done his internship at UCLA. Not too shabby either, I thought. He was clearly bright—not just anybody got into Stanford, and UCLA was pretty high-flying as well.

Going further down the Google rabbit hole, I discovered that his father was a well-known, highly sought-after surgeon at UCLA, so money to educate Ted probably hadn't been an issue. I spent some time investigating Bernard Nichols, MD, FACS, who, from what I read, was a rigidly conservative man active in his church and the Republican Party. Based on several of the articles and interviews I perused, his opinions were what I'd characterize as misogynistic and homophobic, a "my way is the only way" kind of guy. He didn't sound like a great dad to have, particularly for someone as quiet and unassuming as Ted.

So what had prompted Ted to come to Denver? Was it the program or a way to escape his father? The University of Colorado med school was a good, solid, well-respected school, but its surgical residency program didn't rank in the top ten like Stanford's did. I figured it was to escape from his father and wondered what Ted's father thought about that or about Ted being so far from his oversight? My guess was he wasn't happy.

I glanced at my phone and gasped. It was almost six, and I was late picking Teo up from his grandmother's. When I got there, she met me at the door and handed me Teo's bag.

"I put some food in his bag for your supper. Since you were so late, I assumed you wouldn't have dinner prepared. I fed Teo when we ate," she said, referring to Angel's father.

Here comes the guilt trip, I thought but tried to tough it out. "Thanks, Sophia, this will come in handy tonight."

She gave me her look—not unlike Teo's belligerent look—and said, "Well, *someone* has to take care of my son and grandson." She held Teo clutched against her chest, as if relinquishing him to me meant his certain death. "You're so busy. You're missing out on being a mother, you know."

I smiled weakly. "I'm sorry I was late," I said. "I appreciate the food and you taking care of Teo."

"You shouldn't be working when he's sick."

"He's feeling back to normal, his symptoms are gone, and his pediatrician said he was fine."

"You put your work over your son. Maybe when you have your next baby, you won't have time to work, and you'll decide to be a real mother."

God, give me patience, I thought. Sophia was the queen of guilt. Before our marriage and for a while afterward, I had mistakenly thought Sophia wasn't quite as bad as Angel often made her out to be. She had welcomed me with open arms, mostly because our marriage had put an end to Angel's single life. She was a bit histrionic and clingy at times, but not a monster. It hadn't taken long for my newlywed rose-colored glasses to disappear and, once she knew I was pregnant, for me to discover she was every bit as bad as he had warned.

Neither Angel nor I planned to tell her there'd be no more kids. We decided to ignore her comments and, if asked point-blank about why we hadn't had a second child, tell her it was God's will that we didn't have any more kids. She could hardly argue against God's will. *Although*, I thought, *I suppose she could pray God would change his mind.* That thought made me uneasy enough to consider talking with Angel about a vasectomy, and that made me smile. I could almost see him going pale and cupping a protective hand over his genitals while he tried to come up with a valid excuse not to get snipped.

When she gave me a puzzled look at seeing me smile, I said, "Gotta go. Thanks again. Come on, Teo, let's head home and see Daddy." I was shocked when he let go of his grandmother's neck and leaned into my arms. Maybe he'd had enough of his *Abuelita* too.

On the way home, as the Wiggles played on the car stereo, I obsessed about all the snappy comebacks I could have said to Sophia and then imagined all the trouble that would have caused. My cell startled me when it rang, and I hit the answer button on my steering wheel.

"Hello?" I asked as I reached out to turn the music down.

"It's … Carol Rogers."

"Hi, what's up?"

"I spoke with Mia, and she said to call you. She thought it might be important."

"I'm driving. Can you call me back in about fifteen minutes?"

When she called, I had given Teo a snack and handed him all his favorite toys. Hopefully, I could take the call and he'd entertain himself.

"What did she want you to call me about?" I asked as I unloaded the food Sophia had sent home.

"I was telling Mia what was going on in the department. It was sort of an update for her, and she thought you and her attorney should know. It's hard to get a hold of him, so I thought I'd call you."

"Okay."

"Nichols is working with Mykowski now to finish out his rotation. I don't think she's all that crazy about having to work with him, but she tolerates him better than Geoff did."

"Well, you wouldn't have to exert yourself to tolerate him better than Hudson did, from what I gather."

"No, I suppose not. He was pretty hard on the guy. I felt sorry for him. Nichols seems different since Geoff's death, though."

I programmed the oven, slipped the casserole dish into it, and leaned against the counter. "Different how?"

"I don't know how to describe it exactly—sort of withdrawn, a little spacey, almost like he's in mourning. That's the best way I can describe it." There was a pause. "He's forgetful. He never forgot things, unless he was assisting Hudson. Then he couldn't seem to remember anything. Hudson made him so nervous he couldn't think straight. Otherwise, he was like a computer when it came to remembering stuff. It's too bad he chose surgery, or maybe it was too bad he was assigned to Hudson. He was gifted with computers. He could probably perform robotic surgery in his sleep, but Hudson never let him do it."

"Really?"

"Yeah. I overheard him talking about creating a new program for his computer. I got lost in all the jargon, but he sounded like an IT guy. He heard me complaining in the lounge about problems with my laptop one day. He told me to bring it in and he'd look at it. I don't know what the problem was, but he fixed it in a few minutes. I guess he did that for others too."

"He sounds like a nice guy."

"Yeah, he is. He's just in the wrong profession. It's sucking the life out of him, as far as I can see."

"You said he's been withdrawn, like he's in mourning. What do you mean by that?"

I could almost hear her thinking, considering what to say. "Well, it must be kinda shocking to have your boss killed, especially one who was as hard on him as Hudson was. Everything's up in the air since that happened," she said at last.

"I mean, he's with Mykowski until his rotation ends, which won't be long now. Maybe he'll have a better experience with her, but Hudson's death has affected everyone in the department. Mykowski is pissed because she can't follow her husband to his new posting. She has her hands full. She's closed the practice to new patients, but she has to complete the scheduled surgeries and follow up—hers and Hudson's— or refer his patients to someone else. Then she's got to find someone to take on what's left of the practice. Realistically? That could take months. Everybody is being weird about everything. But the pressure on Nichols is gone. All he has to do is put in his time now."

"Yeah, that's true. In a way, it's gotten better for him. Hudson's not riding him anymore or making life miserable for him. That's got to be a relief."

"You'd think, right? But he's distracted, doesn't seem to be able to focus well. I mean, he was like that when he was working with Hudson, but you'd think he'd be over that now. Mykowski is easy to work with."

Maybe, I thought. *Unless something happened, in addition to Hudson's death, that traumatized him. It takes a whole lot longer to get over trauma than most people think.* "Did it seem odd to you that he'd speak at the memorial?"

"Not really. What was he supposed to do? I was surprised at how complimentary he was. I don't suppose he had a choice, though."

"Any idea who he's friends with in the residency program?" I remembered what Carrie Saunders had told me, but it was always good to ask.

"He and Chris Johansson are friends. They're both computer geeks, I guess." She hesitated, then plunged on. "I've always gotten a vibe off Nichols and Johansson that maybe there's something more to their friendship."

"More? In what way?"

"Um, you know, maybe gay?"

"As in, they're a couple?"

She hesitated. "I don't really know, and it doesn't matter if they are, right?"

"Of course not. It's just that no one else has said anything like that about them."

"If it's true, they're being careful. I can't prove it. They may just be friends."

"What made you think he's gay?"

"My brother is gay, and my parents can't accept it. I know the lengths he took to conceal that from them for a long time, and I've seen the consequences of coming out when he finally did. I just think it's a possibility, and Nichols may have had reasons to conceal it."

"Did he risk his job if Hudson found out he was gay?"

There was silence on the line for a moment. "I don't … I really don't know. I never heard Hudson say anything overtly antigay, at least not that I'm aware of."

"Is there anybody else Ted's close to?"

"He's close to Mark Gutierrez, the anesthesia tech. Again, they're computer geeks."

"Okay, thanks, Carol. I appreciate you passing the info along."

"Look, I don't want to cause trouble for him—for either of them.

You can't bring up my suspicions, and that's all they are. If he's gay, it's not my place or yours to out him. You have to promise you won't say anything about it to Ted or Chris or anyone else."

"I don't see how that would be an issue. It really doesn't have any bearing on the case. I don't plan to say anything."

"Okay. If it's true … Well, it's a hard row to hoe if you come from a family who can't accept it. I shouldn't have said anything."

"Carol, I'm not going to cause problems for them. I appreciate you letting me know what's going on," I said, and we hung up.

TWENTY-FIVE

ANGEL WALKED IN NOT LONG AFTERWARD. He set his briefcase on the floor and rubbed a hand over his forehead and face as he made his way to our room to shed his suit and get comfortable. I followed him, and as he changed, he asked, "What have you been up to?"

I sat on the edge of our bed and watched him. "I got lost down a rabbit hole of research on Ted Nichols and, by extension, his father. I was late picking Teo up, but your mother came through with food, along with her usual dose of guilt about my parenting skills. At least we won't go hungry."

He smiled and leaned over to give me a quick kiss. He looked exhausted, and lately the dark circles under his eyes never left. I knew, aside from the usual care Angel took with each of his clients, that this was a make-or-break case for him. The consequences of its outcome were anybody's guess, and that had added to both our worries.

"Come sit down and relax. I thought we could eat out on the patio when dinner's ready. Looks like it was a long day." He nodded.

As we returned to the living room, Teo barreled out of his room toward Angel. "*Papi!*" he cried, as if he hadn't seen Angel in years. Angel swung him up in his arms and sat down on the couch. I walked around to the back of the couch and began rubbing his temples as Teo snuggled into him and began babbling about his day at *Abuelita*'s. I felt him relax.

His recount of the day's events over, Teo climbed off Angel's lap and located the little play xylophone resting on the floor near the couch. He began banging on it, sounding like one of those irritating tuneless wind chimes. Sophia had given it to him. She had, in fact, given him most of the toys that made noise. I fantasized about taking them all over to her house so he could entertain her with them.

Angel rubbed his eyes. "*Mijo*, not now. *Papi*'s head hurts." The banging stopped, at least momentarily. Teo looked up from the now silent xylophone and said, "Chill, *Papi*," and then he giggled.

Angel tipped his head back and looked up at me questioningly. "Chill? Where'd he pick that up?"

"Who knows? His cousins are often at your mom's when he's there, and then there's Frost. He's picking up more and more words, so we need to remember that."

Teo climbed back into Angel's lap and settled in. I left them on the couch and set up the patio table for dinner.

Later that evening, when Teo was asleep and things were quiet, I claimed the large lounge on the patio. Angel joined me on it, settling back against me as I massaged his shoulders, enjoying the soft, warm night air and listening to crickets and the occasional dog barking somewhere nearby.

We sat in companionable silence until he said, "Nichols's shoes were brand new. Apparently, he kept shoe covers on, and they had nothing on them. They used luminol to check, and they were clean. Interestingly enough, though, there was a small smear of blood on the carpeted floor in front of his locker that popped up under the light. The forensic bunch took samples and will get back to me."

"We should ask him when he purchased the shoes and why. He could have tossed the shoes he was wearing that night—I would have. Maybe that's why the ones in his locker are clean." As we talked, I massaged his neck and shoulders, which felt like iron bands, and I could feel him gradually relaxing.

I debated about saying anything, then plunged ahead. "Devil's advocate again." I felt him tense. "Nichols admitted he had shoe covers on when he exited the dressing room to get his phone and saw Hudson's body. He stepped into the area and grabbed Mia. It wouldn't be all that surprising if the blood in front of his locker came off his shoe covers as he removed them."

Angel huffed out a sigh. "It's good you point out this stuff, although I'd thought about it. It's like having my own private prosecutor on hand to blow up all my defenses, but not tonight, please. It's been an incredibly frustrating day. Finley's shoes had blood from a number of sources, so the DNA on them is probably so contaminated it's pointless to test it. I won't get the results for another week at least."

"So nothing to incriminate any of them?"

"No, not yet." He sighed heavily. "Maybe we'll luck out with Finley's shoes, but I don't think so. And it's anybody's guess what'll turn up on Harvey's or Johansson's shoes. I need to find out when Nichols purchased his shoes. Maybe, like you said, he replaced the ones with Hudson's blood on them."

"The only shoes or clothes with Hudson's blood on them are Mia's, and she was next to him, so that's not surprising. When this goes to trial, if I can shed enough doubt on whether Mia would murder Hudson, maybe she'll be acquitted or there'll be a hung jury. But a hung jury just means a retrial, so that doesn't solve the problem. All it does is delay the end result."

"Mia's friend Carol Rogers called just before you came home. She gave me a bit of a follow-up on how things have been since Hudson's murder. Nichols has been acting a little odd."

I told him most of what she'd said. He pursed his lips and nodded slowly, digesting the information.

"That needs some follow-up. I'm not surprised he's acting odd. Seeing someone who's been murdered is a shock, even if you're a surgical resident. See if you can talk to Gutierrez and Johansson and get their takes on Nichols. I wonder how they felt about how Hudson treated him."

"I'll see what I can find out. I still have to talk to Nichols again. Teo being sick threw a monkey wrench into that." I didn't want to talk about Carol's suspicions about Nichols and Johansson or whether Hudson had issues with homosexuality and might have used it against Ted. I wanted to talk to Allen Elliott and get his take on what I'd learned. If the suspicions about Nichols were true and might have given him reason to kill Hudson, did that justify Angel airing those suspicions and outing Nichols to get his client off? That didn't feel right to me. I did tell Angel about Ted's dad.

"Not a great family to be raised in."

"No, it's not. The more I hear about Nichols, the sorrier I feel for him. His father must have been horrible to deal with, aside from all the evangelical nonsense. I guess my feeling sorry for him is irrelevant."

"It's not irrelevant. If Hudson threatened to get him thrown out of the program or discuss his performance with the father, that could have given Nichols a motive. I need you to ask around and see what you can find out about whether Hudson would even care enough to get in touch with the father or make any threats. In all honesty, Nichols is the only other person who has a strong reason to want Hudson dead. He just wasn't found kneeling next to the guy."

"Did the deposition with the head of surgery turn up anything?"

"No. I got lots of equivocation and evasion that boiled down to he was a great surgeon, he made the hospital loads of money, and he'd never been disciplined or cautioned about his behavior. I'm waiting for copies of the HR records to see if there's any record of Hudson's behavior with women on file. That might give me some other people to interview."

He leaned back into me, closed his eyes, and pulled my hands from his shoulders to wrap my arms around him. "My brain hurts. Let's not talk about this anymore."

TWENTY-SIX

ALLEN, DO YOU HAVE SOME TIME to go to lunch or meet for coffee? I need to run something by you."

"Sure." He gave me the name of a restaurant near the Cherry Creek Neiman Marcus, where he worked as head buyer. "Let's say noon?"

Sitting in a cozy booth at the small restaurant waiting for our orders, I filled Allen in on what Carol had told me, leaving out the names of those involved. Hudson's name had been all over the media, so that was no secret.

"I don't know what to do with the information. If he's in the closet, and I can see why he'd want to be, then it's not my place to out him. The other side of the coin is, maybe Hudson found out he was gay, knew his father would have a meltdown about it, and threatened his resident with it. It could make him a suspect. Even if there's no proof he killed Hudson, it could add enough reasonable doubt that Angel might be able to get an acquittal."

Allen took a drink of his iced tea. "Have you told Angel about this woman's suspicions?"

"No. I haven't told anyone. I wanted to talk to you first. I have an interview with a good friend of the resident lined up, and I'm trying to get his other friend to agree to meet. I might be able to confirm whether his being gay is true or not. And I still have to talk to him again."

Allen was quiet as the waitress set out food on the table and left. "Here's the problem as I see it," he said, picking up his fork but not using it. "Even now, coming out is never easy, regardless of the family you have, but it's devastating if you have a family like this young man has. It often results in the family totally ostracizing the person. And while he may have a conflicted history with his father, being totally cut off by your family is an emotional blow that not many ever recover from.

"If there is no proof he had anything to do with this guy's murder, and if Angel outs him in court, then you've caused serious family problems for a person based on nothing more than a suspicion by a coworker. She's friends with Angel's client, so there may be an agenda behind her suspicions. If there were proof of his involvement in the murder, or his sexual orientation was openly known, then that's a different story." He thought for a moment. "Of course, if he was openly gay, then the issue of his father's reaction wouldn't be something the surgeon could hold over him."

I sighed and poked at my salad. "I figured you'd say that. I don't know what to do."

"It seems to me, based on what you've told me, the surgeon was abusive and had the power to cause this young man a lot of problems. He wouldn't have *needed* any other reason to kill him. It's not like his being gay is the only motive he'd have."

"True. At the moment, there is nothing other than speculation that implicates him."

"Then you have no reason to pass on gossip. If you discover anything—evidence, mind you, not suspicion—about Hudson threatening him because of his sexual orientation that implicates him, then tell Angel."

Chris Johansson refused to meet with me, saying he didn't have time and didn't have anything to contribute. I'd ask again later and threaten him with a formal deposition to see if that made any difference. If not, Frost could ask. He was good at making it so uncomfortable not to cooperate that people usually caved and talked to him. Years of being a cop had honed that talent to a fine point. If not, Angel could subpoena him.

I met Mark Gutierrez, the anesthesia tech, in the hospital cafeteria the following morning before he was due at work. He was nowhere near as tall as Nichols, probably closer to five foot seven. His dark hair was straight and shiny, and he looked uncomfortable.

"Thanks for agreeing to meet me here before work. I'm sorry it has to be so early."

I smiled, trying to put him at ease. "I have a two-year-old. The days of sleeping past six a.m. are long gone." That got a smile in return.

"What did you need?" he asked, sitting down at the table with a coffee and a muffin.

"I understand that you're friends with Ted Nichols. I'd like to ask you about him."

The smile died. "I don't talk about friends behind their backs."

"Mark, this isn't gossiping, it's a murder investigation. I'm interviewing a lot of people in the department. I'm asking about Ted because of his relationship with Hudson, not to cause problems for him."

"Ted's not accused of murdering Hudson; Mia Stewart is. I know your boss's job is to find a way to get her acquitted, but I'm not sacrificing Ted to do that."

"You're right, Ted's not on trial. I'm not asking you to sacrifice him. I'm just trying to get a picture of what was going on around the time of Hudson's murder. Other people have told me Hudson was stressed about something. I wondered if Ted spoke to you about it."

"Everybody had noticed that. I heard his partner was leaving. That probably played a role in it. Nothing had changed between him and Ted—it was the same abuse as it always had been."

"Did Ted tell you anything about it or mention why he thought Hudson was stressed?"

"No, we tried not to talk about Hudson after a few early conversations. It made Ted anxious, and there wasn't much point in talking about it. Hudson wasn't going to change, and there wasn't anything Ted could do to change the situation."

"Tell me how you got to be friends, what he's like, and what's going on with him now. I've heard that he's different since Hudson's death. I wondered what you thought."

"Wouldn't you be if your boss was killed?"

"Yes, I would. Do you think that's all it is?"

"Other than everybody thinking Hudson's treatment of him makes him a prime suspect?"

I was taking the wrong approach, and he was getting twitchy, so I changed course. "Seriously, Mark, I'm not here to try to implicate Ted. Background information is all I'm asking for."

"Okay."

He didn't look entirely convinced, so I'd softball him a few questions and see where it went.

"How'd you get to be friends?"

He relaxed a bit. "Because of how badly Hudson treated Ted. I came across him sitting in the men's locker room one night after he'd finished a long day of cases with Hudson. He looked … depressed. I was coming off duty, and I'd chatted briefly with him a couple times in the OR, so I asked if he was okay. He didn't reply. He just sat there, staring at the floor. I volunteer for a suicide hotline, and he worried me, so I told him if he wanted to talk, I would listen.

"It took him a minute or two before he said he was no good at surgery and being with Hudson just confirmed it. I was surprised that he volunteered that so quickly. Sometimes it takes a while to get people to begin talking, but it was almost like telling him I would listen had opened the floodgates. He told me he never really wanted to be a surgeon. He said he'd much rather have gone into IT, but his dad—Bernard Nichols—wanted him to go into medicine. His father's a bigwig surgeon who works at UCLA, does all sorts of cutting-edge procedures. Anyway, his dad, he said, wouldn't hear of it. He put the pressure on until Ted relented and went to med school.

"We talked about what had happened that day with Hudson, and I suggested we go down to the cafeteria and talk rather than in the changing room, where someone might overhear. We got to talking about computers—they're a hobby of mine—and we clicked. I must have sat there for more than an hour talking to him. He's a nice guy; he just couldn't stand up to his father. Couldn't stand up to Hudson either. I told him Hudson was bullying him and he should file a complaint so someone would force Hudson to stop. I told him if he stood up for himself, Hudson would have more respect for him, but that isn't Ted's nature.

"In retrospect, reporting Hudson probably wouldn't have been a good idea. It would have given him more ammunition against Ted. I shouldn't have said anything. I meant well, but things are never as cut-and-dried as you think, and it put pressure on Ted. He didn't need that."

"Do you have any idea what Hudson disliked about Ted?" He shook his head but wouldn't look at me. "Mark, sometimes the smallest thing can help shine a light on events. Other than Ted's skills as a surgeon, was there any other reason Hudson might have disliked him? Maybe something personal."

He gave me a cautious look. "Like what?"

"I don't know, maybe something he found out about Ted? If you know about anything, it could be important information."

"Ted's my friend. It's not my place to talk about his personal life."

"Is there something about his personal life that Hudson would object to?" I felt like I had stepped out onto a slippery and dangerous ledge.

"Not that I know of. Hudson just didn't … I don't know." He sipped his coffee as he looked around the cafeteria. After a moment or two, it seemed he made up his mind and began to talk. "I overheard a couple surgeons talking not long after Ted began his rotation with Hudson. One mentioned that the surgeon Ted had been assigned to for his previous clinical rotation had been pressured into taking him on. According to the person I overheard, it was the talk of the department. That rotation was at another facility, so it was the first I'd heard of it, but I can imagine, if it was true, how much resentment might be turned on Ted. It may have been part of what Hudson held against him."

"Who pressured the surgeon?"

"The program chief at the other hospital. The person I overheard thought the program chief was being pressured by Ted's father." Mark frowned. "If that pressure was put on Hudson, it would have pissed him off. But I think Ted's passiveness and hesitancy was what irritated Hudson. It made Ted a perfect punching bag. You know how some kids in school become victims of bullies because they're different? Hudson was a bully, and I think in some twisted way he wanted to see how far Ted would let him go before he pushed back."

"I've done a little research on Ted and his family. His father sounds like a really unpleasant person."

He pushed his coffee away and watched people coming and going in the coffee shop. "Listening to Ted talk about his father, he sounded a lot like Hudson, actually," he said at last.

"Was there anything in particular that Ted wanted kept from his father?"

"I know what you're fishing for. Ted's father is an evangelical, gay-hating monster, and I'm guessing that you think Ted is gay because of his friendship with me or Johansson and that's what Hudson found out and was holding over him."

"Well, that would certainly be something Hudson could use to hold over him. If Ted is gay, Hudson might have used that against him."

"Ted's not gay. He's shy and socially awkward, especially with women. He's much more relaxed and comfortable with me and Chris. That doesn't make him gay."

"Of course not, and it's fine if he is, or it should be. With a father like he has, though, if Ted was gay, it would put him in a difficult position and might have given Hudson something to torment him about. The only reason I asked about personal issues is that Hudson's abuse seemed so personal, from what I've heard. I wondered if you knew what might have been the cause."

"I'm not sure what was at the heart of Hudson's behavior. It's possible Hudson was pressured into taking Ted on. I have no idea. As far as what he wanted to hide, Ted wanted his entire life kept from his father. The threat to get Ted thrown out of the program—if that's what Hudson was doing—would have caused a lot of problems for him. Hudson wouldn't have had to threaten him with anything else. But Ted never related any threats like that to me."

I wasn't sure whether he'd say anything further, but I waited giving him a chance to continue. I sipped my coffee and waited.

"I don't think Hudson would have cared about someone being gay, but Ted couldn't afford to have Hudson get him thrown out of the program," Mark said at last. "If Hudson was holding anything over him, it was the threat to get him thrown out. Ted used to joke that his father would 'cast him out' if he didn't conform to his wishes. I don't think he was joking."

"What about Johansson?"

"They clicked pretty quickly—both like computers, and they're pretty tight. They spend a lot of time together. Ted wouldn't challenge or fight back against Hudson, and that frustrated Chris. Hudson deserved it, but I can't imagine either of them killing him." He glanced at his phone to check the time then stood up and gathered his trash. "Mia, on the other hand, might. She's a cold one. Your boss is going to have his work cut out for him. Not many people in the department like her, and from the scuttlebutt going around, pretty much everyone thinks she did it. I have to get to work."

He started to walk away and turned back. "The saddest thing about all this is that Ted was never happier than when we were talking about or working on computers or playing some video game. But he wouldn't walk away from the surgical track and do something he loved. When what happened between him and Hudson is exposed at trial"—he held his hand up as if to stop me from replying, although I hadn't planned to—"and his father finds out, maybe he can get a life and be happy."

"The information about the family is interesting," Frost said over the phone. "Maybe Angel can get a subpoena to have the forensic bunch go over Johansson's locker with luminol and see if there's any blood present. The night of the murder, nobody even mentioned that Johansson was friends with Nichols. He wasn't in the OR that night, so no one interviewed him.

"The forensic bunch went over Nichols's locker, and it was clean. Just that small stain in front of his locker, which, as you said, he could have tracked in after corralling Mia at the scene. If Nichols didn't kill Geoff, maybe Johansson did it for him. If so, he'd have to have stored his shoes and scrubs there until he could get rid of them. That had to leave traces."

"Okay, I'll let Angel know." I called and told Angel what Frost had in mind. "They're close friends, and Gutierrez says Johansson was upset about Hudson hassling Nichols. I know you had his shoes confiscated, but a search of his locker might reveal traces of blood or something incriminating."

I could hear the relief in his voice. "*Chica*, I think you may have hit on something. I'll talk to you later."

"It was Frost's idea—credit where credit is due."

"Tell him thanks."

"How about you tell him?"

"Fine."

Maybe a thanks from Angel would resolve some of the competition and tension between the two. I called Frost back. "Angel will let you know about checking out Johansson's locker. He'll need you there to supervise. In the meantime, I'm going to try to set up an interview with Johansson again. If he blows me off, then I'll need you to go after him. Maybe he'll talk to you."

"Okay, keep me posted."

TWENTY-SEVEN

CHRIS JOHANSSON RELUCTANTLY AGREED to talk to me after I threatened him with a deposition subpoena. We met at a coffee shop on his day off. He was tall, broad-shouldered, and wore his blond hair in a close-cut style. His large hands looked entirely capable of wielding an osteotome with ease. It was clear by the look on his face that he wasn't happy about meeting with me.

"I don't know what you think I can tell you about Hudson's death. It's annoying as hell to be threatened with a formal deposition."

"That's what happens when you won't willingly agree to talk. It's a murder investigation, and Mia's lawyer would have subpoenaed you if you continued to be uncooperative. You were friends with Ted Nichols, and you were the assistant on the ortho case that came up missing an osteotome the day he was killed. That makes you a key person to interview. The best way to get this over is to get on with it."

"What d'you want to know?"

"What did you do when the case you assisted on finished?"

"I went with the patient, Glen Paulson, the circulator; and Bob MacPhearson, the anesthesia provider, to the PACU. Finley headed out to talk to the family while I wrote orders and discussed the post-op care with the PACU staff."

"So you had nothing to do with the instrument set after the case finished?"

"No, as I said, I was in the PACU. I can't even tell you where the instruments go after a case finishes other than to say that the scrub person handles them."

"Okay, that's good to know." I scrolled through my notes on my phone, then asked, "Tell me about Ted Nichols. How'd you get to be friends?"

"Mark Gutierrez introduced us. He heard me talking about a new movie I'd seen. We all like computers, video games, and sci-fi movies, so he introduced us. I like Ted. Regardless of what Hudson thought, Ted's an interesting guy. Smart and surprisingly funny when he isn't at the hospital. He should never have gone into medicine—certainly not surgery."

He took a sip of coffee and looked off into space. "He should have been allowed to choose what he wanted to do, or—and this was highly unlikely—he should have told his father to take a flying leap. He didn't need his father's money. He's bright enough he could have gotten a scholarship to college and any postgrad program he wanted. Plenty of us manage without a parent's help. He didn't have to go into medicine, but Ted wouldn't stand up to his father any more than he would stand up to Hudson."

"He went to medical school in California, did his internship there as well. Did he choose a residency in Colorado to get away from his father?"

"Yeah, pretty much. His father was angry about that, but at least it was a surgical residency, so that appeased him somewhat. He pressured several people in charge of the residency program to get Ted valuable rotations, which pissed people off, and that bounced back on Ted."

"You know that for a fact?"

"Not personally, Ted never said anything, but I've heard other docs and residents talk about it." He sipped at his coffee, and I wanted to keep him talking.

"What did you hear?"

He heaved a huge sigh. "The surgeons who work with residents had heard talk—rumors—about Ted's performance during his internship, which was less than stellar. Imagine how you'd feel if you were pressured into taking him on as a resident. That means they had to supervise him far more closely than normal to make sure he didn't do something that caused problems for a patient. The result was they were harder on him than other residents, which rattled him and made him more anxious about screwing up, which in turn made it more likely he would. It's a vicious circle. Ted's so miserable, and he doesn't have to be. I've tried my best to talk him into doing something else, but he's gone this far …" He shrugged. "And he's afraid of pissing off his father."

"You seem pretty close to Ted—"

He cut me off. "Oh, for fuck's sake. I hear the rumors, the gossip, the speculation that we're more than friends. And I know what you talked to Mark about. Apparently, two guys can't be close friends without people thinking they're gay. I get so sick of this. It shouldn't even be part of the conversation." He glanced at my ring. "Are you married to a man or are you in a same-sex marriage?" he asked angrily. "See how it feels? No one should have to explain or defend their sexuality. It's nobody else's business. I know there were rumors, still are, but he's not gay."

"I'm not assuming anything. I've heard the rumors too—that's why I'm asking. What type of relationship did you have with him?"

"We were friends. That's it." He looked at me with his brows drawn together, then it was like a light went on, and his face went thunderous. "I get it now. Mia's lawyer wants to pin the murder on Ted. You're thinking Hudson threatened him, and he killed Hudson to prevent him from telling Ted's father his only son was gay. It's bullshit. He's not gay, and we're not a couple. He's just too nice, incredibly awkward with women, and he put up with too much crap from Hudson and his father. Hudson was a bastard, but Ted wouldn't even stand up to him let alone kill him. He wouldn't hurt a fly, and don't you try to pin it on him just to get that bitch off," he said angrily, stabbing a finger at me.

"Sounds like you don't think much of her. Why's that?"

"She didn't treat Ted any better than Hudson did."

"She says she tried to help him and suggested he file a complaint. She said she felt sorry for him."

Chris laughed. "Yeah, she talked long and hard to try to get him to file a complaint. Mark suggested it to Ted as well, but when I explained the consequences to Ted, he backed off. Mark meant well and didn't realize what the consequences would be. But Mia knew the kind of trouble it would have caused for him and tried to get him to do it anyway. I never saw her help him, and I don't like her much. He's never told me she helped him either."

"How would she have helped him, especially during surgery?"

"There are some scrub nurses and techs who are really good at anticipating what a surgeon needs. They know the procedures, they watch what's going on, and they often give the surgeon what they need before they ask. Mia is that good. It's why Hudson liked working with her. She could have handed Ted what he needed to help cover for his uncertainty, which might have given him some confidence. She could have done that and helped deflect some of Hudson's abuse. He and I talked about it; she never did that. Urging him to file a complaint wasn't to help, it was so Hudson would get pissed off enough to get rid of him."

"Why would she do that?"

"She was infatuated with Hudson and probably thought he'd thank her for it, but if Hudson wanted to get rid of Ted, he'd have done it early on. His rotation was nearing an end, so there was no point trying to get rid of Ted now, but I doubt if she thought that far. She thought no one knew she was involved with Hudson, but it wasn't hard to figure out. Rumor is, she dumped him when she found out he was married. I think it's far more likely he dumped her, and she was the one pursuing him. I've never known Hudson to stick with one of his extracurricular playmates for long."

He finished his coffee, and it was clear he was done with our conversation. "I know how defense lawyers work when they can't find proof that their client is innocent. They throw doubt on whether the accused actually did the crime and try to find other people who might have done it. They make it so there's enough reasonable doubt that they get an acquittal or a mistrial."

He stood up and again thrust an index finger at me. "Do not go there. Ted and I are friends. He never mentioned Hudson threatening him about anything, including thinking he was gay. All the fucking bastard did was destroy what little confidence Ted had and make him miserable. He deserved what happened. I don't know who killed him, but it wasn't Ted."

Interesting take on things, and a part of me, not unlike Hamlet's mother, thought that when it came to Ted's sexual orientation, Chris Johansson protested too much. But the reality was, Ted had more than enough motive to have killed Hudson without the issue of his sexual orientation having anything to do with it. He'd been bullied by his father and bullied by Hudson, and mild-mannered or not, everyone has a tipping point. The question was, had Ted Nichols reached his tipping point, and was he the one who stabbed Hudson?

Ted Nichols agreed, reluctantly, to speak to me again when the cases he was assisting on had finished for the day. As a result, the interview would be after six. I touched base with Angel, and he came home early to relieve his sister Gabriela, who was babysitting, and get dinner on. I had won the husband lottery, no doubt.

The cafeteria was quiet when I walked in and spotted Ted sitting in an isolated corner.

"Thanks for agreeing to talk with me again."

"Chris told me that her lawyer would just subpoena me for a formal deposition, so here I am."

I wanted to warn him in case he thought talking to me would put an end to interviews. "He may still do that, if your testimony helps his client."

"I figured that was the case." He sighed dispiritedly. "What do you want to know?"

"Hudson, from all reports I've heard, was horrible to you. It seemed … personal. Why do you think he behaved like that?" I'd asked him about this in our first conversation, but with Mark Gutierrez's input, I wanted to see if Ted would open up more.

He shrugged. "Who knows? My father has thrown his weight around trying to influence what rotations I'm assigned to, and that hasn't gone over well at all. Because of it, people see me as an overprivileged legacy who's being forced down their throats. It was worse in California. I'd hoped it would be better here, but he has a long reach.

"I doubt my father managed to make anyone take me on, but being related to him has annoyed most of the surgeons I've worked with. They know who he is and probably have run into him at conferences. He's not very likable, which may have turned them against me. Most surgeons don't take to people who they think got where they are by riding someone's coattails. Hudson was the only one who took it out on me in an obvious, public way."

He paused and stared off into space. "I … I don't know why he did that. I irritated him, that was clear. I wasn't like him and never will be. I think he felt like I was a millstone around his neck. I don't know. Whatever the reason, I was never right or fast enough or decisive enough to suit him."

"And you didn't feel like you could ask to be reassigned?"

He gave me a disgruntled look. "Right. Gee, why didn't I think of that? What d'you think would have happened? If I couldn't be reassigned, I'd have just made my life absolute hell." He gazed down at his hands that rested on the table. "It wasn't that bad to begin with. I knew he didn't like me but it was tolerable. By the time it became really bad,

I only had a little over three months left. I just had to endure it until the year's rotation was over and hope my next assignment was better."

"Mark Gutierrez and Chris Johansson tell me you're a computer whiz, and neither of them can understand why you didn't go into that field. They said it makes you happy, and you're really good at it. Why surgery?"

"It was expected, and you don't defy my father."

"What would've happened if you had?"

"He'd have cut me off from my family and his support."

"I get why it'd be painful to be cut off from family—that'd be hard. But even without family financial support, lots of people get scholarships or take out student loans to get through school. From what Chris Johansson said, you're smart enough you could have gotten scholarships for undergrad and graduate school."

"You have all the answers, don't you?"

This was not going well, so I backtracked. "I'm sorry, I don't mean to make light of your situation. I've never experienced a parent that domineering."

"If I'd known what residency would be like, I'd have told him to go to hell. At least, I'd like to think I would have. But I've gone this far; I may as well finish."

"Would Hudson have given you a bad evaluation or tried to get you thrown out of the program?"

"He hadn't yet, but he could have. With only three months or so to go, he probably wouldn't have bothered. I think he enjoyed tormenting me and holding that possibility over me too much to actually do it. Getting rid of me would have inconvenienced him—talking to the program coordinator, explaining the problem, and then being without a resident to take care of all the minutiae and late-night calls he didn't want to deal with. We only had a relatively short time to endure each other. I doubt it would have been worth pursuing."

He leaned forward, elbows on the table, and said, "I talked to Chris, and he told me what you asked. To be clear, we're good friends but not romantically involved. The last few years, and especially recently, I haven't had the energy to date or try to pursue a relationship with anyone. I also know it's your boss's job to muddy the water for the jury to try to get Mia Stewart off, but he better not make up stuff about me."

"He would never do that." I decided to forge on, despite his anger. "I'm surprised at the animosity you and Chris have toward Mia. She claims she tried to help you—"

He barked out a laugh. "Of course she'd say that. Chris told me what Mia said to you. She never helped. I think she enjoyed what Hudson was doing as much as he did. I agree with him—I doubt if she dumped Hudson or that he was pursuing her. Far more likely it was the other way around."

He pushed back from the table and stood up, glaring down at me. "I didn't kill him because of his treatment of me or threats to get me thrown out of the program or over revealing any imagined gay relationship to my rabidly evangelical father. I didn't kill Hudson, but I wouldn't be surprised if Mia did, so take that into consideration when she tells you anything." And he stalked off.

I didn't like Mia at all, and it was far easier for me to believe she killed Hudson than not, but it wasn't my job to believe or not. It was Angel's job to get her off. However, when I told him what I'd found out, I wasn't going to sugarcoat it.

TWENTY-EIGHT

S HE'S NOT WELL LIKED BY MOST PEOPLE. Johansson and Nichols both said Hudson probably dumped her, not vice versa, and they think she's capable of killing him. For what that's worth," I said.

Angel coming home tired and irritable had become the new normal, and tonight was no different. He'd come home early to find Teo tired and overindulged by Gabriela but had managed to feed him and put him to bed before I got home. He'd waited to eat, and based on his mood, I was glad we didn't have to deal with a fussy toddler. I hoped I could get Angel to eat and go to bed as well. Sometimes, it felt like I had two toddlers to raise.

He sighed and shook his head. "It's not worth much. There's no proof that he dumped her—no one really knows—and she denies it. All of us can kill if pushed the wrong way. Fortunately, most of us don't. She's not a likable person, but I don't think she's a killer. You don't like her, but mutual dislike doesn't prove anything."

"Yeah, I know."

"Trust me, I have to keep reminding myself that it's not my job to like her, and I don't," he said as he stopped putting food on his plate and frowned at me. "My job is to represent her to the best of my ability and get her acquitted. But one thing's for sure, I will never represent the relative of any person in the firm from here on out."

"Good. It's a no-win situation, as far as I can tell."

"Owen's driving me nuts, and so is Mia. I'm not even close to forty yet, and look," he said, running his fingers through the hair at his temples. "I'm getting gray hairs!"

"There are only a couple. It's not like you're salt-and-pepper all over yet. Besides, I like it. It adds some gravitas to your pretty-boy looks."

He snorted. "It just means I'm getting old, and this case is responsible."

I sang an off-key version of the refrain from the Beatles' "When I'm Sixty-Four" and made him laugh. "I'll still need you and feed you, and I think it looks kinda hot, so you'll still be getting laid as well."

"That's a relief. The feeling's mutual, by the way." He said, grinning and raising an inquisitive eyebrow in my direction as he ate. Nothing improved Angel's mood more than food and sex.

I managed to arrange a time to speak to the OR director and met her in her office just outside the main OR. She looked to be in her fifties, and she looked tired. Her brown hair had gray woven through it, and there was a droop to her eyes. Her desk was piled with folders and papers. I knew the job was heavy on the administrative side of things rather than the clinical, but most people in similar positions were nurses and kept their finger on the pulse of the OR they ran. She did as well.

"I don't know Mia well, personally. She's good at her job, and there have been no complaints about her. I know there are several surgeons who often request her to either scrub or circulate their cases, as did Hudson. That speaks well of her skills and teamwork." She seemed to hesitate.

I smiled. "I feel like there's a 'but' in there somewhere."

She tipped her head to the side slightly and shrugged. "I don't get the sense that she has a lot of friends, and what friends she does have are primarily surgeons."

"Was she involved with any of them?"

"Not that I know of. There were rumors about her and Hudson, just rumors as far as I know. She's one of those women who seem to relate better to men than women. In my experience, that doesn't endear you to other women. There's nothing wrong with getting along with the men you work with, but when you appear to exclude the women you work with, it can cause problems."

"Did it cause problems?"

"Not overtly, but as I said, she doesn't have a lot of friends and never really fit in with the group. I can't tell you much more than that. Feedback from her last employer was good as well. That probably isn't much help."

"It provides background, and that's always good. Thanks for your time."

It did provide background. She was one of a small group of people who had anything good to say about Mia Stewart. And despite that, there always seemed to be that inevitable "but" that arose when anyone talked about her.

Angel asked that I go over the clothes Mia had picked to wear in court. He wanted her to look confident, capable, and honest, a nurse who could be trusted.

"Nothing flashy or tight or low cut, nothing obviously expensive, and keep the jewelry minimal. She needs to look like someone the jurors can relate to, someone who can be trusted, someone they'd feel safe with if she was caring for them. That's what we're going for. I don't want any surprises on that front. If you have any concerns about what she plans to wear, let me know, and I'll talk to her," Angel said before I left to meet Mia at her apartment.

I had a lot of issues with the practice of dressing a client up to appeal to a jury, especially if they were criminals currently in jail or repeat offenders. But as Angel often told me, showing up in an orange jumpsuit was prejudicial and, in Mia's case, so was wearing clothes that reeked of privilege. I'd never seen her in anything other than jeans or summer pants and nice tops since we first met her in a jail scrub outfit. This would be court, though, so I hoped her clothes would fit Angel's requirements.

I wasn't sure what would make Mia look honest or trustworthy, but I knew what would make her look like the entitled little rich girl she was. We spent an hour looking at the outfits she'd chosen and going through her closet for a couple substitutions. The problem was, most of her clothes and jewelry were obviously expensive, thanks to her family's wealth, but at last we had five conservative outfits chosen.

I picked out a couple pairs of simple stud earrings and advised her not to wear her ten-thousand-dollar Rolex to court.

"I don't understand why you don't want me to wear my watch. It was a gift from my parents when I got my BSN. How could that possibly cause a problem?"

"Jurors come from all walks of life, but my guess is none of them wear a watch that costs ten grand. Most probably know what a Rolex looks like, however, and they know they're expensive. That makes you different from them. You want them to relate to you, not see you as rich or better than they are."

"It's a watch, for God's sake."

"You're right, but it's an expensive one, and it marks you as having the expendable income to buy one. They won't know it was a gift for graduating, and if they did, it might still work against you. There's a lot of antipathy toward wealthy people these days who are seen as having privileges the rest of us do not, including a legal system weighted in favor of rich white people. You don't want that. The fact of the matter is, trials are like movies or plays in some ways. If you set the stage right, people buy into what's being presented."

"Fine," she said with an irritated look on her face. As we headed back to the living room, she surprised me by asking, "Would you like something to drink?"

"No, thanks. I need to go."

"Oh, come on. I'm tired, and I'm going to have a gin and tonic. All this talk about the trial and picking out clothes makes me anxious. I don't want to drink alone. I spend most of my time alone these days." She hesitated. "And I thought, you know, maybe we could put some of our differences to rest over a drink."

I watched her for a minute, looking for an ulterior motive. "Okay," I said at last. It seemed rude to refuse. "But just tonic water for me, please. I'm driving."

She left me in her living room and returned several minutes later with two glasses. "I didn't add any gin to yours," she said, holding out a crystal glass with a lime wedge in it.

I accepted the glass she held out and took a cautious sip. "Thank you." I couldn't taste any alcohol. I looked up and caught her watching me.

"There's really no alcohol in it," she said, rolling her eyes.

"Thanks."

We sat quietly for a minute or two before she said, "Maybe you're used to all this, but the closer the trial gets, the more anxious I get. It's finally gotten scarily real. My life and freedom will depend on a group of people I don't know and probably have little in common with who might judge me by my clothes and jewelry."

"I'm sure it is scary. At this point, I guess you have to let go and trust that the system will work in your favor." I smiled in an attempt to make her feel better. "If it's any consolation, Angel will do everything possible to get an acquittal."

She gave me a half-hearted smile in return and sipped at her drink. I had no real way to reassure her. You could be as innocent as the day you were born and still get convicted. My guess was she was remembering her short stay in the Denver Detention Center awaiting her bond hearing. That was a taste of what awaited her if convicted, and it was unsettling. If it were me, I'd probably be weighing whether to run or tough it out and go to trial.

"I just think it's absurd that how I dress could influence the jury," she said at last. "For that matter, how in the world am I not supposed to react when awful things may be said about me?"

"Look, I get you're anxious, and some of this does seem absurd, but juries are influenced by things like this. You don't want to distract them with something trivial. They need to be listening to what's presented. You want them to see you and not get triggered by your clothes or your attitude."

I hesitated, trying to decide whether to say what I thought or just let it pass. Making up my mind as I finished my drink, I said, "Mia, you may not be aware of this, but you give off some seriously entitled vibes. You don't have a lot of friends among your colleagues. Some of them will be witnesses at your trial, and some of them believe you have the capacity to have killed Geoff Hudson. It'd be to your advantage to watch how you behave in the courtroom. Sit still, pay attention, and keep your face neutral. Watch the witnesses, not the jury, so you don't make them uncomfortable." I shook my head irritably. "A lot of it is a performance just for them."

A scowl appeared, and her lips thinned. "You really are a bitch. I'd think you'd have some sympathy for what I'm facing. I can't for the life of me understand what he sees in you."

She was mercurial; one minute she was trying to mend fences, and the next, when she heard something she didn't like, she attacked. I stood up and smiled, ignoring her comment about Angel. "I am a bitch when it's called for, and I do understand what you're up against. That's why I said what I did. And if you do what you just did in court, you're likely to piss off the jury. Angel can only do so much to try to defend you. Talk to him if you don't believe me."

"Fine, have him call me and set something up."

"Call his secretary and set something up yourself," I said with a tight smile.

Standing there, I felt a little dizzy, but it eased and I left, much relieved to be done with her. As I drove away from her parents' property, the dizziness again swept over me, and my vision blurred. I'd had one glass of tonic water that I was sure had no alcohol in it, but I felt as if I'd had several fully loaded drinks. I pulled over to the curb and parked, thinking the dizziness would resolve, but it didn't. Had she put something in the drink other than alcohol?

Angel was tied up with depositions all day, so I called Frost. "Hey, would you come pick me up? I'm near Mia Stewart's place," I said, giving him the address. "I'm not feeling well. I don't want to drive, and I don't want to call for a ride with a strange driver."

"What's going on?" he asked. I could almost hear the frown on his face.

I hesitated. I didn't want to tell him I thought she'd put something in my drink. It sounded paranoid even to me. "I think I may be coming down with something. I met with Mia to go over her court outfits; I was fine when I arrived and have been all day, but as I left, I started feeling weird."

"Okay, sit tight. I won't be long."

TWENTY-NINE

A FEW MINUTES AFTER FROST HAD HELPED ME into his car, I lifted my head from the headrest, and despite the dizziness, I realized he wasn't heading toward our house. "Where are you going?"

"I'm taking you to urgent care."

"No, Frost, just take me home. I'm probably coming down with something viral. I don't need to be seen."

"Did you have anything to eat or drink at Mia's?"

"A glass of tonic water. Why?"

"Maybe she slipped you something."

"Don't be silly. Why would she do that?" Telling Frost that I had begun to wonder that myself sounded nuts.

"She doesn't like you, and she enjoys rattling your cage and Angel's and then watching the reaction. Because of his boss, Angel's stuck with her. She's playing with both of you and enjoying it." He turned into the urgent care parking lot and stopped. Turning to me as he pulled the keys from the ignition, he said, "It may have nothing to do with her, but I want to make sure you're all right."

"I'd almost rather not know if she dosed me with something. It'll only add to Angel's stress—and mine, for that matter."

"Well, I want to know, and I don't want you having any further contact with her. If your boy needs someone to deal with her, I'll take care of it, and I'll be present when he sees her in the office."

"Maybe Angel could get out of representing her if he knew—"

Frost cut me off. "No, he can't. I wanna know if she slipped you something, but there's no proof she did anything other than offer you a drink. You can be sure, though, if she did dose you, that glass of yours has been washed and there'll be no evidence left. Angel can't accuse her, and he can't use something he *thinks* she did to get out of representing her. He's being paid, and she's cooperating—on the surface at least. Her other shenanigans aren't verifiable and don't rise to the level of refusing to represent her." He gave me his cop look. "But at least if we know what happened, we'll all know who we're dealing with."

"Lord, I hate her."

"Same here, kid. This could be nothing, maybe just some sort of unrelated dizziness, but you need to be assessed to make sure you're not in danger of a serious reaction. Let's wait until we hear the results before we say anything to your boy. No point in yelling 'Fire' until it's necessary."

The urgent care staff collected blood and urine specimens and kept me for almost two hours, assessing my blood pressure and other vital signs. Most of the caregivers came and went without comment, but eventually the attending doc returned.

"I can't say for sure until we see the toxicology results. It could be viral labyrinthitis. But if you ingested something, my guess is it's a high enough dose to cause problems—like the dizziness—but so far I'm not seeing anything worrisome. You're alert and oriented, your vitals are stable, and your symptoms are resolving, so I'm going to discharge you." He looked at Frost. "You need to drive her home and stick around until there's someone who can stay with her, just to be sure."

"No problem," Frost replied. The frown hadn't left his face since he'd picked me up.

"We'll call with the test results, but I think your symptoms will disappear in another couple hours. Lots of fluids to keep you hydrated and help flush any medication that may be on board out of your system. Take it easy—no alcohol, don't drive, don't operate any machinery, don't go skateboarding or operate a blender." He laughed. "You know, the usual 'don't be an idiot' instructions."

I grinned at him. "Sounds like a plan. Thanks."

On the way home, I debated about saying anything to Angel. I'd feel like a paranoid idiot if the drug screen was negative and the dizziness was just some random event. More to the point, I didn't want to add to his stress. He had to work with her. If she'd dosed me with something, knowing Angel, he'd have a hard time keeping his anger about it under control. If he confronted her she'd deny it, and he couldn't prove it. His job was to do his best representing her, and if he knew, it'd make doing that almost impossible.

The house was quiet when we walked in. Gabriela was babysitting and wouldn't bring Teo back until I called and told her I was home. It was a relief to be home, and all I really wanted was to lie down on the couch and take a nap. All I had to do was convince Frost to leave.

"I'm fine, Frost. I'll call Gabriela in a little while to bring Teo home. I won't be alone. You don't need to stay."

"I said I'd stay, so I'll stay. She may not be able to stay once she brings Teo home, and you don't need to be here with my grandson and nobody to help."

There really was no point in arguing with Frost when he'd made his mind up, but I gave it a shot. "If you're here hovering, though, Angel will know something's up. He'll push for an explanation."

"I'm staying. Your car's over by Mia's and will need to be picked up, so it makes sense that I stayed to drop him off at the car so he could bring it home."

"I think you're right about not saying anything to Angel about the possibility of Mia dosing me with something until we know the results of the tests. I don't know what to tell him though."

"All we have to say is you didn't feel well and leave it at that."

"Okay."

By the time Gabriela dropped Teo off, I was feeling pretty much back to normal and Frost had dozed off on the couch. I'd looked up a couple of likely drugs online and figured if she'd given me something, it was most likely a benzodiazepine. I'd never taken Xanax or Valium, and one of their side effects was dizziness. They weren't that hard to come by. Mia's mother probably had a medicine cabinet full of various antianxiety meds. The bitterness of a pill dissolved in a drink would be perfectly covered by the bitterness of tonic water. Assuming that's what she'd done.

The question was, Why? As a way to mess with my head—that was entirely believable. But I'd discovered that since Teo's arrival I had developed the ability to catastrophize. If he fell and bonked his head, I was sure he needed a CT to rule out intracranial bleeding. A stomachache meant a ruptured appendix, and so on. Naturally, I began to wonder if she'd dosed me hoping I'd get in a wreck and conveniently die, leaving her to enjoy Angel minus my presence.

"Don't be ridiculous!" I muttered aloud.

"Be dickless!" I heard Teo say and had to laugh. He was going to be the death of me.

"You sure you're okay? Should you call your doc?" Angel asked after he returned to the house with my car.

"I'm fine. I feel back to normal. I wouldn't have called Frost, but I couldn't drive with the dizziness. I didn't want to call a ride service and be with someone I didn't know, and I knew you were tied up. The dizziness is gone now."

He handed me one of the containers of Chinese food he'd picked up on his way back to the house. Teo was occupied with his cut-up chicken and rice and was ignoring both of us as he fingered food into his mouth. I smiled as I watched him pick up rice grains one by one and pop them into his mouth instead of using his spoon. Then, frustrated with the time and effort involved, he grabbed a fistful of rice and crammed it into his mouth.

"Take it easy, little man. Use your spoon so you don't choke," I said, anxiously watching him to make sure he wouldn't need to be resuscitated. He looked up at me and grinned as the rice stuck to his chin fell onto the table.

"I dickless," he declared.

I looked at Angel and said, "Don't ask." *Angel isn't the only one who is going to go gray early*, I thought.

"How did the clothes selection go?" Angel asked, trying not to laugh at Teo's comment.

"Not bad. I substituted a couple tops for less flashy ones, but it's hard to disguise that her clothes and jewelry are expensive. What we picked out is low-key, though. I told her not to wear her Rolex. Just FYI, she's annoyed with me about that. She said it was a gift from her parents when she graduated from her BSN program. I told her it'd give the jury the wrong impression. They wouldn't know it was a gift, and wearing a ten grand watch wasn't a good idea. I also talked to her about how to behave in court." I decided not to mention the exact nature of the conversation I'd had with her. If she called to talk to him or set up an appointment, I doubted she'd say anything about our confrontation.

"Good, I'm glad you mentioned that. I'm going to meet with her and go over it again closer to trial."

"Not much longer until we're done with this case—and her."

"Yeah, that'll be a relief. The case has kind of soured me on working with Owen. I just hope he backs off when the trial is over. If she's convicted, I may have to look for another job."

"I know he's been micromanaging things. Is it getting worse?"

"You don't know the half of it. If I lose this one, it's pretty much history for me." He ate for a bit, then said, "He seems anxious. I get that it's his niece who's at risk of going to prison, but his behavior puzzles me. It's like there's something more he's worried about. I dunno, maybe he'll calm down regardless of the outcome, but I've been thinking about options just in case."

"Like what?"

"I could run for Denver DA. That election is coming up next January."

"Seriously?"

He shrugged. "It's always an option. I've got the experience on both sides of the aisle. No idea if I'd win, and the political side of it isn't all that appealing. I could find another criminal defense group to work with or see if the DA's office would take me back." He could see the scrunch of my eyebrows, put down his fork, and reached out to grasp my hand. "Don't worry about it, *chica*, This whole thing with Owen will probably all blow over once the trial ends. I'm just thinking about options."

I nodded, but I'd lost my appetite. Mia Stewart was fucking up everything.

THIRTY

IT WAS XANAX. If her motive was simply to mess with my head, I couldn't see how she thought dosing my drink would benefit her. She obviously didn't know Angel well. If I told him, he'd try to find a way to stop representing her, even if it meant quitting his job. I wasn't sure of all the legalities, but I didn't think lawyers could simply decide they didn't like their clients and quit. If he knew what she'd done, it would create a huge problem for us. It would also cause problems for her, and I didn't understand why she'd done it.

It was possible the drink was payback for the run-ins we'd had. If so, it was impulsive and a risky way to handle what had happened. Neither of us liked the other; maybe it was just a way to jerk me around. Perhaps she hoped it'd be enough for me to ask Angel to handle things, or she hoped I'd avoid her. Being with him without interference from me made sense. Her comment about not understanding what he saw in me made me wonder if she wanted me out of the picture completely.

The thought of a fatal car accident floated through my brain again. I brushed it aside. The dose hadn't been high enough to be dangerous, but then I hadn't made any attempt to drive home. Attempting to drive with the dizziness could have had serious consequences. Trying to get me killed seemed totally paranoid, but being stopped and arrested for driving while impaired would have caused huge problems for me and taken me out of the investigation permanently. I decided not to tell

Angel and not to stop handling things he needed me to do. Why give her the satisfaction?

"I think you should stay as far away from her as possible," Frost said, a scowl on his face as we sat in our office.

"If I do that, she'll know why. She'll know I know what she did, and she'll have scored a point and gotten what she wanted—me out of her life. I'm not going to give her the satisfaction."

"If she'd do that, what else would she try?"

"Well, forewarned is forearmed."

Frost shook his head. "You are the most bullheaded woman I've ever known, not counting Evie," he said, referring to his wife. "If Mia hadn't pulled this on you, I'd be history. I'm not sure she's guilty, but there's something not right about her, and I don't want to help her in any way. I'm sticking around for you. You and your boy should be very careful around her."

"I think she's just an entitled rich kid who doesn't like me because I've stood up to her. Honestly? I think she's got a thing for Angel and wants me off the case. She knows he can't stop representing her without losing his job or worse, and I think that makes her feel like she can control him. She really doesn't know him. He's being polite and professional with her, but he's no pushover, and he has a temper. She just hasn't seen it. I've not been as manageable as she'd like, which probably pisses her off. She's just flexing her muscles."

"Maybe you should tell Angel."

I sighed and made a face. "Frost, I've thought about it, but that'd be a nightmare. As logical and practical as he is, when it comes to me and Teo, all that flies out the window. He'd be furious and do something rash. As far as I know, the only way to get out of representing her would be if she was doing something illegal or asked him to, wanted him to mislead the court, was refusing to cooperate, or wasn't paying his fees. She hasn't done any of that, and like you said, there's no proof of what she did to me. I don't think there's any way he can quit in the middle of the case. Telling him what she did would only add to the stress the case has already caused. We need to tough this out, hope for an acquittal, and then be done with her."

Frost shook his head. "I'm not so sure that'd get rid of her, kid, but let's hope. She's got a touch of the Glenn Close character in *Fatal Attraction* about her."

I snorted a laugh. "At least we don't have a bunny."

"No," Frost said. "You have a two-year-old."

And with that, the laugh died in my throat.

I headed to Angel's office, planning on taking him out to lunch or, if he couldn't leave, fetching something and sharing the food with him while he worked.

"Is he free?" I asked Kelly Evans, the receptionist, as I pointed toward Angel's office door.

"He's with a client."

"Is it Mia Stewart?" She nodded. "Okay, I'll knock first."

His door was closed, but I heard his voice, and it didn't sound happy. I tapped quickly and opened the door without waiting. It was intrusive, and had it been anyone other than Mia, I'd have waited in the reception area until the client left. I found Mia with her hand reaching for Angel's face, stopped only by his hand grasping her wrist in midair.

"Am I interrupting something?" My question came out more sharply than I had intended. Mia whirled around with a surprised look on her face and pulled her hand out of Angel's grasp.

"This is a private appointment. Do you always walk in on his clients?" Despite her imperious response, her face was red as she moved away from him.

Before I could reply, Angel said, "It's okay, Annie, the meeting's over. Mia, I'll have Kelly let you know if I need to set up any more appointments."

She gave Angel an annoyed look. "Fine." Turning to me as I stood at the door, she said, "You're looking well."

"Never better, Mia, thanks for asking." I smiled and stepped out of her way as she brushed past me and left. Closing the door, I turned to Angel. "What was that all about?"

"A misunderstanding on her part."

"Some misunderstanding."

He shook his head in annoyance and gave me his "Really?" look. "She thinks that because she's Owen's niece, she's entitled to overstep. I was disabusing her of the idea when you walked in."

"Overstep in a physical way?"

"It didn't get that far."

"That's good to know, but it's a little worrisome." I walked over to him and wrapped my arms around his waist. "I'd like to ask a favor. Whenever she's here, I'd like Kelly or one of the paralegals to sit in on the appointment, or let me or Frost know and we can be here. I don't trust her. Kelly said she was with you, which is why I walked in without waiting for you to respond to my knock. She could easily say you came on to her or assaulted her if you don't play her games. Without a witness, you'd be in trouble."

"After today, that's a good idea." He leaned in and kissed me.

"I came by to see if you wanted to go to lunch, or I could get some takeout, or we could lock the door and just make out." I grinned at him.

"I like that last idea, but not here. Would you mind going and getting takeout? I have some catching up to do on the case that's going to court next week."

"Of course."

I stopped at the reception desk. "Kelly, I'm picking up lunch for Angel and me. Can I get you anything?"

She smiled. "That's so nice of you, but I'm meeting a friend for lunch at one."

I nodded, called in an order, and headed out of his office. As I turned the corner toward the elevators, I was surprised to see Mia standing there. I raised my eyebrows. "Waiting for me or the elevator?"

She made a half-hearted effort to smile and tucked a piece of her hair behind one ear. "You. I didn't want you to get the wrong idea about what you saw. I was going to brush—"

I didn't let her continue. "Mia, don't. I know what you were up to, and so does Angel. Not sure what your goal is, but he's not a pushover, and I can spot bullshit a mile away. Angel's far more forgiving than I am, but he keeps his relationships with clients strictly professional. You may have carried on an affair with Geoff Hudson, but you won't be doing that with Angel." I stared at her and waited.

She scowled. "You clearly don't like me, and I think you could screw up my case. I'm going to ask Uncle Owen to make sure you're not involved in it."

I laughed and shook my head. "Little girl, you're in for a rude awakening."

I turned and chose to use the stairs to avoid further contact with her. Seventeen flights would be good exercise, and I wasn't sure I would be able to stop myself from punching her in the face if I rode down in the elevator with her. More and more of late, I found myself hoping she'd be convicted and sent to jail.

We sat around his desk, eating the sandwiches I'd brought back. Angel frowned as he took a sip of water and gazed out the window behind his desk. I had related the conversation with Mia, and he wasn't happy.

"I thought I should tell you so you can be prepared if Owen confronts you about me."

"I don't think he will. He's not that stupid."

"He might, and then what?"

Angel put his sandwich down and slumped back in his chair. "I haven't said anything, because in a way it's been helpful, but ..."

"But?"

"I've been busy with other clients and their trials since taking on Mia, and every time one finishes up, Owen doesn't assign one to take its place. I'm down to Mia and one other case that goes to trial next week. When I questioned him about it, he said he wanted me to be able to focus on her case. I think he's worried I won't get her off."

He bent his head into his hands and scrubbed at his face. "And then there's the weirdness that you walked in on. She flirts a lot when we meet, likes to touch my arm, link hers with mine on the way out of the office. Then it escalated today. I feel like I'm walking a tightrope—I don't want her attention, and I can avoid it by having another person in the office when she's here, but I can't really say anything about it to Owen. He told me she complained about how I reacted to her 'investigating' us.

"We nearly got into it, because when he called me on it, I told him it wasn't his place to talk about my private life with her or anyone else. I told him all he was entitled to do was talk about my professional qualifications and the info in my bio. He backed down and apologized, but I feel like I'm burning bridges here. I will be so glad when this is over and she's out of my life—one way or another." He paused and then said, "There are times, like today, when I don't care if she's out of our lives because she's in prison or acquitted, which is not good. I've never run up against this with any other client. I owe her the best defense I can give her. I can't let personal feelings interfere with that."

"I'm leaning more and more toward hoping she's convicted," I said and watched Angel grimace. "I don't suppose there's any way you could foist her off on one of the other lawyers in the practice?" He shook his head. "Well then, we'll both just tough it out. If she comes on to you again, let me know, and I'll take care of her."

He laughed. "Please don't. I don't want to have to visit you in prison."

"I'd be careful. Orange really isn't my color." We ate in silence for a bit. "Seriously, though, be careful around her. Don't put yourself in a position to be alone with her."

He reached out and took my hand. "I won't, *Corazón.*"

THIRTY-ONE

I DISCOVERED MIA HAD WORKED at a hospital in New Mexico for several years after graduation before returning to Colorado. It didn't relate to her current case, but I wanted to know how she'd fit in there. I admit it was personal—I'm not above that—but perhaps if there was a pattern of behavior, it might be good to know. I didn't know whether it would help or cause more problems, but I wanted to dig. I called the hospital's OR and asked to speak to the supervisor. It was anyone's guess whether I'd get what I wanted, but it was worth a try.

"I'm working for the lawyer representing Mia Stewart. I understand she worked at your hospital up until last year."

There was a pause. "Why does she need legal representation?"

I sighed. "Perhaps you're unaware of it, but she's been accused of murder and goes to trial in three weeks."

I heard a sharp intake of breath. "I had no idea. Good lord."

"I'd really appreciate any background information you can give me about her."

"What kind of information?"

"Anything, really. Where did she come from, did she talk about family, how'd she get along at your hospital, were there any problems?"

"She did her job well."

"And how did she get along with other employees?"

"Fine, as far as I know. There were no complaints."

"No liaisons with men in the department or surgeons?"

"I can't remember hearing about anything like that. But I'm a supervisor—unless it caused a departmental problem, I'm not sure I'd even know about it."

"Can you put me in touch with one of her coworkers at the time? I'd like to talk with them."

"I need to ask around and see whether there's anyone who'd be willing to contact you. If not, I'll call you back."

"Of course. Please give them my number and ask them to call me directly." I gave her my number and disconnected. I figured it was fifty-fifty whether anyone would call back.

It was nearing eight o'clock. I'd given up on anyone calling me back. People often left for jobs at other facilities or other departments; maybe there wouldn't be anyone to talk to who knew her. A lot of turnover could have happened in two years. I wasn't sure it was worth pursuing, but I never knew what would come through when talking to people or how what they told me would relate to whatever case Frost and I were working on. It might be a waste of time, or it could provide something crucial.

I sat on the bathroom floor, supervising Teo's bath. Angel had yet to come home and the house was quiet. The only noise that could be heard was the splashing going on and Teo's conversation with me and the toys that floated in his bathwater. Bath time, generally speaking, had always been a happy time. As a baby, if he was colicky or unhappy, a stint in the tub made things better. I enjoyed sitting next to the tub and watching him play, sneaking in attempts to clean the day's accumulation of debris off him.

At last, his face, hair, and bum clean, I called an end to it and lifted him out of the tub. After I wrapped him in a towel and carried him into his bedroom, he wriggled free and ran around the room naked, giggling and shrieking as I played keep-away with him. He was so like his father; there was nothing Angel enjoyed more than being free of clothes, although I never had to chase him when he was naked—if anyone was being chased, it was me.

I could see how Sophia had let Angel get away with murder growing up. I was inclined to play with Teo rather than enforce bedtime. I had finally corralled him and got him into his pj's when my phone rang.

Teo had settled and was playing with his stuffed dog, so I sat in the rocker and picked up the call. "Hello?"

"Is this Annie Collins?"

"Yes, who's this?"

"Erika Zamora. My supervisor said you called asking about Mia Stewart. I'm sorry to call so late, but I just got off shift."

"No worries. Thanks for calling. Your supervisor probably told you, but she's been accused of murder and goes to trial in three weeks."

"Yeah, she did. That was quite a surprise."

"So you worked with her?"

"Yes, for the two years she was here."

"Were you friends or just coworkers?"

"Coworkers. I don't think she had any friends." There was a pause. "What exactly do you want to know?"

"Background information. It helps with a defense if we know as much about a person as possible."

"She wasn't one for talking about personal issues. In fact, she never really shared much at all. She did a few things with the group outside of work, but she wasn't really close to anyone. In fact, after she quit, I don't think anyone ever heard from her again."

"Any conflicts with staff or docs?"

"No, not that I'm aware of. She got along with the guys—surgeons and other men that came to the OR. Women, not so much."

"Do you know if she was involved with any of them?"

"Not that I ever knew."

"Where there other problem?"

There was silence for a bit. "If something went wrong or got lost or damaged or there was a misunderstanding, it was never her fault. She always had an excuse and a story about how the other person on the case or someone involved hadn't done something right and had contributed to the problem. Because of that, she really didn't have friends."

"But otherwise, no complaints?"

"None from the head honchos. She didn't endear herself to the staff."

"Okay, thanks for your time. I appreciate the effort."

"No problem. Now that I know what's happened, I'll follow the trial. It'll be interesting to see how it pans out. Hard to blame someone else for murder."

"You can blame, but it doesn't work unless there's evidence," I said.

That had been a waste of time—nothing that was much different from what I'd heard so far from her colleagues here. But I'd learned working with Frost that private investigation was a lot of work and often didn't result in much return. I'd also learned that it never hurt to ask.

It was annoying, though. I wasn't sure what I'd hoped to discover. If I had found something damning, what the hell was I going to do with it? Angel was stuck with her. If he were still with the DA and I'd discovered that she'd had an unhappy relationship with a married doc or had stalked someone, that would help build a case against her. But with Angel as her defense attorney, all it would do is make his job much harder.

I'd been engrossed in the conversation and my thoughts while I checked messages on my phone, never a good idea when in charge of supervising a two-year-old. Looking up, I saw Teo had wandered off and heard the front door open. I leaped up from the rocker and ran into the living room in a panic, sure he'd managed to open the front door and disappear.

"*Mijo*, did you escape from *Mamá*?" He grinned at my sudden panicked appearance in the living room. The sound of his voice shut down the panic, and I smiled back. He shrugged out of his suit jacket, tossed it over the back of a chair, and picked Teo up.

"He scared the life out of me. I was on the phone, and I heard the door open. I thought he'd escaped out the front door." I walked over to them and held out my arms for Teo. "Let me get him settled, and we can sit and talk."

"No, let me. I don't get to do this a lot."

Angel disappeared into Teo's room, and I heard them talking quietly. Peeking around the doorframe, I saw that Angel had turned the lights down low. He sat in the rocker reading a favorite book to Teo, who was curled up in his lap, one small arm lifted to hold on to Angel's earlobe, as was his habit, and the other hand holding his stuffed dog.

Watching them, I teared up a bit. I was always surprised at how deep the feelings ran for my husband and our son. I had never really thought about having kids. I liked them, had a vague idea that eventually I might have one, although if I'd never had a child, I would have been okay with that as well. I had never felt strongly one way or the other about it, mostly because I had never expected to find someone who'd stick around or who would love me enough to make having a child seem possible. Yet there they sat, two unexpected gifts that had been dropped into my lap. Sometimes you hit the jackpot.

"Let's go sit outside. It's nice out tonight. Long day?" I asked, handing Angel a glass of wine when he emerged from Teo's room. He declined dinner, saying he wasn't hungry, which was happening a lot lately. He was tall, and exercising kept him lean and muscled, but he'd lost weight, which worried me. He couldn't afford to lose much.

"They all seem long these days." He walked over to one of the patio lounges and sat down, sighing in relief as he relaxed back against it. "It is nice out here. We should do this more often."

"We should. It'll be fall soon enough. How'd the trial prep go?" His remaining client's trial would begin in several days' time. It wasn't a murder trial, but it was a serious criminal fraud case that could land his client in jail for a long time if things didn't work out as Angel and the client hoped. Angel never disclosed a client's name or privileged information unless I was investigating for him, but he liked to talk about strategy with me. It seemed to be a release valve. I mostly listened and hoped it helped.

I sat down in the lounge next to him and watched as he let his head drop back against the chair and stared up at the patio roof. "He wants to testify at trial, and I had to talk my head off before I could convince him that wasn't a good idea, but I don't think he's given up on the idea. He's the client, and if he insists on testifying, I'll let him after I go over all the reasons he shouldn't do it—again. I may actually have one of my colleagues come in, and we can put him through a mock cross-examination. Maybe that'd terrify him enough to change his mind."

"I think people always want to tell their side of things, and they forget there's a prosecutor waiting to tear them to shreds."

"Yeah, a lot of clients do, but at least I can talk the majority of them out of it. Not sure I can with this guy." He sat up and sipped his wine. He reached for my hand and ran his thumb over the back of it absently. "Then I got a call from the ADA who'll be handling the prosecution, and he offered a plea deal. They're pretty confident they can get a conviction but would like to avoid a trial."

"Was it a good offer?"

"Yeah, pretty damn good, but he won't take it. He insists he's innocent and shouldn't get any jail time. I can't force him, but I went over the situation with him and the risk that a jury would convict him. Still no go, so we go to trial next week. No telling how long the trial will last, but I'm thinking two weeks at least." He took another long sip of his wine before he let his head fall back against the chair again. "I've been at this for two years now, and I'm beginning to think I'm not cut out for this type of work."

"I thought you enjoyed it."

"Conflicted, I guess. Sometimes I think I should have just toughed it out at the DA's instead of taking Owen's offer. But I was so frustrated being there after the insanity surrounding Ian Patterson's revenge and getting put on the back burner because of it that I jumped ship."

I raised my eyebrows at him. "Is it because of Mia's case?"

"Some. I cut my teeth being a prosecutor, and this side of the courtroom has never been completely comfortable. The money's good, and it's made our lives easier—"

I interrupted. "Angel, look what Mia's case is doing to you. The money is nice, but in the grand scheme of things I prefer you happy and poorer rather than unhappy but well paid."

He laughed and took another drink, letting go of my hand. "I'm just tired, *chica*. Don't pay any attention to me."

I sat up and reached for his hand, stroking it. "Here's my two cents: Do what makes you happy, whatever that ends up being."

"You're probably the only woman who'd say that and mean it." He smiled softly at me. "When this case and Mia's are done, we're going on a vacation. Just the two of us. Maybe *Mamá* would take care of Teo for us."

"I'd like that," I said, grinning at him. "I promise, no antibiotics, and I'll bring several boxes of condoms if you want me to."

He barked out a laugh. "No condoms, please, just no antibiotics. I love him to death, but one's enough for me."

"Same here." We sat quietly for a few minutes, listening to the night sounds around us. "I'm superstitious enough to worry about your mother praying for another grandchild. Do you think we should do something permanent about it?" I asked, breaking the silence.

"She can pray all she likes. I've never known it to help. We can talk about it if you want." He set his wineglass down on the cement patio floor and reached for me. "But tonight, let's go inside and practice for the vacation."

"Good idea. You know what they say … Practice makes perfect."

THIRTY-TWO

ANNE, I WAS WONDERING IF WE COULD MEET for lunch today. Would that be possible?"

I was surprised to hear Owen Cameron's voice over my phone. And, as always, I was somewhat apprehensive when someone called me Anne. It never boded well, in my experience. "Okay, has something happened?"

"With Mia? No. I simply want to chat with you over lunch."

He suggested a time and a restaurant located in the lobby of the building that housed his law firm. I warily agreed, wondering why he wanted to meet. I'd never met with him without Angel being present, and those meetings had only been at social events. With huge misgivings, I dressed with care and headed to the restaurant.

Angel was in court for the first day of his remaining client's trial, so I had no way to touch base with him to see if he knew what was going on. I had an uneasy feeling that, despite his denial, it had to do with Mia and our last interaction. The restaurant was quiet and private, just the spot for a little tête-à-tête, and my anxiety ratcheted up a notch.

A hostess escorted me to a table in a secluded nook of the restaurant where Owen sat. He looked dressed for court, wearing a sharply tailored suit and a muted tie, his silver hair perfectly cut and groomed. I joined him, trying to maintain an open friendly manner when I was not feeling open or friendly or at ease.

"Thanks for meeting me. I ordered a bottle of wine. I hope you don't mind," he said, offering me a glass.

I rested my hand over the empty wineglass. "It's a bit early in the day for me. I'll be fine with the water. But thanks," I quickly added, not wanting to offend him.

"My philosophy is it's five o'clock somewhere and life is to be enjoyed. If you change your mind, just let me know." He smiled and replaced the wine bottle in the bucket at the side of the table.

I'd always liked Owen. At least, I liked the Owen I knew—the public, suave Owen who was Angel's senior partner, who'd always been pleasant and chatty with me. The man who sat across from me, however, held Angel's job in his hands, and based on what Angel had been telling me, things were tense between them.

Not wanting to prolong the agony, I said, "So, to what do I owe the pleasure of lunch?"

He tipped his head at me and smiled. "Angel has always said you're direct."

"I find it wastes less time that way." I took a nervous sip of water and stared at him. "Frankly, I was surprised by the invitation. I'm curious what prompted it."

"I wanted to talk to you, as it happens, about just that. Apparently you've been direct, troublingly so, with my niece Mia. She says she doesn't appreciate many of the things you've said to her and wants you off her case."

"I see you can be direct as well."

"As you said, it wastes less time." His smile was far less friendly.

I watched him for a bit until I saw he had become uncomfortable with the silence. A lifetime of dealing with surgeons had given me a backbone, so I said, "What your niece may not have told you is that my directness has been in response to her being evasive and not entirely honest with Angel or me. She's withheld—or tried to withhold—important information, and I think she assumes she'll get off based on the status you and her aunt hold in the legal community. You and her aunt were able to get her bail when anyone else would have been denied or been unable to post it. Most of our conversations have been me trying to get her to tell the whole truth about her role in this debacle and convince her to cooperate. She doesn't like that."

My heart was pounding in my chest, and my hands had gone cold. I hoped like hell I hadn't just gotten my husband fired.

"Still, I think it would be best—"

I had a brief thought that I probably shouldn't say anything further, but I didn't let him continue. I held my hand up to stop him. "What I don't like is her invading our privacy, which you helped her do. I'm sure she didn't tell you, but she has tried to intimidate me by threatening Angel's job, and the private information you gave her about us has made her think she owns him, which includes unwanted physical advances toward him.

"I don't like being intimidated, but I'll happily withdraw from her case. I think Angel has a say in this, though, and I think you should have had this conversation with him, not me. I also think you should trust that he will do the best job possible and let him do it. You're not doing her any favors by interfering and trying to control how he handles the case."

He sat back in his chair, a look of surprise on his face, and took a sip of his wine. "I see."

"I hope you do." I pushed back from the table, stood up, and shouldered my purse. "Thanks for the invitation, but I think I'll pass on lunch." I turned to leave, then turned back to him. "The case against your niece is pretty daunting, but if anyone can get her off, it's Angel. My suggestion is to talk to Angel about me and Mia and then let him do his job. That is, if you want her to have any chance of being acquitted."

My exit was surprisingly controlled despite my shaking hands and how furious I was with Owen Cameron and his damned niece.

"Oh my God!" I shouted in frustration at Frost when I returned to our office and filled him in on the conversation. I'd made the mistake of getting lunch at a drive-through. I'd ordered onion rings, one of my weaknesses, despite knowing my stomach would rebel. In addition to being totally pissed off, I was slightly nauseated, which didn't help.

"That entitled little bitch. I can't believe Owen would even broach the subject with me. He and Angel have already had a confrontation over his telling Mia all about us."

"You should know by now that the rich are different. They play by their own rules, but I gotta say what he did surprises me. You gonna tell your boy?"

I plopped down into the chair behind my desk, ran a hand through my hair, and gathered it up in a ponytail using the covered rubber band from my pants pocket. It was ninety-five degrees outside. Our little AC unit was doing its best to cool things down, but couldn't quite keep up.

"Yeah, I will. I can't just stay out of anything to do with her and hope he doesn't notice. He will—he's not stupid."

"No, he's not, but knowing what his boss did isn't going to help. If he confronts him and it goes south, that won't be good. I'd wait and see if Owen says anything to Angel and let him take care of it."

Frost stretched back in his desk chair and linked his hands behind his head. His jacket hung over the back of his chair, and he'd rolled his shirt sleeves up in deference to the heat. "My guess is he won't after how you handled it. At this point, there isn't a whole lot more we can do. We've talked to everybody who might have had information or a grudge against Hudson. It'd be pretty easy for you to stay out of it."

I rolled my eyes at him. "Frost, I have to tell him. He needs to know what he's up against. I don't want Owen ambushing him. That's when he's likely to blow up. If I tell him, he'll have time to think about what to do.

"Besides, I don't want to withdraw. I want to rub her snotty little nose in the fact that she doesn't control what we do. What's Owen going to do? Get rid of Angel at this late date?"

"You know, you and Evie are almost twins. She's the same as you … stubbornness personified."

"I don't like it when someone tries to manipulate me."

"Your boy looked a little on the skinny side last time I saw him," Frost said, changing the topic. Frost was like that; he didn't beat his head against brick walls. He knew talking me out of something, especially this, wasn't going to happen. "Might be because I haven't seen him in anything other than a suit in a while. His T-shirt was looser than I remember seeing. Everything okay?"

"He's not eating regularly or sleeping all that well. I've never really seen him like this. He gets caught up in cases, but it usually has the opposite effect—it energizes him. This is eating at him. God, I can't wait until it's over. Angel may have to find another job depending on the outcome, but all things considered that'd probably be a good thing."

"Speaking of eating," Frost said deflecting the conversation again. "Evie's been wanting to have you guys over. She keeps reminding me to ask, and I keep forgetting. How about tomorrow night? Bring the little one. Evie will love having him to spoil, and Angel can relax and eat. I'll talk to her and find out a time."

I brought home dinner from one of Angel's favorite restaurants. I had been weighing how to time telling him about what happened. I wanted us to have a quiet dinner so he could relax and put Mia and Owen out of both his mind and mine, but telling him was likely to blow that all to hell. I asked Allen, who was babysitting, if he and Phil would mind keeping Teo for a sleepover, and he readily agreed. The evening, while not a total blowup, had its bumps. Best laid plans, as they say.

Angel walked in around seven and dropped his briefcase near the door. I'd thought for a while about getting him something to deposit his briefcase on or in rather than dropping it on the floor but decided he probably wouldn't use it. He was a creature of habit and had done this for as long as I could remember. It seemed to be his way of leaving work at the door. He walked quickly to the bedroom and changed from his suit to jeans and a T-shirt. Returning, he went into the kitchen and pulled a beer out of the fridge.

"Where's Teo?"

"At Phil and Allen's for a sleepover. I brought dinner home from the Bistro, and I thought we could have a nice night, just the two of us." I started to reach for his hand to tell him what had happened, but he stepped back, leaned against the counter, and took a long swallow of beer, an annoyed look on his face.

"Owen had a chat with me this afternoon. Said he felt you shouldn't be involved with Mia's case going forward."

"I wanted to talk to you about that. He invited me to lunch today. He told me Mia felt I was too direct, didn't like me, and didn't want me working on the case any longer." Angel's brows drew together in a hard scowl. "I told him she'd been evasive and difficult to deal with and thought she'd get off because of who he and her aunt are."

Angel started to say something, and I cut him off. "I told him he should talk to you and then leave you alone to do your job if he wanted Mia to be acquitted. It's up to you how you want to handle it. I'll happily bow out if you want me to. I don't want to cause problems for you."

He slammed his hand on the countertop, then turned and banged out the back door into the yard. I poured a glass of wine for myself and found him stretched out on the lounge on the patio. I sat down on the lounge next to him and sipped my wine in silence.

Several minutes went by before I said, "It's so nice out here this time of night."

"Don't try to change the subject," he snapped.

Okay, there will be no avoiding this, I thought. I hoped it was Owen he was mad at, not me. "Look, I don't care about working on this case." Not true, but I'd forgo my need to get in her face to protect him. "I don't want it to become a bone of contention between you and Owen. I'll just drop out and go back to the PI stuff that Frost's been dealing with alone while we've been working on Mia's case. It's no big deal—"

"It *is* a big deal. It's a damn big deal. He has no right to try to dictate how I work unless I've done something stupid or damaging to the practice. But interfering because his entitled niece doesn't like you is absurd." He slugged down the rest of his beer, got up, and retrieved another from the kitchen.

Instead of returning to the lounge, he paced in front of me. "I told him after his little 'counseling' session that I was at the point of petitioning the court to stop representing her. That I'd had enough of her and his interference, and unless he stopped what he was doing and tried to talk some sense into her, I would withdraw from the case and he could represent her."

I was glad he wasn't mad at me, but my heart had begun to race as I listened to him. He was treading on thin ice. I was just as fed up as he was with the whole thing, but the problem was that Owen could make professional trouble for Angel, and I didn't want that to happen.

"This is not the hill to die on right now, Angel. I know you're furious—I am too—but the trial will start soon, and then it'll be over, and you never have to deal with her again. When the trial ends, you can decide what you want to do. You've said your piece to Owen. He knows where you stand, so let it go. Me working on the case shouldn't be what screws up your job."

"It's more than that. It's that he had the nerve to think it was his place to even broach the subject with you behind my back that pisses me off. He never mentioned the lunch with you."

"Well, to be accurate, I never had lunch. I said my piece and left."

"Good. He's been treating me like a first-year hire since he dropped this case in my lap—hovering, intruding, questioning, suggesting. I'm dead serious. If he doesn't back off, I will petition the court to stop representing her and I'll quit."

I heaved out a breath. "I hoped he wouldn't say anything to you before I could tell you what happened, but he did. It's a done deal, babe. A cooling-off period over the weekend can't hurt. Let things settle down before you return to work on Monday." I sat up and grabbed his hand, pulling him toward me and down onto the lounge. "It's Friday night, and we have it all to ourselves. Dinner's ready to go, and then we can decide what we want to do with the rest of the night." I leaned over and kissed him. "We should take advantage of a night off from parenting, don't you think?"

He smiled, stroked my face, and kissed me. "You arrange a night off from parenting, bring home dinner, listen to me rage on about Owen and Mia, and then talk me into a time-out to keep me from committing professional suicide. I love you." He stood and pulled me up off the lounge. "Let's eat dinner. I have some ideas for later."

Angel's client insisted on testifying, despite Angel doing his best to dissuade him. Listening to an accused testify under oath and tell his side of the story should, in theory, work out well. That rarely works in the defendant's favor when the prosecution has presented a bulletproof case. According to Angel, the prosecutor took the client apart, had him stumbling over his answers and coming very close to perjuring himself. The defendant merely prolonged the inevitable and in the end probably wished he'd taken the deal offered by the DA's office.

"Sometimes I feel like I'm talking to my clients in a foreign language. He wouldn't listen, even after the fake cross that the lawyer

I work with put him through. During that, he kept his cool and came off pretty good, so when he insisted on testifying, I went over all the reasons why he shouldn't, then I quit trying to talk him out of it. It fell apart in the courtroom, and all it got him was a sentence twice as long as the DA offered him."

"I'm sorry." We'd met at a bar near the courthouse for a drink before heading home. I'd thought it might help Angel let off some steam. I wasn't sure if it was working.

"Well, he is too, and pissed—at me!"

"Will he appeal it?"

"Hell, who knows?" He took a generous swallow of his scotch. "I wonder what else I could do with a law degree that doesn't involve clients?"

"You could run for public office. You wouldn't have clients, just constituents."

He rolled his eyes and shook his head. "And donors who expected something in return. No thanks."

THIRTY-THREE

ANGEL PLANNED TO COACH MIA ON HOW she should behave in the courtroom. She was disconcerted when she arrived to find me there and glared at me and, surprisingly, glared at Angel. It seemed even he could piss her off.

"My uncle assured me she wouldn't be present going forward, and I—"

Angel cut her off. "He should have waited until we talked, as I have no intention of letting you or him dictate who I employ. I'll be blunt. Do you want another lawyer?"

She shook her head. "I just don't want her here."

"You don't always get what you want, and if you continue to cause problems and not cooperate, that's grounds for me to ask the court to let me withdraw. The decision is yours—work with me and my employees, do what I ask, or get another lawyer to represent you. I'm sure your uncle would be happy to help you find another lawyer while I ask for a continuance and file the necessary papers to relieve me of my duties to represent you."

"No, I-I don't want to get rid of you. Just keep her away from me." Angel sat and stared at her until finally, a deep frown on her face, she blurted out, "Fine, let's just get on with it."

He gave her a curt nod and began. "Your behavior in this office is a good example of what I do not want you to do in court. No glaring at witnesses or the prosecution under any circumstances. You follow my directions in court without question, understood?"

She nodded.

"Things will be said that you won't like, and you can't react. No sighs, no huffed-out breaths, no displays of frustration, no head shaking or looks of anger or disdain or any other obvious reactions.

"No staring at the jury or the prosecution team at their table. Keep your comments to me to a minimum. There will be reporters in the courtroom watching you. Juries can assume a lot of things—most of them negative—if a witness says something and you lean in and make a comment to me or glare at the witness. Watch the witnesses when they testify, but once they leave the witness stand, they're off limits. It looks like witness intimidation if you stare at them or frown at them, and you do not want that. I don't plan to call you as a witness. If the prosecution tries to, you have the right to refuse. We'll go over how to handle that closer to trial."

"I'm just supposed to sit there?"

"Yes, you are. We want the jury to like you, to think you wouldn't kill someone, or at the very least we don't want them to get negatively triggered by you. If you come across as you have to me and Annie, they're not going to like you."

She let out an exasperated breath and crossed her arms across her chest.

Angel shook his head and pointed at her. "That's what I'm talking about."

"So now I can't even express my opinions in front of you?"

"I'm merely pointing out what I see and how it will affect a jury. You can express yourself however you like in this office, but if you aren't aware of what you're doing, you'll be causing problems for yourself." He plowed on. "You need to understand that juries are human, and they react in unpredictable ways. During jury selection, the prosecution and I have a way of weeding out jurors we don't want on the jury. But we can't be sure what any of them will ultimately decide, so you need to cooperate."

After he finished and she left, I said, "Boy, you have your work cut out for you. She lives in her own little world, like Alicia Harvey. Honestly? I don't think she realizes how easily she could be convicted."

"I think you're right. The prosecution might try to call her, but she can't be compelled to testify. She can also take the fifth under questioning, but most people assume that means you're guilty. I may do what I did with my other client and stage a prosecution interrogation to open her eyes."

"That would be an excellent idea. It might wake her up. I'm going to make a trip to the ladies' room, but how about stopping for some dinner on the way home?"

His face was drawn into what seemed to be a permanent frown these days, and he carried exhaustion around like a millstone around his neck. He gave me a small smile. "How about I pick up some food, you pick up Teo, and we eat at home?"

I smiled and gave him a hug. "Sounds good to me. I'll see you at home."

To get to the reception area from the ladies' room, I had to pass Angel's office. As I neared it, I heard a low-pitched conversation. The door to the office was partly open, so I slowed and stopped short of the door when I heard Owen's voice.

"Angel, all I'm asking is for you to ease up on her a little. She said you threatened to withdraw from representing her."

"I didn't threaten her. I told her it was up to her to decide if she wants me to represent her. If she does, then she needs to trust me, accept how I practice and who I employ, and cooperate. I don't think she has a clue how badly this could go. I've tried to school her on her behavior in court, and she seems to think I'm doing it to annoy her."

"She's scared, and she doesn't trust your wife."

"Annie has gone out of her way to talk to people and use her OR nursing experience to help Mia. Without her help, I'd have wasted a lot of time and energy trying to sort through all the intricacies of this OR. She knows how ORs work, who to talk to, and what to ask. She's come up with several avenues of investigation that I probably wouldn't have thought of, so you can tell Mia her antipathy toward Annie is misplaced. And you might want to talk to her about how to behave in court. She's her own worst enemy, Owen, and that could end up getting her a one-way ticket to prison."

I heard Owen mumble something. "I'll keep you posted," Angel said, and it seemed as if the conversation was over. I turned and walked back down the hall so Owen wouldn't catch me eavesdropping. He walked quickly out of Angel's office without glancing in my direction, and he did not look happy.

"Um … I overheard the conversation," I said, entering Angel's office. He started to say something, and I stopped him. "You don't really need me on this case anymore, and you shouldn't have to spend your time justifying my participation to Owen or Mia, so I'm bowing out. My presence is causing problems for you, and I don't want that. Just promise me you won't meet with her alone, here or anywhere. I don't trust her or what she might do if I'm not around when you meet. I want you to promise me you will have someone who works here or Frost present whenever you meet with her."

He reached for my hand and pulled me into an embrace. "I promise. I'll see you at home."

THIRTY-FOUR

IT TOOK SEVERAL DAYS TO CREATE A JURY from the pool of people who'd been summoned. Angel employed a jury consultant who helped prepare questions he would ask during the *voir dire* process. She also watched and listened to the jurors and identified ones she thought ought to be eliminated. It was a fascinating process. Sometimes the reason for dismissing a potential juror was obvious, but at times it puzzled me.

We didn't talk about it when Angel came home. He had once said it was like playing armchair quarterback. What had happened in court had happened, and he didn't want to reexamine it. Angel seemed to have gotten some energy back now that the case had gone to court and was in full swing, but it was more like he was wired than enthusiastic.

I didn't intend to be there for the actual trial itself. The game playing and verbal fencing that went on was too frustrating, too nerve-racking, to watch on a daily basis. Frost, however, planned to attend every day and would keep me posted. I did plan to be there for closing arguments. If Angel was wired, I was on pins and needles, and I hoped the trial would go quickly. I didn't think either of us were tolerating the tension well.

I didn't ask about the trial, but it wasn't hard to tell Angel was unhappy about the way it was progressing. Most nights, he spent time after dinner out in the backyard with Teo, playing games or just hanging out. It took his mind off the trial, but once Teo was down for the night, he worked in his home office until late in the night. I would often hear him practicing his closing argument as he paced in front of his desk. At midnight or one a.m., I would finally convince him to come to bed. Some nights he fell asleep, his head cradled in his arms on his desktop. I knew if I woke him to come to bed, he'd be unable to sleep, so I waited until he woke himself up and decided to come to bed or, as he had taken to doing, sit out on the patio until he fell asleep on the lounge.

The night before closing arguments would take place, he surprised me by inviting me to sit with him on the patio. The house was quiet; Teo was spending the next few nights with Angel's parents. Sophia's request was a relief. Angel and I were both stressed, and a couple nights off was a gift. We'd had a late dinner because he hadn't gotten home until nearly nine. It had been a subdued event.

Standing up from the table, he picked up the half-filled bottle of wine and collected our glasses. "Let's go outside for a while."

I followed him out the back door and watched as he pulled one of the lounges out onto the grass and let it recline as far as it would go. After placing the glasses and the bottle next to it in the grass, he sat down and held out his hand. "Come here. I want to lie in the dark, drink some wine, and hold you. I want to shut my brain off and feel you next to me. I want to hear the crickets and see the stars."

He lay down, and I stretched out next to him. "That sounds wonderful." I wrapped my arm around his waist and rested my head on his chest. I closed my eyes, lulled by the rise and fall of his chest and the deep thump of his heart. Faint strains of Jimmy Buffett's "Margaritaville." drifted to us from somewhere in the neighborhood, and it made me smile. "I haven't heard that tune in a while. I'm more familiar with the Wiggles."

He laughed. "You poor thing. Maybe we should go somewhere by the sea for that vacation. We could sit on the beach and have margaritas."

"Mm, that sounds perfect."

"Do you want your wine?" he asked, searching for the glass.

"No, I want you."

I nestled my head into the crook of his neck and ran my hand over his chest and belly, undoing the buttons on his shirt and enjoying the warmth of him, the feel and scent of his skin. He ran a hand down my back until he found the hem of my T-shirt and pulled it up and off, undoing the front clasp on my bra and finding my breast with his hand. His hand dropped and took hold of the waistband of my leggings. Sitting up, he pulled them off and dropped them on the grass.

"No panties?" he asked, surprised.

I grinned. "I try to avoid panty lines with leggings."

He quirked his eyebrow, and a slow smile spread across his face. "Sure you didn't plan this?"

"No, you just got lucky."

He stood and shrugged out of his shirt, then dropped his jeans and briefs on the grass and stretched out next to me. "I did. I'm lucky to have you." Propping his head on his hand, he ran his other hand down my body, finding spots that still surprised and aroused me. "You are so lovely. I never tire of seeing you, feeling you lying next to me, making love to you."

I traced his face with my hands and pulled him down for a kiss. "Then stop talking and make love to me."

Faint refrains of Buffett's "Cheeseburger in Paradise" and occasional laughter drifted to us on the air. He wasn't a cheeseburger, but I was in paradise. When at last we returned to our bedroom, Angel curled up around me and slept more deeply than he had in months. Maybe life would return to normal once Mia Stewart's case was over.

THIRTY-FIVE

SAT IN THE COURTROOM GALLERY, WAITING for Angel's closing argument to begin now that the ADA had at last sat down. While the prosecution's case against Mia Stewart was largely circumstantial, it was damning. The ADA had presented his case well throughout the trial, according to Frost, and the jurors had listened closely. Angel had held his own during the trial, and Frost thought that he'd done a good job of sowing reasonable doubt. Apparently, Mia had been on her best behavior. I wondered which side would win. If the jury convicted her, I wondered what the consequences for Mia and Angel would be.

It'd been a while since I'd watched Angel in court, but I wanted to hear his closing argument. I wanted to watch the jury and Mia and see what happened. I hadn't been this nervous over one of his cases in ages. The jury held not only Mia's future in their hands but ours as well.

Angel stood, buttoned his suit jacket, and walked toward the jury, stopping a few feet from them. He always looked well dressed, but he saved three expensive bespoke suits—a navy, a gray, and a charcoal one—for court. One perk of his private-sector job was the ability to indulge in his clotheshorse tendencies. Standing there, he looked professional and understated, someone who could be trusted. I hoped he'd had that effect on the jury all along.

He paused as if deep in thought, then said, "The prosecution's job in this trial is to *prove* that Mia Stewart committed the crime of which she has been accused—with evidence not supposition—and they have failed to do so.

"To convict Mia Stewart, you must weigh the evidence and the testimony presented during this trial and be convinced of her guilt beyond a reasonable doubt. *Beyond a reasonable doubt*," he repeated, emphasizing each word. "That means there must be no question in your minds that someone else could have perpetrated the crime she is accused of and no question whether the evidence brought by the prosecution has *proven* her guilt, and it hasn't.

"In our judicial system, people are innocent until proven guilty. That foundational belief sometimes gets lost in the chaos of a crime, an arrest, and the publicity surrounding it, but it's something each of you must keep in mind as you consider what has been presented during the trial.

"You've heard the circumstantial evidence the prosecution has presented, none of which *proves* that Mia Stewart killed Geoff Hudson." He raised a finger. "She carried out an affair with him until she discovered he was married and ended it. This was a decision he wasn't happy about, and he pursued her despite her repeatedly telling him she wasn't interested in continuing their affair. The prosecution would have you believe that this harassment fueled her motive to kill him."

Angel smiled at the jury. "A cheating spouse, however, is far more likely to be killed by the spouse to whom they were supposed to be faithful." That got a subdued laugh from several of the jury members. It had always been hard for anyone to resist one of his smiles. Apparently, even jury members were susceptible. I'd never been in court when he was prosecuting someone; listening to him now had shown me a new side of him.

Angel paced the length of the jury box. He stopped and raised a second finger. "Mia had a confrontation with Geoff Hudson in the hospital's cafeteria, where she again told him she wasn't interested, and because of his ugly response, she slapped him. The prosecution would have you believe her reaction demonstrates her increasing hostility toward Geoff Hudson and reinforces Mia's motive to kill him. It's not uncommon for a woman to slap someone who calls them a bitch, but killing someone for that seems a little over-the-top. More importantly, the prosecution cannot *prove* that's why she slapped him or that it gave her a motive to kill him." I saw a woman in the jury box nod as she wrote something in a notebook she held.

He raised a third finger. "And of course, Mia was at his side when he died, trying to help him. The prosecution maintains that she stabbed him and stayed with him because she wanted to make sure he was dead. But theories are all they have about what happened and what Mia Stewart's intentions were. They have provided no proof of why she was there or what her intentions were.

"Ask yourself, why would Mia Stewart stab Geoff Hudson, remain at his side, and risk being discovered? The stabbing wasn't witnessed—the prosecution never found anyone who saw it. If she was the killer, why would Mia Stewart stay at Geoff Hudson's side? If she was the killer, she wouldn't have needed to stay to make sure he was dead, which is the prosecution's explanation for her being found next to him. As an OR nurse, she knew his wound was fatal. If she'd been the one to inflict it, she'd have known she didn't need to stay. If she was the killer, common sense and survival instinct would have urged her to leave. But she didn't, because she isn't the killer.

"She was by his side trying to save him, like any nurse would. Do you know any nurse who would refuse to help a victim found bleeding to death, regardless of what they thought of that person? Refuse to help because of anger and frustration with the person's behavior? Nurses often care for people who are quite vocal about their bigoted, racist, or misogynistic beliefs. They provide care even for people who are abusive and offensive. They may not like those people, but they do their job. And doing their job resulted in approximately fifty-seven assaults on nurses per day in 2022, not fifty-seven murders per day committed by nurses. The prosecution has been unable to prove any motivation for Mia Stewart to remain with Geoff Hudson other than to try to save him."

Angel continued. "You've heard Ted Nichols testify that Mia was holding the osteotome when he saw her and that he heard her say Hudson 'deserved' something. Eyewitness testimony is important, but remember that Nichols did not hear the entirety of what she said. He can't testify about what she was referring to when she said 'deserved it.' That was what he *thought* he heard, and there is no one who can verify what he saw or what he thought she said. Mia, the only one who knows what was said, maintains she told Geoff Hudson that she was there and that he didn't deserve what had happened.

"Ted Nichols also testified that Mia looked angry to him. Again, that's his interpretation of what he saw. In an emergency, people often look angry when they're upset, when they're focused on the emergency and not how they look. And remember, no one else saw any of what Ted Nichols has testified to—it's his word against Mia's."

Angel resumed pacing in front of the jury box. "I would ask you to consider that there are a number of factors that raise enough reasonable doubt about Mia Stewart's guilt for you to acquit her. Geoff Hudson repeatedly cheated on his wife and had been involved with several women in the department. One of those women, including his wife, may have had a reason to kill him.

"Ted Nichols must be considered a suspect as well. As you heard during testimony, Hudson bullied and tormented him from day one. By all accounts, Hudson resented having to work with Nichols and took that resentment out on him. Nichols had to have been afraid that Hudson would get him kicked out of the residency program. If that happened, he'd be forced to face his domineering father as a failure. It was entirely likely that his father would have cut off all association with him, including his financial support. And Ted Nichols didn't like Mia Stewart."

Angel lifted a shoulder and dropped it. "Ted Nichols had ample reason to want Hudson dead, and he had the opportunity to kill him. After Hudson told him to 'get out of his sight,' Nichols says he was in the dressing room getting ready to go home, but no one can back that up. There was time for him to wait for Hudson's return from speaking to the patient's family, stab Hudson when he returned, and retreat to the dressing room in time to emerge, find Mia Stewart bent over Hudson, and accuse her of stabbing him. Everyone has a tipping point. Perhaps Ted Nichols reached his that night."

Out of the corner of my eye, I saw Nichols get up and quickly leave the courtroom, his face pale, obviously shaken by the accusation. He couldn't have been surprised by it, as both Angel and the prosecution had covered what he had endured from Hudson during their questioning. Hearing Angel's accusations now would have been difficult. Frost said he'd looked defeated and lost during his testimony and cross-examination, but this must have been hard to hear. I wondered why he had bothered to come today. Perhaps he wanted to hear the closing arguments to see whether he would become the prime suspect if Mia was acquitted.

Angel continued. "And then there's Nichols's friend, Chris Johansson, who'd watched what Hudson put his friend through. He'd tried to convince his friend to do something else that would make him happy, to no avail. I'd remind you the murder weapon was an osteotome—an instrument often used during orthopedic surgery. It belonged to a rack of osteotomes in the instrument set used the day of Hudson's death. A case Johansson was assisting on. It's entirely possible that Chris Johansson killed Hudson as payback for what he had put his friend through."

Angel walked over to the defense table and pointed toward Mia. "The prosecution must prove, *beyond a reasonable doubt*, that Mia Stewart killed Geoff Hudson and has failed to do so. They have provided no concrete, irrefutable proof that Mia Stewart took that osteotome from the instrument set, and as presented during the trial, there were opportunities for someone other than Mia to have taken it from the set. The prosecution can't prove she wielded it, nor have they provided anything other than supposition for why she might have done so.

"Even the handprint on the osteotome can't be definitively identified as Mia Stewart's, and there were no identifiable fingerprints on it. Mia admits pulling the osteotome out from under Geoff Hudson, a logical first step to providing compression to try to stop the bleeding. The handprint most likely is hers, but not because she stabbed him. Her handprint may have actually covered over that of the killer. We'll never know.

"Something else to consider when you begin your deliberation—the women's dressing room was less that twenty-five feet from where the stabbing took place. If she'd stabbed him, all Mia Stewart had to do was step inside the dressing room, change into her street clothes, and leave. No one would know she'd even been there, but she didn't. She found him and tried to help him, despite there being little that could have been done to prevent his death."

He dropped his hand. "I would ask you to remember that there are no witnesses, no one who can confirm what happened that night. The prosecution has offered no evidence to *prove* what is, at best, their theories about what happened. We may never know who killed Geoff Hudson, but it wasn't Mia Stewart, who is innocent and deserves a not-guilty verdict." He paused to let that sink in, then said with a respectful tip of his head in the jury's direction, "Thank you for your time and attention."

When Angel's closing statement was over, I slipped out of the courtroom and left to pick up Teo and head home. There was no telling when the jury would come back with a verdict, and the fireworks were over for now. Angel had done his best, and despite my bias and as much as I disliked her, I'd have probably acquitted her based on the closing argument he'd presented. I only hoped the jury would feel the same—for his sake, not hers—and that we'd be done with her. I didn't think either one of us would survive an appeal if she was convicted.

⌒

"So, nothing from the jury yet?" I asked as Angel walked in the front door. He took a deep breath and let it out, his shoulders drooping, the anxious frown leaving his face.

"No. Court was adjourned after the judge gave his instructions to the jury and they were dismissed to begin deliberations. They were let go at five, and they'll return tomorrow morning. I'd have been home sooner, but Owen wanted to obsess about my closing argument—what I did right, what I should have done—and debate how the jury will vote." He rolled his eyes in frustration. "*¡Ay Dios!* I hope to God she's acquitted."

"What's your guess? Will they acquit?"

He shrugged. "Lord only knows, *chica*. Maybe. I've thrown enough reasonable doubt at them that I hope they won't convict. The prosecution's case was built on testimony from Nichols, who had a strong motive to kill Hudson, and no one witnessed or heard what he says he heard. The rest is circumstantial evidence. But it's anyone's guess.

"Juries are always a crapshoot. There could be a juror who's been cheated on who takes against Mia for her liaison with Hudson. There could be a juror who cheats on his wife and is worried about his mistress enough to think Mia probably did kill Hudson. There could be a juror who hates nurses. Regardless of them being asked to be impartial, we all filter facts through our own biases, same with juries, so Christ, who knows? I did my best, and I hope she's acquitted, but mostly I just want it to be over."

He dropped down onto the couch and let his head drop back against it. I sat next to him and brushed a lock of hair off his forehead.

"If it's any consolation, I'd acquit her based on your closing argument, and I can't stand the woman." That earned me a slight smile. "It'll be over soon enough. Let it go tonight and try to relax."

He tried. He waved off the dinner I'd saved for him, saying that Owen had food delivered while he was grilling Angel about the trial, and had wine instead. We watched a comedy on BritBox. I hoped it would distract him, but he was restless. I could tell his mind was elsewhere. Finally, at about ten, we went to bed. I woke around three in the morning to find his side of the bed empty and found him sitting in the rocking chair beside Teo's bed, watching him sleep in the soft, faint glow from the night-light.

I walked up behind the rocker, bent, wrapped my arms around his shoulders, and gave him a kiss on the cheek. "Come to bed, love, and try to get some sleep."

"He's so beautiful, so peaceful when he's asleep."

Teo's arms lay flung out from his body, his stuffed dog clutched in one small hand. The faint glow of the night-light cast a shimmer of soft light over his face. His eyes moved rapidly from time to time under his closed lids, their lashes spread gracefully across his cheeks, his dark curls in disarray. He looked like a very young version of his father, the man whose mother called him *Angelito*—little angel. We had our own little angel, I thought, watching him sleep.

"Thank goodness," I said. "He's not all that peaceful when he's awake."

Angel laughed softly. "No, he's not. Since he arrived, I have more sympathy for my mother." We watched our son for a few silent moments before Angel continued. "I haven't slept like that in months, not since taking this case. It's like it's cursed. I'm exhausted and so ready to be done with it."

"Come back to bed and try and get some sleep."

I led him back to our room, hoping that a verdict—whatever it turned out to be—would be the end of this whole debacle. But life was never that simple. I woke to my phone vibrating against the bedside table several hours after Angel had dropped off to sleep. I scrabbled for it, hoping the noise wouldn't wake him, but I felt him stir as I answered.

"H'lo?"

"Annie, it's Frost. Is your boy handy?"

"What's wrong?"

He hesitated and then said, "Roberts called me just a bit ago. Nichols hung himself. His friend Johansson found him."

"Oh God …"

"Annie, what is it?" I heard Angel ask sleepily.

"Here, talk to Frost," I said, handing him my phone. "I'll go make some coffee."

It was nearly five, might as well get up for the day, I thought. As I listened to their muffled conversation, I pulled my robe on and headed for the kitchen. This case was cursed.

THIRTY-SIX

FROST SHOWED UP ABOUT AN HOUR LATER, after having spoken further with Paul Roberts. He accepted a cup of coffee and sipped it as we sat around the kitchen table.

"Any idea why he did it or when?" I asked.

"The ME said it was sometime last night. According to Roberts, Johansson talked to Nichols around four yesterday afternoon, and Nichols told him he had left the court to go home after Angel's closing argument." Angel flinched at the mention of his closing argument.

"According to Johansson, Nichols was pretty upset. Because of the trial publicity, his father had heard about what was going on between him and Hudson and was furious. He called Nichols and apparently said some really hateful things, according to what Johansson told Roberts.

"Johansson planned on going over around six after his cases for the day were finished, but there was an emergency case that got added, and he was delayed." Frost took another sip of coffee. "He texted Nichols a couple times before his last case began, and he tried again after it finished. When he got no reply, he was worried enough to go over. He got to Nichols's apartment around seven thirty and found him. Nichols left a note that said 'I'm sorry,' and that was it. No one's sure what he was referring to."

Frost shook his head and blew out a tired breath. "Christ, it could be an apology to his father for not living up to his expectations, he could have been sorry he killed Hudson, or it could be an apology for everything his suicide would do to his friends and family. There's no way to know. Maybe he'd just had enough of everything."

I watched Angel carefully, and he seemed stunned by what had happened. The stricken look on his face worried me, and I wished Frost hadn't mentioned that it had happened after his closing statement. I wished he'd simply blamed it on the call from Nichols's father, but the cat was out of the bag.

"Will they tell the jury?"

"No," Angel said. "They're not supposed to be aware of news or current events that relate to the trial to avoid it influencing their decision. It's just as well. He deserves some peace."

Nichols had deserved far more than peace. He'd deserved a chance to be happy, and it seemed to me the only ones who'd cared about that were his friends Chris Johansson and Mark Gutierrez. If there was a hell waiting for us in the afterlife, then I hoped Hudson was there. If, as I've often suspected, hell was here on earth, then I hoped that was where Ted Nichols's father was. And I desperately hoped Ted was happy, or at least at peace, wherever he was.

Angel was worryingly quiet after Frost left. I knew Nichols's death had hit him hard. I wished there was something I could say to erase that stricken look I saw on his face when he thought I wasn't looking. He dressed for work, refused breakfast, and said as he kissed me goodbye that he'd let me know when the jury had reached a verdict.

The jury deliberated most of the day, which didn't seem like a good thing. Nichols's death stayed with me, the sadness and worry enveloping me. I didn't hear from Angel, and the waiting was torture. No doubt it was worse for Angel and Mia Stewart. After all, I wasn't the one going to prison if the jury returned a guilty verdict.

Angel's face was deathly pale, his tie askew, his collar undone, and his jacket missing when he burst through the front door. He dropped his briefcase on the floor and rushed past me toward our bedroom. I followed and saw him disappear into the bathroom and slam the door closed. I gave him a minute and then hesitantly knocked on the door.

"Angel?" I waited and got no response. "Is … Is everything okay?"

"I'm fine." He didn't sound fine. I heard him retching through the door followed by the sound of the toilet flushing. "Just give me a minute, Annie."

I heard Teo come up behind me and clutch my leg. "*Papi?*" he asked, tugging on my jeans, asking to be picked up, obviously unsettled by his father's surprising behavior. I picked him up and walked back into the living room.

"*Papi*'s tummy's upset, baby. How about I turn *Sesame Street* on, and you can watch it until dinner?" I set him down, and he walked over to where his favorite stuffed dog was and picked it up. He sent an anxious glance in the direction of our bedroom and then at me, ignoring the TV.

"*Papi* will be fine, sweetheart. I'll go check on him."

He nodded and sat down in front of the TV, clutching his dog to his chest. The dog had become his security blanket. Given to him by Frost and Evie for his second birthday, it was a favorite when things were going well and a comfort when they weren't. I could see he was unsettled, so I crouched down next to him and kissed his pudgy cheek. "I'll go check on him, sweetheart, don't worry. *Papi* probably ate something yucky for lunch." That got a faint smile but didn't do much to take the worried look off his face.

I heard Angel open the bathroom door, and I went back to our bedroom. I found him sitting on the edge of the bed, pressing the back of his hand against his mouth, opening and closing his fingers into a fist, a frown on his face and his eyes tightly closed.

Four hours earlier, he'd called to let me know the jury had reached a verdict. As he drove to the courthouse, Angel said he'd let me know the outcome, but I'd heard nothing further from him. Worried that something had gone wrong and she'd been convicted, I called his phone. When he didn't pick up, I left a message asking him to call me when he had a minute. Unable to stand not knowing, I checked the local news station online and saw that the jury had returned a not-guilty verdict.

Against the odds, he'd succeeded in getting her acquitted, so what had happened? I texted him twice, and he didn't text back. Finally, I called Frost and asked if he'd talked to Angel. He was with several cop buddies at a local bar and told me everyone was trying to digest the news about Nichols and the acquittal. He hadn't had a chance to talk to Angel after the verdict was rendered and didn't know where he was. The only bright spot, he said, was Mia had been acquitted and Angel was off the hook with his partner.

Time had passed slowly, and I assumed he was celebrating with her and her family. He didn't like Mia, but he could hardly refuse to celebrate with her family or Owen, if invited. I thought that was why he was late coming home. It had been a difficult, frustrating case, but he'd won. That didn't warrant how he looked now. I stood in the doorway of our bedroom and waited, hoping he'd talk to me.

At last, he let his hand fall and said, "I can't do defense work anymore."

"What's happened?"

He shuddered. "As we left the courtroom, Owen and Mia's family congratulated and thanked me. Owen asked me to meet him back at the office and left. Mia told her parents she'd meet them at home later, then invited me out for a drink to celebrate—just the two of us. I declined. There was no way I was going anywhere alone with her, and she wasn't happy about it.

"Before I could walk away, Johansson surprised me and Mia in the hallway. He grabbed me, shoved me up against the wall, and shouted at me that it was all my fault Nichols was dead and that I had sacrificed his friend just to 'get that bitch off.' One of the court security officers pulled him off me and escorted him out of the building. The whole time the security guard was manhandling him down the hallway, he kept shouting that I had killed his friend and Mia and I would be sorry."

That worried me. Angel looked away from me and down at his hands that now draped limply between his knees. Without looking up, as if looking me in the eye was too painful, he said, "Mia said not to let Johansson get to me. I started to walk away, and she took me aside where we couldn't be overheard. She leaned in and said, 'I hoped you'd get me off. I was worried for a while, but you did it. I shouldn't have wasted time watching him die, but I had to have a chance to tell him he deserved it. He looked so shocked when I stabbed him, I wanted him to know why. He dumped me and took up with Alicia. Nothing I said could convince him to come back to me. He didn't touch my face and say sorry. He was trying to push me away. He called me a bitch again right before he died. I never expected Ted to pop out of the dressing room. I thought he'd gone home already.'"

Angel swallowed convulsively, as if on the verge of throwing up again, before he continued. "She smiled at me, Annie. *She smiled at me.* She was so smug. She said, 'I don't mind telling you I did it. It's privileged communication, and there's nothing you or anyone else can do to me. Double jeopardy, right? So thanks.' She laughed at me. 'Don't look so shocked, Angel. I'm sure you've gotten plenty of other guilty people off.'

"Before I could stop her, she kissed me on the cheek. She told me she chose the osteotome because she knew Nichols and Johansson were friends and it would point a finger at Johansson. She said … said Nichols was a waste of space and not to take it so hard. Then she laughed and walked away."

He rubbed the side of his face hard, as though he could still feel the kiss. Closing his eyes, he fisted his hands in his lap. "And she's right.

She can't be retried for Hudson's murder. I got … I got a cold-blooded murderer off."

"Oh God, Angel. Are you sure she's telling the truth? There've been so many times she hasn't, so many times she's caused problems. Maybe she's just messing with your head." I moved from the doorway to sit next to him on the bed.

"You didn't see her face or her smug, self-satisfied smile or hear her laugh. She wasn't lying this time. She planned it, and she killed him, all because he didn't want her. I sat in the parking lot near the courts and tried to think of a way to rectify it. I can't turn her in to the cops or tell Owen. It's privileged communication. I shouldn't even be telling you. Even if I told the cops, she can't be prosecuted for the murder, but she or Owen or her parents could get me disbarred." He gave me a hopeless shrug. "I wouldn't care if I thought she'd be held accountable, but she's untouchable."

I rubbed his back. "There's nothing you can do, then."

He shook his head emphatically. "You're wrong. I finally headed back to the office to talk to Owen. When I got there, he congratulated me again and said he planned to make me a full partner because of the way I handled the case. He kept going on about it, wouldn't let me get a word in edgewise, and offered me champagne to celebrate. It was … weird. He was nervous and couldn't seem to stop talking. I think he knows Mia is guilty. I think that's why he got so involved in the whole case." Angel grimaced and shook his head as if to clear it of the memory.

"So I did the only thing I could do. I shouted at him to stop him talking and told him I was resigning, effective immediately. I told him I'd had enough, that I couldn't do defense work anymore, not after Nichols … I used Nichols as an excuse. I cast aspersions on him in the courtroom to get her off, and then I used his death as an excuse to resign. It's despicable.

"Owen's furious. He tried his best to talk me out of it. Christ, he's as bad as Mia. He said Nichols wasn't my fault and he probably did kill Hudson. This job has turned me into someone I don't recognize anymore. I can't risk becoming Owen."

He sat so still, looked so distraught, and I couldn't think of any way to help. At last, he said, "I've never had a case turn out so disastrously. I can't take the chance I might help someone else get away with murder. I can't justify it."

"But you haven't up till now—"

"*That I know of*," he hissed. He squeezed his eyes closed and took a deep breath. "Jesus, Annie, I probably have. That's my job—get the client off regardless of their guilt or innocence. I thought I could justify that. I have done, but Mia … After Mia, I won't—can't—risk it."

"What will you do?"

He shrugged and sighed. "I dunno." He ran a hand tiredly over his face. "It's been a while, but maybe the DA's office will take me back."

I took him in my arms and held him. "I'm so sorry, love."

"Nichols." He choked out the name. "The worst part is, I'm responsible for what Nichols did. He's dead because of me."

"No, Angel, no. There were so many things that poor man was dealing with—his father, Hudson—"

"And me," Angel said, cutting me off and pushing away from me. "I made it all worse. I brought it all out in the open to save a psychopath, a killer, and now he's dead."

Teo had come quietly into the bedroom, a questioning, worried look on his face. He hesitantly approached and placed his small hand on Angel's thigh. Angel scooped him up and held him to his chest tightly. I wrapped my arms around both of them, and Angel broke down and began to sob.

Early the next morning, I sat nursing a cup of coffee at the kitchen table. It was barely light out, and the house was quiet and dark. It had taken Angel hours to calm down enough to try to sleep, and at last he had dropped into a restless sleep about one a.m. The bedroom door was closed, and I intended to let him and Teo sleep as long as possible. Teo, who'd never seen his father so upset, had refused to leave Angel's side and had fallen asleep between us after I finally convinced Angel to lie down. I had woken at four and debated carrying Teo to his room, then decided it would be comforting for both of them to wake up next to each other.

After the verdict, Angel had been bombarded with calls from the press, and when contacting him via his phone didn't work, they somehow discovered mine. I silenced my phone and turned Angel's phone off; the only people trying to call him were reporters. There were two emergency contact numbers on my phone—Angel's and Frost's. Frost's number would ring through regardless of whether my phone was on silent mode or not.

The house had been so quiet and still that when my phone vibrated in my bathrobe pocket, it jolted me. It was Frost, so I picked up.

"Hey ..." There was a long pause. "I wanted to let you know the latest. I figure better from me than the TV or online. I wanted to warn you there'll be press hounding you guys, maybe showing up at the house."

"What's happened?" My heart began to race. I knew it wouldn't be good news.

"Chris Johansson confronted Mia as she and her family were coming out of a restaurant last night. I guess they were celebrating her acquittal. He shot her, and she didn't make it."

"Oh my God."

"He didn't run, didn't put up a fight when the cops showed up, and the scuttlebutt from Roberts is that he refused a lawyer and confessed. He says he doesn't want a trial. Says he did it for Nichols. Things are insane right now, and the press is going nuts. I wanted you to know so you can avoid them. I'm just glad Angel wasn't there. In his current state, I think Johansson would have shot Angel too."

A wave of nausea washed over me as I took that in. Thank God Angel had refused to have anything to do with her last night and that Chris was in custody. The case had been a nightmare from start to finish, and it felt as if the nightmare had turned into a full-fledged night terror.

"Thanks, Frost. I'll let him know." I lay my phone on the kitchen table and disconnected. Holding my head in my hands, I wondered how the hell I was going to break the news to Angel. He'd been inconsolable the previous night, and I worried this would be the final straw.

I'd read somewhere that cops called what Johansson had done a brass verdict. When a friend or relative believed the legal system had failed them, a bullet became judge, jury, and executioner. Chris Johansson had given Ted Nichols the justice he deserved and, unintentionally, had given it to Geoff Hudson as well. He was right—Mia was guilty—and he'd made her pay for what she'd done. While she deserved it, Chris had thrown his life away. It was such a waste, and I wasn't sure Ted Nichols would have wanted that.

I had willingly placed my life and future on the line for Angel when confronted by Ian Patterson and hadn't cared about how it might affect my life. All I'd wanted was for Ian to pay for what he'd done. Fortunately for me, Ian had tried to kill both of us, and it was self-defense. Chris couldn't claim that, but perhaps, in a twisted sort of way, killing Mia had given him some peace. I hoped so.

THIRTY-SEVEN

TWO MONTHS LATER, THE GUILT OVER MIA'S ACQUITTAL, Ted Nichols's suicide, and Johansson's revenge had taken their toll on Angel. Some would say he was naive, that being a criminal defense attorney meant it was quite likely you'd get a guilty person acquitted at some point in your career, maybe many times, and there would be times when you'd know in your heart that they were guilty and still work to get them acquitted. Early on, one of his colleagues had told him that everyone was guilty of something; worrying about whether a client was guilty or not didn't figure into the job, and he needed to let it go. All defense attorneys were required to do was try their best to get the client acquitted.

Others would say he had nothing to feel guilty about. He'd done his job well, and he should accept that it was "better for one guilty person to go free than for an innocent one to be convicted," as the saying went. What most never said was that to be a criminal defense attorney, you had to live in a gray area of life where guilt or innocence was irrelevant and shouldn't be a factor. All you needed to focus on was providing your client with the defense they were entitled to and hopefully getting them—even the guilty ones—off. And Angel had discovered he couldn't do that.

All that ethical debate paled in comparison to Ted Nichols's suicide, and no amount of talking could convince Angel he wasn't responsible.

Piled on top of that, he felt he was to blame for Johansson's revenge. It was a ten-ton weight that quickly pulled him into a depression so severe I feared he'd end his life before he could find his way out of the deep dark hole he was in.

"How're you managing, kid?" Frost asked as he sat across from me at a table in the hospital cafeteria, where we were each nursing a cup of coffee. Neither of us were really drinking it. Frost knew that Angel felt responsible for Ted's suicide and its consequences, but he also suspected something else had happened. I couldn't tell him, to protect Angel from legal repercussions, but Frost had put two and two together like he always managed to do and knew that Mia Stewart had fucked Angel over somehow.

He'd been a detective for years, and I think Frost knew exactly what she'd done, but he never asked. He'd always believed that something about Mia was off and hadn't been totally convinced she was innocent. Mia had paid for it, and in his mind, the proverbial scales of justice were balanced. Maybe her death had helped balance the scales for Nichols's death, but nothing made up for the loss of Ted Nichols or Chris Johansson, and Angel felt responsible for all of it.

I had stopped the private investigation work with Frost and was working in the OR full time to support us until Angel returned to work—if he returned to work—and that was a huge worry at the moment. After Angel had taken the job in Owen's firm, we were smart enough to resist upgrading to a more expensive home—we could have easily—and socked away a decent portion of the large salary Angel had earned during the last two years. Both of us were pretty conservative as far as money went, and I was grateful for that. But most of the money had gone into IRAs and an education fund for Teo, none of which were easily tapped or without huge tax consequences.

There might or might not be a severance package from Owen's firm. I hadn't asked, and Angel was in no condition to ask. Owen had left several messages, and I had yet to return them. Finally, a thick official-looking envelope arrived in the mail from Owen. It sat unopened on Angel's desk behind closed doors. Angel showed no interest in it, and I was afraid to open it.

With Angel not working, my salary as a PI would have barely paid for basic necessities, let alone our mortgage, and we would have exhausted our savings accounts in short order. My salary as a nurse kept us going, but I was losing hope that he would recover enough to find a job and return to work, and I was terrified that he would do something to end his life.

He refused to get help, saying that nothing would make him feel better about what had happened and confession wouldn't absolve him of it either. Aside from the guilt Catholicism induced, I was glad he'd been raised Catholic and had been indoctrinated enough to believe suicide was a mortal sin. I hoped, if nothing else, that belief would keep him safe.

I lied to people for a while. I couldn't tell anyone the real reason behind Angel's abrupt departure from the law firm, and I wanted to keep his depression private. I told them Angel and his senior partner had gotten into a serious disagreement that concerned the practice, which I was not privy to, and Angel had quit.

When he lost the ability to put on a relatively normal public face in front of his family during the short contact we had with them, and when the seriousness of his depression became clear, I told friends and family that he was upset about Nichols's suicide, Johansson's revenge, and the difficulty he was having finding another job.

No one in the family asked further questions and, oddly enough, rather than overwhelming us with offers of help or invitations to do things, they withdrew. Depression made people uncomfortable. They didn't know what to say, or they were terrified that it'd rub off on them or that they'd say the wrong thing and make it worse.

But his family's abandonment was hard to take. It was as if his misfortune and depression were contagious. Their golden boy had lost some of his shine. The abandonment was a relief, in a way, but it isolated both of us. We had a few friends who were there for us. My friends Chip Elliott and Maddie Doyle checked in on us periodically. Frost and his wife, Evie, never probed—they were simply there when I needed help, a shoulder to cry on, or someone to watch Teo for a day or two. Chip Elliott's dads babysat Teo as well. I suspected Phil, the lawyer, knew something serious regarding the case had happened, but neither he nor Allen ever asked.

This small group of friends was simply there for us, and I would always be grateful, but I was exhausted and stressed to the max. I reluctantly left Angel at the house each day and held my breath on returning home, worried about what I might find. He didn't look like the man I'd married, the man I'd always known. He'd lost weight, his face was gaunt and pale, his eyes lifeless, his hair shaggy and riotously curly from lack of a barber. He'd stopped shaving, so his face was covered in a dark, unkempt beard that made him look feral, and he did as little as possible.

I sighed. "I don't know anymore, Frost. There's a pall hanging over our house. Teo is confused and upset. He doesn't understand what's happened to his father, and he's acting out because the whole thing scares him. He behaves at daycare and I know he behaves for you and Evie, and Phil and Allen, but that's because you're normal and familiar and haven't changed.

"Angel's not the father Teo knew, and he can't figure out what's happened. I've tried talking to him, telling him his father's sad, but he's two—all he knows is the dad he knew isn't there anymore. The man I've always known isn't there either." I twisted my coffee cup around and around, not unlike my life, which was going around in circles, heading nowhere. "Angel's just a shell of himself."

"Have you been able to get him to see a therapist?"

I pressed my fingers over my mouth and closed my eyes to try to stop the tears that threatened. When I had that under control, I said, "I can barely get him to eat. God, I wish his grandmother were still alive. Maybe she could force him to see someone. He sits in the room he uses as an office and drinks, or he sits out in the backyard and just stares at nothing, or he sleeps the day away and prowls the house at night. I've never seen him like this."

"D'you know anyone who could prescribe an antidepressant for him? Once those kick in, maybe he'd go talk to someone."

"No one will do that without seeing him, and he won't go. He won't talk to me about it. He won't even talk to that priest we know who offered to meet with him. He could talk to Father Giraldi or go to confession, and what he talks about in the confessional would never be mentioned to anyone else. But he won't. He says he can't be forgiven so there's no point."

Frost took a deep breath. "Call the therapist he saw after the shooting and get a psychiatrist's name. Call and make an appointment, and I'll come over and help you get him there."

"I don't know …"

"Something has to be done—and now, kid—or you might not have a husband to worry about."

"I don't want to go anywhere. Just leave me be, both of you."

I was afraid to tell him where Frost and I were taking him, afraid he'd revolt and refuse to go. But Frost took over. "Come on, let's get out of the house. You've been sitting around here for too long."

"No, just leave me alone."

"Not an option, *amigo*. Let's go."

Frost took hold of Angel's arm and walked him to the door like he was walking a perp to booking, and surprisingly, Angel didn't resist.

Maybe the authority in Frost's voice and his attitude made resistance too hard for Angel to summon, or maybe under all the depression he wanted help and didn't know how to ask for it. If life had been at all normal, I would have laughed as Frost loaded Angel into the back seat of his car with a "Watch your head" comment and a protective hand on top of his head. A classic cop maneuver. He came around and got in the driver's seat and surreptitiously used the parental control to lock the doors. Nobody was getting out until he unlocked the car.

When we reached the psychiatrist's office and Angel realized where we were, he said in a resigned voice, "I figured this was what you were up to. I don't want to do this. It won't help. Nothing will help."

I turned in my seat and watched him. "Do it for Teo. He loves you, and he's scared. If you won't do it for yourself or me, do it for him. He needs you … and so do I."

THIRTY-EIGHT

I WASN'T SURE IF IT WAS REGRET OVER what had happened or curiosity that made me visit Chris Johannson in prison. Maybe it was simply a way to make sure he was okay. That seemed ridiculous—how could you be okay after what had happened? But I wanted him to know he wasn't forgotten. I wanted him to know he hadn't been wrong about Mia, that he hadn't wasted his life for nothing. I had yet to figure out how to do that without compromising Angel.

It was a long drive to Florence, Colorado. It was in Fremont County, where fifteen of the prisons in Colorado were located. I wasn't sure why this particular area had so many, but I knew there had been a prison in the area since the 1800s. Now there were so many, it was known as Prison Valley.

The most notorious of the federal prisons was ADX Florence, also known as Supermax and the Alcatraz of the Rockies. It was a maximum-security facility that housed many notorious, violent, high-risk, high-profile inmates. Chris Johansson, however, was housed in Fremont Correctional Facility, a medium-security Colorado prison. It might have been less forbidding than Supermax, but it was still a prison. Sitting waiting for him in the visitors' room, I tried to imagine spending years in a place like this and couldn't. I was sure I wouldn't survive a month, let alone a life sentence.

At last, the door opened, and he was escorted to the table where I sat by a guard, who then retreated to the area by the door. Seeing me, Chris looked a bit puzzled as he took a seat opposite me. His face was pale, the inmate uniform he wore adding to his paleness, but he looked much the same as he had when I interviewed him.

"I wasn't expecting to see you. Thought it was probably a journalist."

"I wanted to check in and see how you're doing."

"Not bad, all things considered. It's prison, so there's that." He gave me a half-hearted smile.

"No huge problems, though?"

"It took a while to settle in. You get a lot of shit initially, but you know what the hardest part is?" he asked, a faraway look on his face. "I dream about doing surgery and being in an OR again. I can feel the tools, feel the tissue and the hardware, the stitching, then I wake up and it's gone. I'm here and won't ever be doing that again."

"I was so sorry to hear what happened, so sorry that you're here—"

He cut me off. "I knew what I was doing and what the consequences would be, so don't be sorry. I'm not. Ted didn't deserve what he went through with Hudson or Mia or your boss. Hudson was a bully and used people, but he didn't deserve to be killed. Your boss was doing his job. He's paid to defend people like Mia Stewart, although I don't know how he lives with that. She was guilty. She helped Hudson chip away at Ted's confidence. Ted was depressed and discouraged because of both of them. Then she kept trying to throw him under the bus for Hudson's murder."

I nodded. "I'm sorry."

He watched me carefully for a moment. "At least I did something to defend him. She would never have paid for what she did to Ted or what she did to Hudson. I guess it doesn't matter now, but I'd have done anything for him. I loved him. He should never have been tormented like he was by his father and Hudson."

"Were you lovers?"

He looked off toward the door, where the guard sat. "I wish we had been, but we were friends. I hoped in time that would change, but I was happy to just be his friend. He didn't have many, didn't have much happiness in his life. If my friendship gave that to him, then that was all I needed." He shifted in the plastic chair, huffed out a breath, and frowned. "I hope his father is suffering and regretting what he put Ted through, although knowing what Ted told me about him, he's probably not. Self-righteous religious pricks like Bernard Nichols rarely face up to their own mistakes."

He swiped hastily at his eyes, looked at the ceiling, and sighed. "And Mia Stewart? You'll never convince me she didn't kill Hudson. I saw the look on her face as she walked out of that courtroom with your boss. She didn't deserve to walk free when Ted was dead. I think the shade your boss threw on Ted to get her off was what broke him."

The weight of guilt settled on my shoulders as I watched him. He didn't seem angry, more resigned to his fate. I knew he had done what he felt was needed, and I couldn't argue with that. Mia had been dealt a swift and final justice for what she'd done.

"I regret the pain I've caused my parents, but I'm not sorry I killed Mia. She deserved it."

I held his gaze and said, "You're right, she did."

"I knew it," he replied, watching me carefully. Relief swept over his face. "Thank you."

I leaned close to him, holding a business card under my hand. "Chris, if you ever need anything I can help with, or you want to talk, please let me know." I slid the business card across to him, and he palmed it.

"Thanks, but I'm fine."

I wasn't sure that was true, and I was even less sure what I could do for him, but he had my number and could call if he wanted to. I watched as he got up and walked toward the guard at the door and they left.

Love could be noble and foolish, and there was no telling what side you'd end up on given the right circumstances. His sentence included the opportunity for parole in ten years' time, but that was a long way off, and I wondered whether Chris would think killing Mia had been worth it. I didn't think it was what Ted Nichols would have wanted for him.

THIRTY-NINE

ARE YOU READY FOR THIS?" I asked Angel as he dressed for the first day of the job he'd accepted at the DA's office. I wondered if he was ready to resume practicing, but he thought he was.

"It'll be good to get back to work and not have to worry about having another … Mia for a client," he said as he stopped sliding the tie around under his collar and began to tie the knot. "Joe," he said referring to his therapist, "thinks going to work will help me focus on other things."

It had been several months. We were nearing Thanksgiving, and I had a lot to be thankful for. Angel was better. His hair was now back to his previous carefully tended style, the beard was gone, and he wasn't so thin. He was more himself now and able to function. He was still living with the guilt, but he'd agreed to take medication and see a therapist.

He had made a serious effort to reconnect and reassure Teo. It had been a slow process for both of them—but he had made the effort despite his depression, and Teo had cautiously, then enthusiastically, welcomed it. It seemed to lighten the weight Angel carried, and it soothed Teo. Life had begun to feel nearly normal. It was as if I had sighted land after drifting for an eternity on a vast empty ocean. Maybe we'd make it to shore after all.

Teo heard us talking and came into the bedroom, catching the tail end of Angel's statement. It had been a while since his father had dressed up and left for what he knew we called work. I doubted he knew for sure what that entailed. All he knew was that his father hadn't gone to "work" in a what, for a toddler, was probably an eternity.

"Work?" he asked. "Me go to work too!"

Angel smiled at him and picked him up. "You have to grow up a little more, *mijo*, before you can go to work. But since you're a big boy now, I'll take you to the office one of these days so you can see what I do."

That made Teo grin and nod. We'd celebrated his third birthday two weeks ago, and he had declared at the party that he was a big boy now. God only knew what that meant in his mind, but I was sure we'd find out. Parenting was an ongoing adventure. I'd decided to just let go—celebrate it when it was good and muddle through it when it wasn't. I was pretty sure that was what most parents had to do.

I was glad Angel's therapist had urged him to return to work. It had been six weeks, and he was more outwardly engaged, the episodes when he got caught up in the disaster that Mia Stewart had caused had lessened significantly, and we were able to talk about them.

Angel finally opened the packet Owen had sent, and after signing a multipage document and returning it, his severance package arrived. Owen had held up his end of Angel's contract, and that was a relief, but there had been no further contact from Owen or anyone in the firm. The case had ended so disastrously that no one wanted contact, least of all us. That was also a relief. I didn't think I could look Owen in the eye and not berate him for his treatment of Angel or be civil.

Despite all the encouraging developments, what we had been through with Mia was still deeply affecting our lives. Since the trial ended, we hadn't made love. Angel allowed me to curl up against him, hug or kiss him, hold him if it was a bad night, but he seemed unable or unwilling to respond any further. When the depression had overwhelmed him, he had taken to wearing a pair of boxer briefs and a T-shirt to bed. It became a not-so-subtle barrier that made an unplanned physical reconnection difficult.

I was afraid to make any sexual overtures, casual or otherwise, and I ruthlessly repressed the fear that nothing would change. I took comfort in the fact that he was alive and getting better. I hoped, eventually, we'd be able to reconnect. Nothing could change my loving him, but our physical connection had always been an important part of the foundation of our relationship, and it broke my heart to think it might have been irreparably damaged.

EPILOGUE

I T WAS LATE, I WAS TIRED, AND I HAD an early-morning shift the next day. Angel was in his office organizing things for work in the morning when I announced I was going to go to bed. I gave him a quick kiss on the cheek and headed for our bedroom. I no longer worried about him sitting in his office drinking and ruminating about what had happened. His office was back to being a workspace, not a hiding place. I turned the bedside lamp off, closed my eyes, and was nearly asleep when I felt him ease into bed beside me.

He slipped my sleep shirt off my shoulder and touched his lips to my back between my shoulder blades, then he softly kissed his way up onto my neck, brushing my hair aside and kissing me behind my ear. I sighed with pleasure and, as I turned toward him, pulled my shirt off over my head and dropped it on the floor. The boxer briefs and T-shirt were gone. He braced himself on his elbow and caressed my face, letting his hand trace it softly. Leaning down, he kissed my lips, my eyes, my cheeks, as if he was starving.

"I need you, Annie," he murmured. "I've always needed you, for so many things, and you're always there. You'll never know how much that means to me. I'm so sorry for what I've put you through, so sorry for what it's done to Teo."

I reached up and caressed his cheek. "Don't apologize, please. There's no need to."

He kissed me longingly. I fought against the burning tears that threatened to fall. I felt him harden against me, and I reached down and stroked him. He kissed his way down my neck, and I heard him sigh softly.

"I've missed you," I said, surrendering myself to his touch and kisses, reveling in the sensation and the feel of him that I had missed so badly, that I thought was lost to me. When he entered me, I pulled him in deep. I traced his face and shoulders with my hands, starved for the feel of him, while he moved slowly and tenderly, his eyes locked on mine.

When at last he came, I followed him. He lowered himself onto me, and I could feel hot tears on my neck. His breath shuddered near my ear, and his shoulders shook. I held him tightly, stroking his back, and whispered into his ear, "Welcome home, my love."

THE KILLER WITHOUT A FACE

PROLOGUE

THE SOUND OF HIS VOICE RAISED THE HAIR on the back of her neck. He made small talk as he drove, and the more he talked, the more insistently a warning alarm deep inside her sounded. It was nothing he said, really, and she couldn't figure out why she was having a hard time breathing or why her heart had begun to race.

She turned toward him as he pulled up to the junction that would take them to the interstate. He looked to the left for oncoming traffic, and the alarm went ballistic. *Get out,* she thought frantically, *get out now!* She quietly unlatched her seat belt, gripped the backpack that sat on her lap, and, as he pressed the accelerator to merge onto the highway, grabbed the door handle, jerked it open, and bailed out of the SUV.

He lunged for her but missed. In his attempt to grab her, he jerked the steering wheel and lost control of the car as it slid on the icy pavement. He overcorrected, which sent the car into a 360-degree spin across the highway and off the opposite edge. She landed hard on her left shoulder and hip and rolled several feet before coming to a halt. Despite the searing pain in her shoulder, she staggered up, pulled her backpack onto her other shoulder, and took off running into the snow-shrouded trees without a backward glance.

CHAPTER ONE

THAT STUPID FUCKER TULIO. *Listening to the voice on the other end of the burner phone, he squeezed his free hand into a fist and bounced it against his thigh, keeping time with the headache that pulsed in his head. Tulio had been released from the county jail after serving six months on an assault charge and had gotten high as a kite. He was stopped for speeding and tried to pull a gun on two cops. For Christ's sake, what the fuck had he thought he was going to do? Shoot two police officers? And then what? Benny Tulio liked to brag. He had a record an arm long, so he would want a deal, and that would require naming names.*

He should have taken care of Benny a long time ago. This wasn't his first screwup that had landed him in trouble with the law. Well, it was a done deal, and now the cleanup had to begin. Benny was just one of many things that he needed to take care of. He would, but the next couple of problems, he'd take care of himself.

"Major fuckup on Tulio's part. See to it before he decides to talk to anyone." The man disconnected. On his way across the street toward his car, he removed the SIM card, dropped the phone in a garbage can, and ground the SIM card under his heel.

Lieutenant Kaye Jagerski's phone vibrated in her pocket. She sighed. It was late. She'd actually thought she'd be able to eat and maybe get some sleep, but apparently not. Head of Vice meant long hours and disrupted plans. She reached for her phone as she walked to her car in the precinct parking lot, the cold wind of an October evening in Denver playing with her dark, curly bob. She was a woman who might, at first glance, make you think she was harmless, but she had served her time on the streets and in Vice and had made a name for herself for all the connections she could tap. At last, she'd been rewarded with her boss's job when he retired. Kaye wasn't sure it was a reward. A promotion yes; a reward not so much.

Raising her phone to her ear, she got in her car and answered. "Jagerski." Kaye listened intently, a frown on her face. "What the hell happened? Where were the guards?" She listened for a few seconds longer. "I'll be there shortly. Separate the guards who were involved, if you haven't already, and put them in different interview rooms. I want to talk to them. Keep the inmates involved isolated. I'll want to talk to them too."

Benny Tulio had been arrested earlier in the day during a traffic stop. It had ended in a charge of carrying a concealed, unregistered weapon and possession of a shitload of meth and fentanyl. He'd been booked and sent to the Denver Detention Center, where he'd been found in the men's showers with a bar of soap shoved down his throat. No one saw anything or heard anything, if the guards and the inmates were to be believed. The guards had been standing outside the shower area while Benny and four other men showered.

Everything had sounded normal, both guards claimed—no noise or indication of trouble—until Tulio didn't exit the showers with the others. In the chaos that ensued, the remaining inmates claimed to know nothing. With a smirk, one inmate had actually suggested that Tulio had committed suicide. The inmates were involved, little question about that, but the guards had to be complicit, Kaye thought. The task ahead would be proving it.

There were no injuries to the inmates or the guards, but the marks on Benny indicated he'd been restrained while the bar of soap had been shoved down his throat. Figuring out who was to blame would have to rely on forensics, assuming there was anything that was usable. It was doubtful; Tulio had been left under a running showerhead. None of the inmates involved were talking, other than to claim innocence, without their court-appointed lawyers present.

Inmates got injured occasionally at the DDC or died from other causes as they waited to be sentenced and transferred to the Department of Corrections jail. There'd been an inmate who died as a result of a confrontation years ago. He'd been put in a headlock, sat on, and tasered. Kaye couldn't remember what had caused that confrontation. Despite the coroner's ruling of homicide, prosecutors hadn't filed charges. But intentionally killing an inmate at the DDC had never happened.

After the interviews, she sent the guards home on suspension pending an investigation, and the inmates involved were isolated until their bond hearings. The incident report would be included for the judge to rule on whether any of them got bail. It had been a long shot whether they would have been offered bail, but this incident had ended that possibility. Kaye planned to press the inmates, and after a conversation with the DA's office, perhaps offer a deal that would encourage one of them to give up the guilty parties.

Locking the barn door after the horse has escaped, Kaye thought on her way home from the DDC. The guards had been involved, had to have known what was going on, and stood outside the shower area, pretending not to hear or see anything. Kaye didn't see how it could have happened otherwise.

She'd have to do a deep dive on the guards to see how they'd been compromised and vulnerable to someone on the outside needing a favor done or whether they had a side hustle to pad their wallets. She'd get warrants to have their bank accounts searched for any unusual spending or the appearance of unexplained money in their accounts and get their phone logs to review all calls.

Any of the inmates showering with him could have held a long-standing grudge, seen him as a rival, or been asked to take care of Benny in return for favors of some kind. The end result was somebody hadn't wanted Benny Tulio to talk to anyone. Now he couldn't.

She wasn't even sure he'd had anything to talk about. He wasn't a major player in the local drug business, just a low-level repeat screw-up, but she'd hoped to interview him and see what he could tell them. He'd been too high when arrested to bother trying to interview him, so he'd been charged and sent to the DDC.

The stash of drugs found in his car, though, represented a lot of money. Someone might not be all that forgiving when an employee fucked up and lost that much product. Benny was in serious trouble legally, and he might have volunteered to rat out the higher-ups in exchange for a lighter sentence, or, depending on who he ratted out, no sentence at all.

She sighed as she let herself into her small bungalow, locked the door, reset the alarm, and made her way to the bedroom. She thought about a shower, but with the shower death fresh in her mind, she decided to pass until morning.

ACKNOWLEDGMENTS

FIRST AND FOREMOST, THANKS TO THE FANS who buy and read my books—I couldn't do this without you.

Thanks to my beta readers, Lois Miller and Mary O'Neale, you always keep me focused. Thanks to Erika Zamora, RN, who helped answer questions about the OR that have changed since I practiced clinically, and Raven Avellino, MA, who offered suggestions for Angel's closing argument. Big thanks to Carlos Obrey-Espinoza for his help with the Spanish (and yes, even when referring to a boy, it's *mierda pequena*).

Thanks to my editor, Julie Cameron, for her guidance, astute comments, and her humor. Thanks to KB Jensen, for her help with all the details that need doing to publish a book, and thanks to Victoria Wolf, Wolf Design and Marketing, for the great cover.

This book is a work of fiction, people, names, and places are in my imagination alone, and any mistakes are mine.

ABOUT THE AUTHOR

COLORADO NATIVE AND FORMER OR NURSE, Helen Starbuck, is an award-winning author of *The Annie Collins Mystery Series* and contemporary romantic suspense. Sadly, being no relation to the coffee bunch, she doesn't get free coffee. When she's not writing, you can find her ballroom dancing  and reading books about strong women and interesting men who find themselves in suspense-filled situations.

Follow her on Facebook (facebook.com/helensstarbuck), Instagram (instagram.com/helenstarbuck/), Threads (https://www.threads.net/@helenstarbuck_author), and BlueSky (@hstarbuck-books.bsky.social). You can sign up for her newsletter to be the first to hear about new books, events, and cover reveals on her web site (helenstarbuck.com).